LINEAR TACTICAL SERIES

EAGLE

USA TODAY BESTSELLING AUTHOR
JANIE CROUCH

EAGLE: LINEAR TACTICAL

CHAPTER 1

TODAY WAS THE DAY.

Charlotte Devereux just needed this *one* thing to go right.

She rested her head against her hands on the steering wheel. Was it so much to ask, after everything that had happened, to catch a break?

She dragged her head up and peeked out her windshield. Not that she'd thought she'd find it here in Oak Creek, the town she'd fallen in love with when she'd moved here at fourteen years old. At the time, she'd planned to live here the rest of her life, get married and raise half a dozen kids. She'd had it all worked out, right down to the father of those six kids.

But sometimes real life got in the way of your inner fourteen-year-old's plans.

And once she'd left Oak Creek with such fanfare eight years ago, she'd never thought she would be back. Especially under these circumstances.

But it was fitting that this town, which had once held so

much promise and heartbreak for her, would be the place that would allow her to start again.

This was the job she wanted, the one she had worked so hard for and discovered she had such a natural talent and passion for.

The one that had been snatched away from her at every opportunity.

But not today. Today she had circumvented the powers-that-be keeping her from her dream by discovering a way around them. Maybe it wasn't the prettiest way possible, or the cleverest, but she'd done it.

And this was just the beginning. She would prove herself here, and then slowly things would build.

She straightened, ignoring the exhaustion that pulled at her. She'd worked a shift last night at her other job until after three o'clock in the morning and then had been unable to sleep. She wouldn't deceive herself into thinking that, after today, she could give that other job up. Not yet.

But it would build, though slowly. Things didn't change fast, but God knew she'd become patient. When you didn't have any other choice, it was all you could be. Otherwise you just went bat-shit crazy. She'd been there too.

But not today. Today was going to be good.

She opened the door and got out, grabbing the blazer she'd paid to have pressed with money she couldn't spare. But looking professional—that difficult-to-obtain mix of friendly and capable—was more important than anything else she could have used it for. Like food.

There wasn't a stitch of designer anything on her body, but hell, it had been so long since she'd worn a name other than Walmart's Faded Glory that it no longer even fazed her. She had real battles to fight, which meant she had no time for the cosmetic ones.

Taking a deep breath, she turned and faced the Frontier Diner. She'd spent so many hours hanging out here during high school, her only cares those of any privileged, happy girl her age. Gossip. Friends. Boys.

Finn Bollinger in particular.

God, how she wished Finn was her biggest concern now.

She pushed the thought of him from her mind because that would derail her faster than her exhaustion or nervousness. *Ethan*. Ethan was the name of the person she was to concentrate on today.

She grabbed her tote bag from the back seat, wincing at everything else stuffed in her car. But that didn't matter either right now.

Today would be the start. One step at a time.

She smoothed nonexistent wrinkles from her blazer, locked her car, and turned toward the Frontier. It was time.

Opening the door, she stepped inside. Eight years later and it was all still the same. The smell of pies, the low murmur of voices, the burble of coffee brewing behind the counter. She closed her eyes just for a moment to take it all in. God, this was home. These smells, these sights, these sounds. . . Her mind associated this with home even more than the eight-bedroom mansion she'd lived in on the outskirts of town.

This had been where her heart desired to be. Not because of the building, but who'd always been by her side.

She opened her eyes, looking around once more. She'd left of her own accord. She couldn't deny that, nor that she'd been the one to walk away from everything—*everyone*—here.

And she'd do it again, given the same circumstances.

But the price. . . It had been so high. So much higher

than she'd expected. And she was still paying it.

Today she had to keep her soul from withering any further. Hopefully, someday, she would trace her new start all back to now.

She looked around for her prospective client. All she knew about him and the family she'd be working with was that his name was Ethan—his last would be withheld until the parents approved her as a tutor—and that he was almost eight years old. He had some neurologically based processing disorders, including dyslexia and possibly more.

It felt good knowing that she would be able to help him.

All of her college professors had told her she had a gift in working with children with these types of learning disabilities. It hadn't been one she'd expected, but she'd fostered it all through her bachelor's and master's degrees in education. So, she had the training to help Ethan. She was almost buzzing in excitement to get to use it.

If she could, she would've already been working full-time for a school system. But forces stronger and more financially equipped than her had made sure that wouldn't happen. She was done trying to fight them; she'd just go around them.

Ethan. Seven. A little small for his age. She scanned the restaurant.

She took a breath. This was the day. The start.

"Your Royal Highness."

She didn't have to turn around to know who that voice belonged to. Her entire body—*every single place*—tightened at the sound she hadn't heard in eight years.

Finn Bollinger.

She stiffened, steeling herself as she turned. Finn was here, of course. This had been his hometown long before she'd arrived and then again after she'd left.

The sight of him was like a sucker punch, a blow she would've done just about anything to avoid had she seen it coming. At least the air hissing out of her lungs was silent, rather than the explosion it sounded like in her mind.

He hadn't changed eight years later. Two-hundred-plus pounds of muscle rested on his broad-shouldered, six-foot-three frame so easily that it might have just floated down from the sky and decided to attach itself there.

She knew his strength from experience. That he could hold her full weight with one arm until they both. . .

He could hold her weight for a long time.

His raven hair was cut military short, just like the last time she'd seen him. His chiseled jaw, strong nose, and full, sensual lips were all the same. But it was those eyes, those sea-green eyes that gutted her. They always had.

But now they were as hard as emeralds before he bowed with an exaggerated flourish.

"On behalf of the peons and plebeians of Oak Creek, we welcome Your Majesty into our humble abode." Sarcasm dripped from his deep voice. His buddy, Zac Mackay, was standing just over Finn's shoulder, his eyes just as cold.

She stiffened further. She didn't want to fight, not only because she wasn't emotionally equipped to handle Finn right now, but she needed to not make a scene. But if he wanted to treat her as the high-and-mighty mistress of the manor, she certainly remembered how to play the role.

"*Plebeians.*" She raised an eyebrow. "Wouldn't have expected you to know that word, Bollinger."

Finn's eyes narrowed. "Why are you here, Charlie?"

Charlie. She almost smiled. God, how her parents had hated when he'd given her that nickname in high school and everyone had begun using it. She'd reveled in it.

But she forced the smile away and lowered her volume.

"I didn't realize it was a sin to enter a public restaurant here."

Finn crossed his arms over his huge chest, shaking his head. "It's not, just in bad taste."

That would be his stance, wouldn't it? And she couldn't blame him for it. But she just needed him to stand down this one time, to not ruin this for her. She'd beg if she had to, take him outside and explain that she needed this break. If he'd just back off this one time, she'd gladly let him publicly humiliate her for what she'd done. Just not today.

Today was *the day*. It had to be.

"Look, Finn, I'm not here to see you, okay?" Her voice was barely more than a whisper now. "I'm here to meet a family to help their son with some tutoring."

Now those green eyes nearly bugged out of their sockets. "*You're* the learning specialist Mrs. Johnson suggested for Ethan?"

She'd forgotten how information flowed in a small town. Very little remained private. "Yes, I'm here to meet a child named Ethan. The agency doesn't give me a last name until after the parents have approved me as a tutor. Do you know his family?"

He stared at her for so long she didn't think he was going to answer. Finally, he said, "Ethan is right behind you at the bar."

She turned to find the boy.

"And he's *my* son."

Another sucker punch.

"You have a *son*?" The words were out of her mouth before she could stop them. She stared at the young boy sitting at the bar, talking to Finn's sister, Waverly, for a long moment. Finally, Charlie turned back to Finn.

"Sure do, sweetheart." He smirked. "And you think

you're getting near him? That would be a *hell no* with a side of *no chance*. I don't know what your game is or who you paid to make Mrs. Johnson think you're a specialist at anything, but you need to leave. Now."

For just a second, she thought she might do something terrible—Vomit? Beg? Fall on the floor and just start sobbing at the unfairness of it all?—but she strangled the need with ruthless efficiency.

She would not break. Not here. Not in front of Finn, his friends, and family. He wasn't going to listen to her, no matter what she said. He had no interest in knowing that she was indeed a special education teacher and might be able to help his son. And she couldn't blame him.

All she could do now was get out of here before everything inside her crumbled. No doubt Finn would report back to Mrs. Johnson that Charlotte was not an acceptable tutor. That would effectively end the possibility of using her skills in Oak Creek.

"I see," she finally said, keeping her chin as high as possible. "Goodbye, then."

She half expected Finn to toss some sort of verbal grenade at her as she left. Somehow the silence that followed was even worse. Finn didn't give a damn about her.

Nobody did here, not anymore. She'd do well to remember that.

The door closed behind her and she walked back to her car. She eased her blazer off, folding it carefully over the seat to prevent as many wrinkles as possible, although it didn't matter now.

She rubbed her chest, fighting back the fear, desperation, and weariness, trying not to let it crush her. But she didn't cry. Charlotte Devereux did not cry. Ever.

Even when today was not the day.

CHAPTER 2

FINN SAT at the large table of the Linear Tactical conference room, arguably his least favorite place in their entire facility. He'd much rather be outside teaching one of the classes he and his partners provided here. Their years in Special Forces had taught them how to adapt, defend, and survive almost any situation. They'd used that training and knowledge to develop this company and share those same survival intelligence skills with others.

Sitting around a conference table wasn't Finn's forte. But for US Army Major Mark Pinnock, his former commanding officer, he would do it. No doubt the two men sitting with him, Aiden Teague and Zac Mackay, felt the same—about the man, and conference table.

"I need people who can fit in without standing out, who are smart, and who I can trust." The major was currently stationed at Hill Air Force Base a few hours west of Oak Creek, but was working with NORAD, the North American Aerospace Defense command. "You guys fit the bill for all three."

Finn looked across the table at Aiden and Zac. All of them had served under Major Pinnock when they'd been in the Army, as had their other partners, who would be here if they were in town. Zac was here out of respect for the man, even though he was currently taking time off with his girlfriend, who was recuperating from being attacked two weeks ago.

They would all do anything for the major.

The fact that the older man had come to Oak Creek to enlist their help, rather than asking them to travel to Hill AFB, spoke to the gravity of the situation.

"As you know, after 9/11, NORAD took over monitoring any large or small aircraft entering into American airspace. We work with them on a daily basis," the major continued. He turned to the man sitting next to him. "This is Henry Nicholson. He came to me last week concerned that his boss is selling ways to get around holes in our air defense."

Finn nodded to the man who had been sitting silently up until now, just observing the situation. He could appreciate those who monitored and took in information before launching into speech. That was someone you wanted on your side of a battle.

Major Pinnock gestured for Henry to continue. "My evidence is not conclusive, but I discovered some pretty damning transmissions from my boss. Tracking small aircrafts in US airspace is an important part of the battle against drug, weapon, and human trafficking. Providing intel on how to avoid detection would be a valuable commodity to the right buyers."

"And that's what your boss is allegedly providing?" Finn asked.

Henry nodded. "Gordon Cline. Yes, I've tracked down

some of the contacts that received the incriminating transmission from him. None are terrorists or known enemies of the US, but most are certainly criminals. Smugglers, from what I could tell. Cline should not have been in contact with these people."

Zac turned to the major. "We'd be the first to agree this is suspicious and that you should look into it. But you probably have more resources equipped to handle this than we do."

Major Pinnock nodded. "I do, but I still need your help. We're keeping Cline in play at the base to catch the people he's in contact with, or at least gather more intel about them. Henry will be tracking things from his end to see what he can discover."

Henry's jaw clenched. "I know Cline is setting up meetings, but the locations are constantly changing, and we don't know what's happening there. I can't go because I'll be recognized immediately."

Finn leaned back in his chair, stretching his long legs out in front of him. "What about law enforcement? Federal or local. Get someone to go undercover."

"That was our first inclination," Pinnock said, "before we discovered a man named Stellman was involved."

Finn looked over at Zac and Aiden, who were both shrugging. None of them had ever heard of Stellman. "Should we know who that is?"

Pinnock rubbed the bridge of his nose. "That's just it. Nobody—at least not in law enforcement—does. But everyone knows he's near the top of the criminal food chain. He's got his fingers in just about every sort of illegal pie there is: trafficking, weapons, extortion, information brokering. If we can grab him at the same time we bust Cline, we'll be doing everyone a service."

"All reasons to get law enforcement in on this, Major," Zac said. "We want to help, but there's only so much we're trained to do."

"We know Stellman has some law enforcement in his pocket, so we're not sure who can be trusted," Henry responded. "That's why the major wanted to come to you guys. He knows you can't be bought."

Major Pinnock nodded. "When the time is right, and we know who can be trusted, law enforcement will very definitely be involved. But all I wanted to see from you guys today is if you're even interested. We don't have specifics on the when or where yet, but we will soon. If you're not available, I need to find someone else."

"We'll help." Aiden was quick to jump in. "Whatever it is you need, you can count on us. You know that, Major."

Zac and Finn agreed. This man had commanded them at their best, worst, most wounded, and their most triumphant. Finn in particular. If it weren't for Major Pinnock, Finn probably would've been court-martialed and dishonorably discharged eight years ago.

"Yeah, Major, we're in." Finn grinned. "Even if Uncle Sam has an Army man like you working at an Air Force base. What's up with that?"

The major stood, shaking his head ruefully. "Trust me, I'd much rather be back in Stuttgart or Fort Bragg, but all in all, working with the airmen—guys like Henry—isn't too bad. We'll be in touch soon with more details."

Henry stood also. "If everything follows true to form, this shouldn't interfere with your jobs or the day-to-day running of Linear Tactical. It will be more nighttime work—probably a lot of nightclubs. So far that seems to be where Cline is setting up meetings. It may result in just showing up and keeping your eyes and ears open."

Finn, Zac, and Aiden got up to walk Major Pinnock and Henry to the door. The major slapped Finn on the back. "You guys can get in and out of places around most of this part of the state without anyone batting an eye."

"Just let us know what you need, and we'll be there," Zac said, and once again everyone nodded. They all shook hands.

The major's car had barely left the drive before Finn's son, Ethan, came zooming around the corner, followed by little Jessica. At four, Jessica was three and a half years younger than Ethan, but she was big for her age and he was small, so the age gap wasn't very apparent.

Except to Finn.

He didn't give a shit if his son's best friend—that his *only* friend—was a girl. In his mind, that just proved the kid had good taste. But the fact that Ethan needed someone so much younger to relate to. . .it ate at him. Ethan never wanted to play with kids from his own grade, even when Finn tried to arrange play dates.

Ethan only wanted to be around Jess. Granted, she was one of their closest neighbors and her mom worked at Linear, so Jess was around a lot. Were they so close because of that or the intellectual challenges facing his son?

"Come on, Jess," Ethan said. "Dad's done. Let's go build Legos!"

Jess roared her answer in a voice twice as loud as Ethan's. "Yeah, Legos!"

On his way out, Zac laughed and waved as, without even stopping the children streaked past Finn and Aiden and into the office in the back room where the toys were kept. A German shepherd puppy, which Ethan had named Sky—short for Skywalker—scrambled in after them.

A few seconds later Jessica's mom, Peyton, rounded the

corner, looking tired and worn out. "Sorry, Finn." The pinched look that always seemed to blanket her features was even more pronounced than usual. "They got away from me while I was cleaning the sparring area."

Finn smiled. "No harm. We were already done. Plus, I'm pretty sure babysitting Ethan is not included in your agreed upon duties." Peyton was, for all intents and purposes, Linear's janitor. She came in four days a week and cleaned a different area each day.

Her smile was brief and tight. Her eyes darted back and forth across the yard, as if she was on the lookout for something. "But keeping my Jess under control is."

"They're in playing Legos, so I think we're all safe for a while. I'll make sure they don't burn down the place, so no worries."

"Okay, thanks." She grabbed her bucket of cleaning supplies and turned toward the large barn they'd turned into a sparring and workout area when they'd first opened.

Standing on the wrap-around porch, Finn could hear Ethan and Jessica talking in the playroom. Was he perpetuating the problem by allowing Ethan to spend so much time with the preschooler? School was out for summer, so his son was relatively happy spending all his time with Jess, Finn, or Finn's mom. But things would change when school started again in the fall.

Ethan hated school. Finn knew it was because his son felt like a failure when it came to learning, particularly reading. He was too young to understand that part of the problem was because of choices his mother had made when she'd been pregnant and when Ethan had been a baby, before Finn had even known he had a son.

"What's that look about?" Aiden asked.

Finn rubbed the back of his neck. "Ethan. Knowing that

school will start in the fall and he'll still be behind."

"What about that tutor Ethan's teacher found?"

Charlie. Finn had spent the past month specifically trying not to think about her. "Yeah, that didn't work out."

"Ethan didn't like her?"

Finn shrugged. "He never actually met her. I found out the tutor was my ex. . ." Ex what? Love of his life? Woman he thought he would spend forever with? ". . . girlfriend. Just thought it would be better to forget the whole thing."

"The rich ex-girlfriend?"

"Yep. The princess of Oak Creek."

"You think she's not good at her job?"

To be honest, Finn couldn't imagine Charlie as any sort of education specialist, particularly working with kids with disabilities. But he'd never been able to think straight when it came to her. "I think Charlotte Devereux is unreliable. She might be okay as a tutor, but it won't take long before she gets bored and takes off. What happens when Ethan comes to depend on her and she decides this little hobby isn't worth her time? I don't want her near Ethan at all."

Didn't want her near him either.

Liar.

Finn pushed that voice out of his mind the same way he had the thought of her the last few weeks. But like it or not, the fact was, Ethan needed help. They'd been working with Mrs. Johnson, the county special ed coordinator, all summer, but it wasn't enough. Ethan needed someone who specialized in his particular learning disabilities.

Nobody in Teton County had really been able to make a difference for Ethan. Hell, that was true even for the people they'd traveled outside of the county to see. And now there was talk about putting him in a special class. When the kid had heard that, he'd just about lost it.

Ethan had already been through so much in his short life and had come so far. Both Finn and Mrs. Johnson had tried to explain to Ethan how a special class might help him, might make things easier for him to learn. But Ethan didn't want that. He just wanted to be a normal kid in a normal class. He didn't want to be someone the other children made fun of.

Kids could be cruel.

But Finn couldn't let him just continue to flounder academically. He was going into third grade, and his learning problems would compound if they didn't manage to teach Ethan some coping strategies. Soon he wouldn't be able to successfully pass each grade.

His kid needed help. Finn scrubbed a hand across his face again. If Charlie could possibly provide that, didn't he owe it to Ethan to give her a chance?

Maybe. But he just couldn't see Charlie having the patience and tactics to provide Ethan that sort of help.

He didn't even know if she was around anymore. He hadn't seen her in Oak Creek since that day at the Frontier Diner a little over a month ago. She may have already gotten bored with her little foray into special education.

"I'm sure you'll figure it out, man," Aiden said. "You are coming out to The Eagle's Nest tonight, right?"

"Are you kidding? Annie would kill me if I didn't. Plus, my mom already agreed to let Ethan stay overnight. So yeah, some adult shenanigans sound good."

He was happy for Zac and Annie, he really was. His friend had finally found happiness, even if it was with someone Zac had never expected to wander back into his life.

Finn just didn't hold out any hope it would happen the same way for him.

CHAPTER 3

CHARLIE NEEDED A THIRD JOB. Although, honestly, as there'd been no more tutoring opportunities since the one with Finn's son had gone down the drain, it was only a second job.

She didn't want to take a full-time job during the day because it would mean having to say no to any tutoring jobs. If any actually ever came her way again.

Nothing quite like trying to keep a dying dream—one gasping its last breath—alive. Yet she couldn't bring herself to put it out of its misery. Every day she prayed another call would come. Another chance. But, so far, nothing.

Hopefully she could get a job at The Eagle's Nest. A few day shifts per week would be flexible enough to allow her to take any education assignments that came her way. She was here now on a Wednesday night, thinking it might be a good time to talk to the manager. The bar shouldn't be very crowded, and maybe they'd let her go ahead and start tonight.

Because she needed money desperately. It was the first

of the month, so the payment was due next week, and once again she wasn't sure she was going to have enough.

Forty-five hundred dollars, an amount that at one time she wouldn't even have batted an eyelash at, was now the sole focus of her day-to-day life.

She realized her mistake the moment she walked inside the bar. It might be Wednesday, and The Eagle's Nest could definitely use some waitressing and bartending help, but it was way too crowded for her to be able to talk to the manager.

Some sort of celebration was going on. A guy was sitting at a booth near the front, arm in a sling, a big grin on his face even though he looked like he was in a little bit of pain. Everybody was stopping by his table, shaking his hand, and generally cooing over him. It was packed.

A lot of these people were ones she remembered from high school. Just for a minute, her reality seemed to shift.

This would've been her life. This was what she had *envisioned* for her life. She would've been one of the gaggle of women buying shots, planning to flirt, dance, and drive the guys a little crazy. She would've been one of those hugging, smiling, and bumping hips casually with others as they walked by, laughing out loud at a joke that wouldn't even seem funny tomorrow. This would've been her tribe. This town would've been her home. They had been meant to be hers.

But they weren't.

She walked over to the bar, grabbing a stool in the far corner, ignoring whatever was roiling and twisting in her gut. She sat, just watching.

Just *wishing*.

It was Riley Wilde, the little tomboy who had grown up into a gorgeous woman, who saw Charlie and waved to her.

Before Charlie could even decide how to respond, Riley was making her way over.

"Charlie Devereux! Come join us for shots!" The woman already had some sort of bright blue concoction in a glass in her hand.

But damn if it wasn't nice to have someone just pull her right into the fold like that. Maybe Riley had already had a couple, or she was just as friendly as she had been when they were younger. But either way it was nice to be invited. To not be on the outside.

What the hell, ten dollars' worth of drinks wasn't going to make the difference in whether she could make her payment this month or not.

She slipped off her lightweight jacket and let Riley pull her into a group of other women. They all started talking to her and seemed to be celebrating something to do with Anne Nichols, who was evidently a doctor now and had said more in the last two minutes than Charlie had heard her say during the entire four years of high school. Anne looked so pretty, soft, and happy. A glass of the blue stuff in her hand, she glanced over at a table across the bar. Her pretty features softened even more with happiness as she did.

Charlie followed Anne's gaze, a shot glass in her own hand now, to see what the other woman was looking at.

Not what. *Who.* Zac Mackay. Anne wasn't just pretty, soft, and happy, she was in love. And Zac—unable to tear his eyes away from the woman—was obviously just as in love with her.

It was sweet and beautiful and made Charlie want to drink in their honor.

"Let's go make the guys drink these, ladies!" Riley yelled, and the others agreed.

"Where?" she yelled over the din.

"There!" Riley pointed toward the table where Zac was sitting.

She hesitated. But maybe it would be okay. Zac didn't have a problem with her, she didn't think, even though he was Finn's best friend. She could stay for a little while. Be part of a life outside of just surviving.

Then someone moved, clearing her view. Zac was sitting with a bunch of guys.

Including Finn.

His eyes met hers and she couldn't look away. She didn't know what to do, didn't know how to breathe.

But she couldn't stay.

"Riley." She grabbed the younger woman's arm. "I just remembered something I have to do. I'll catch you guys next time, okay? Don't let those drinks kill you."

Riley was caught up in the women's march toward the table. She yelled something back, but Charlie couldn't hear it. And it didn't matter anyway.

She couldn't stay. She should've known that from the second she walked in. And definitely recognized that a job here was out of the question.

She slipped her jacket back on, consciously not looking over at Finn, and headed straight for the door.

She made it across the parking lot to her car before releasing the breath she'd been holding. She'd escaped without another showdown with Finn. Good. She didn't have the energy.

"You running and me chasing after you. Seems about par for the course."

She squeaked and spun around. "Damn it, Finn, you shouldn't sneak up on people like that. It'll get you punched in the gut."

"Punched in the gut is pretty much what I expect from you, princess. Believe me, I'll never be stupid enough to leave my guard down for it again."

She couldn't blame him for that.

They stared at each other for a long minute before he took a step forward. She eased back, finding herself trapped between him and her car. Something over her shoulder caught his attention.

"This yours?"

"Yeah." The BMW 3 Series was old but paid off. She didn't want to explain why she was driving it. He probably expected her to have something much newer and fancier.

But that wasn't what had caught his attention.

"Geez, princess, what the hell is all this stuff?"

An icy panic seized her. Explaining an older car was much easier than why everything she owned was split between the trunk and back seat.

"Finn. . ." She searched for words, lies, for anything to get out of telling the truth.

But he just laughed. "What, are your maids on vacation? If not, you need to fire them. They are doing a piss-poor job of keeping this car clean."

He thought she was a slob, too lazy to clean out her own car. That was better than him knowing the truth, but it still cut at parts of her she didn't want to acknowledge.

"Just leave me alone, Bollinger. Go back to your friends."

That was a challenge. One of those sexy, dark eyebrows rose. "You know this is where I hang out." He stepped closer, trapping her further. "You following me, Charlie?"

"Don't flatter yourself." He was too close. All she could do was breathe in the woodsy, leathery scent of him. He still smelled the same even after all these years.

She should leave, get some distance between them. But she couldn't seem to force herself to do it.

"Don't you have a husband at home wondering where you are?" he finally asked.

She should tell Finn yes, she was still married, that Brandon was in fact waiting at home for her. It was the surest way to get Finn to leave her alone.

But once again she couldn't. "No. We divorced four years ago."

"Ah, 'the course of true love never did run smooth.'" He didn't even hide his smirk.

Asshole. She responded with her own weapon. "Isn't Shakespeare a little above your pay grade, soldier?"

His eyes narrowed. She'd scored a direct hit. His lack of college education still ate at him. Of course, she'd helped rip open that chink in his armor eight years ago.

He rebounded quickly, as he always had with their verbal sparring. He may not have gone to college, but it hadn't been because he was stupid. "Why are you here, Charlie?"

"I came in for a drink—"

"No, in Oak Creek as a tutor. You never mentioned wanting to help kids when we were together."

That was because she thought she'd have half a dozen kids of her own. It had never occurred to her that she might want a job helping someone else's children.

Yet another thing she was never going to tell him. She crossed her arms over her chest. "We haven't seen each other in almost a decade. I think we can agree that people change in that time. I got a master's degree, found something I was good at. Is that a sin?"

He took that final step so all the ways he *hadn't* been

touching her, he now was. He was pressed against her from thigh to shoulder. Again, she should move away.

Again, she didn't.

She had the strength to survive what would bring others to their knees, but not to move away from Finn Bollinger. She'd done it once, and it had nearly killed her.

"Sin," he whispered, his mouth so close to hers. "You mentioned that last time I saw you. This is the only sin I think about when I'm anywhere near you."

His hands started at her elbows and slid all the way up to her shoulders. She shuddered inside her thin jacket even though the night was mild. His fingers kept trailing up, along her collarbone, then to her throat. He tilted her chin higher as he bent toward her.

And then his lips were on hers, like they belonged there. And maybe they did. She gripped his wrists and held on as the heat surrounding them crackled in the air.

The kiss was lush, open, and hot, the way it always had been between them. It had been a long time, *so damn long*, since she had kissed anyone. Since she had been this close to anyone at all. Her body was starved for it.

But it hungered for Finn most of all. Only he had ever been able to ignite a fire in her with just a kiss. And this one went on and on like it had when they were in high school, when kissing was all they'd known how to do. When they'd been young and hadn't figured out there was so much better.

She would've expected his lips to be hard and punishing, vengeful. But they weren't. They coaxed, slid, nibbled against hers, as if he could sense how alone she had been, how close to the edge she'd been walking these last few months. How close she'd been to breaking.

They both emitted low sounds of hunger as their

tongues met and dueled. His thumbs rubbed gentle circles on her throat, the sensation more arousing than anything she'd experienced in years. The feel of his big body pressing her hard against the door of her car should probably have made her wary. Concerned.

But it didn't. This was Finn. They might tear each other apart, but he would never hurt her. She just wanted to stay here and kiss him forever and forget about everything else that waited, ready to pounce, beyond the two of them.

But it wasn't long before people were coming out, laughing, talking, and very definitely coming within visible range. Finn eased his body back from hers, then took a step away, completing the distance.

She wanted to cry at the loss.

"I've got to go back inside," he said. "We're celebrating and it's important I be there."

She looked down at their feet, his so much larger than hers. "Yeah, no problem. I need to get going." To absolutely nowhere.

"You can come in if you want. Hang out with us."

She swallowed. God, was that possible? Could she actually start over? Reclaim some of what she'd lost here when she'd turned away all those years ago? Friends. *Finn*. The slightest bit of hope bubbled up inside her. *Possibly* she could find her way back.

It wasn't definite, she understood that. But she didn't need it to be definite. Just the possibility was enough.

A maybe.

She tried to keep it casual. "Sure. I guess I could. . ."

She looked up at his face, and the hope that had been building inside her was wiped away in an instant. He was just being polite. The tension in his features was concrete evidence he didn't honestly want her inside with them. She made him uncomfortable.

And who could blame him?

She almost wished she didn't know him so well. But she'd spent so many years studying that face, that body. Most people wouldn't have been able to tell that he was feigning politeness.

She gave him her best smile, hoping it would hold up for just a few more seconds. "Actually, what am I saying? I can't stay. I've got somewhere I have to be."

It sounded like the most pathetic excuse in the history of pathetic excuses.

Evidently to him, too. His features softened. "Charlie. . ."

Oh God, she couldn't stand any kindness right now. She would shatter all over the ground. "We both know I don't belong in there, Finn." Her voice was low, husky.

He rubbed at the back of his neck with one hand. "Yeah, probably not."

And there it was. The truth, stated as gently as possible. But the jagged edge of it ripped across her heart all the same.

She slipped away from him—what she should've done as soon as he'd followed her—opened the door of her car and got inside.

He didn't try to stop her.

Because what else was there to say?

CHAPTER 4

TWO DAYS later Finn still couldn't erase the look on Charlie's face from his mind when he'd told her she shouldn't go back inside The Eagle's Nest.

Not that it had been anything overt. She hadn't flinched. No tears had leaked from those ridiculous blue eyes of hers. Charlie never cried.

It'd been so much subtler. The tiniest glimmer of hope right before it died out. That was almost worse.

He couldn't wrap his head around it. What had she wanted? Why had she been there in the first place? Had she truly wanted to go hang out with his friends?

Like she hadn't shattered his heart into a million pieces eight years ago. As if she hadn't told him she loved him, then married another man despite Finn begging her not to.

God, he'd almost gotten court-martialed for her. For coming back to Wyoming to try to stop her wedding to a man he knew she didn't love. He'd been so sure if he could just talk to her, see her face-to-face, ask her to wait and trust him, she would. She would marry Finn.

But she hadn't.

She'd told him, pretty much in front of the entire town, that she chose Brandon Kempsley. That *he* had the money, means, and education to give Charlie what she wanted.

Finn had been fine to screw around with for a few years, but when it came to lifelong choices, he didn't quite make the cut.

He'd been in love with her through high school and beyond. She'd just been marking time until she had a chance to marry someone closer to her tax bracket.

So, what if she'd gotten her feelings a little hurt at not being invited to hang out with Finn's friends.

But it bothered him. Maybe he was just a sucker, or he'd gone soft after leaving the Army. But that look on her face, of hope being squashed? It ate at his gut.

And that kiss. He'd be lying if he said it hadn't run through his mind on repeat from the moment they'd pulled away from each other.

Maybe the hurt in Charlie's eyes was new and unexpected, but that kiss. . .it had been the same in all the good, bad, and burning-down-the-whole-town ways.

His body remembered everything about the feel of hers. The way her much smaller frame fit against his. The way his fingers automatically dug into that long blonde hair. The sound she made when all she was thinking about was him.

Who knows what would've happened if they hadn't been in a crowded parking lot.

Heat had never been their problem. Not getting burned? That was another story.

If she burned him now, nearly a decade later and hopefully wiser? Well, then that just made him an idiot, didn't it?

He was pulling up to the county education offices to talk to Mrs. Johnson. Because whether he was an idiot or not when it came to the sexual chemistry between him and Charlie, he had to know if she could truly help his son.

Mrs. Johnson was the special education specialist for all of Teton County. She knew about Ethan's situation, what he'd gone through as an infant and toddler, and even before he was born, which was now contributing to his learning problems.

Finn let his fury roll off him as he walked into the school. It was an old anger directed at the woman who had given birth to Ethan and then refused to care for him the way he needed, and it wouldn't help now.

He would give up anything to go back in time and know about Ethan from the moment his beautiful son was born. But he couldn't. All he could do was provide the best available options for Ethan now. Even if that included Charlie.

He knocked on Mrs. Johnson's door and entered at her invitation.

"Finn." The older woman smiled, tucking a strand of gray hair behind her ear. "It's good to see you. How is Ethan? How's your summer going?"

Mrs. Johnson had a calming, friendly way about her—equal parts personality, training, and godsend. Finn had asked more than once if she would consider leaving her administration position and going straight back into the classroom. Ethan's, to be specific. But even the lure of having summers off hadn't persuaded her.

"Everything is going great. I can't get Ethan to come inside until dark almost every day. We're out in the woods all the time or he's playing with Legos. Normal boy stuff."

Except that his bestie was a four-year-old.

"I'm glad he's having fun. That's important. Any luck on getting him to read something?"

Guilt slid through him. "No, but that's my fault more than anything. I'm not much of a reader either, I'm afraid."

Mrs. Johnson didn't tsk or make him feel bad. She just shrugged. "It's summer. The sun's out. I think books take a back seat for most boys Ethan's age." She smiled kindly. "And maybe yours too."

"But school starts in a month and a half." Finn rubbed his fingers over his eyes. "Every time someone mentions it, Ethan gets all tense and nervous. I hate that."

She gestured to a chair, and after he sat, she took the one next to him. "I do, too. We should do anything we can to establish school as a positive place for him, rather than negative. Any stories you can think of from your own school experience, funny, silly, *anything* positive, you should go out of your way to tell him. Or your Linear Tactical friends. Ethan looks up to them all like uncles."

Finn nodded. "That's a good idea. I'll ask my mom too. I'm sure she has a lot. They might be of me causing trouble, but they'll probably be entertaining and positive."

"Good. These aren't solutions, of course, but changing his outlook about school is part of the equation."

"I wanted to talk to you about that tutor you suggested a month ago, the one I refused."

Mrs. Johnson's face lit up. "Charlotte Devereux. Yes. I was really so sorry when that didn't work out."

"Can you tell me more about why you suggested her? Charlotte and I went to high school together, and she never mentioned any desire to study education or work with children. Nor did she ever seem to have the temperament for it. So I'll admit, I was caught off guard when I found out she was the tutor you thought so highly of."

"I see. Well, I obviously didn't know Ms. Devereux

when she was in high school. I can only speak to my interviews and sessions with her currently, which are stellar."

The older woman didn't say it, but Finn heard the gentle rebuke in her words. It was unfair to judge anyone solely by how they'd acted in high school. He certainly wouldn't want someone to judge him that way. Hell, half the older adults in this town still brought up his streaking-through-the-bleachers-naked incident from high school.

"Then tell me what it was about her that made you think she'd be good for Ethan."

"Well, first, I looked into her actual schooling and master's thesis. To be honest, I don't have time to interview a lot of people. I only want to bring in those who are well suited for the kids we have in this county. I won't bore you with the details, but Ms. Devereaux's course choices and master's thesis topic on the use of symbols and codes as a coping strategy interested me. I ended up reading the whole thing." She smiled. "I can't tell you the last time I read an entire master's thesis."

He bit back a sigh. He'd never doubted Charlie was smart. "That doesn't necessarily make her good with kids or as a tutor."

"Absolutely. But it was enough to get her in for an interview. That went really well, so I brought her in for some supervised sessions working with kids. She is exceptional, Finn. And I do not say that lightly."

He just couldn't wrap his head around it. He hated the thought that entered his mind, but he had to ask. "Mrs. Johnson, I respect you a great deal. You know more about Ethan's life and those early years than anyone outside my immediate circle. You worked with him and his regular teachers and I owe you a great debt for that. Without you, I have no idea what state Ethan would be in. Perhaps he'd still be that completely silent kid who came to me when I first got him out of foster care."

"But. . ." Mrs. Johnson stared at him patiently.

He held his hands out in front of him, palms up, a gesture of regret for the words about to come. "But I just have to know if Charlotte offered you money to get you to hire her as a tutor. I don't mean to get to Ethan. She seemed legitimately surprised when she found out it was my son she'd been scheduled to see a few weeks ago. But the Devereuxes owned a lot of Oak Creek and the surrounding area at one time, probably still do. Them throwing money at someone to get Charlotte what she wanted isn't unheard of."

"I see." Mrs. Johnson tapped her fingers on her desk.

"I don't mean that as any sort of slight against you," he was quick to add. "It would not be some sort of shady bribe. More like an offer to provide resources you don't have, but need, if you hired Charlotte. And honestly, if you said yes, I have no problem with that. I truly don't. I say get whatever you can to help the children in your care."

"But in that case, you don't want Ms. Devereux around your son."

"I'm not sure I want Charlotte around my son in any case."

She smiled at him again. "Certainly, with any education specialist, the relationship between them and the parents is critical. If you don't trust Charlotte, then you are right to keep her from Ethan. Your instincts as a father are good. Trust them."

Finn rubbed the back of his neck. This wasn't coming out right. "It's not that I don't trust Charlotte around Ethan. It's really not. I don't think she would ever hurt anyone." That was the truth. "I just don't want to waste Ethan's time"—and force himself to be near her every week—"if this is just some sort of hobby for her and she's not really going to help him."

She leaned her elbows on the table, studying him. "Then I hope you will trust me when I say no money at all was offered or even hinted at during the hours I've spent with Ms. Devereux. No mention of her father or her family whatsoever. There's no hidden agenda here."

"I hope you understand I was just trying to—"

The woman held out a hand. "Let me go on to say that if I could bring on Charlotte Devereux full-time, I would do so without hesitation. I even went so far as to put the initial paperwork in. In my professional opinion, working as a part-time private tutor is a complete waste of her talents. I think she could probably get a job in any school system, not only in Wyoming but the entire country."

He could feel his eyes widening. "Really?"

"But for whatever reason, that's not what she wants. I didn't pry. I thought maybe she had young kids at home and didn't want a full-time job or something like that. You probably know more about that than I do."

No, he really didn't. "I see."

"Unfortunately, we haven't been able to use Ms. Devereux again since we sent her out to meet you. School was ending, so there wasn't as much demand for tutors. Also, any time a family rejects the tutor, we must put an official mark in the file. Then there's a waiting period and a chance for the family to file any sort of complaint."

Shit. "I didn't have one against Charlotte. We just have. . .history and I think we were both caught a little off guard. But I didn't mean to jeopardize her work." Especially if Charlotte was as good as Mrs. Johnson said she was.

"Well, I'm sure we'll be using her once school starts again if she's not swept up by another school system."

He studied the older woman for a long minute. "Would Charlotte really be good for Ethan? Would she be able to help him?"

He didn't ask the question lightly, but it was the one he ultimately needed an answer for. The price for tutoring would be nothing compared to the personal price Finn would have to pay if Charlotte was around all the time.

But he wasn't surprised at Mrs. Johnson's answer. "Academically, I think Charlotte Devereux might be the best thing that ever happened to your son."

CHAPTER 5

CHARLIE WAS out-and-out grinning and flipping her phone in her hand as she walked from her car toward The Silver Palace, her current main job.

Grinning.

She couldn't remember the last time she'd done that.

Mrs. Johnson had called her today. She had three —*three!*—tutoring jobs for Charlie. The woman was confident that all of them would turn into weekly appointments. Not only that, she was positive that once school started and word spread about Charlie's abilities, Charlie would have so many appointments she'd have to turn some down. She found that hard to believe, but it was a fabulous thought.

Mrs. Johnson had asked her once again to consider joining the Teton County School System, had sworn she would be a shoo-in for the job.

It was hard to lie to the other woman, but Charlie had already learned her lesson. There was no way she was going to be able to hold down any job where her ex-husband's family, the very *rich* and *powerful* Kempsleys, had any sway.

That would be all of Wyoming and most of the surrounding states.

They hadn't liked that she'd divorced Brandon after he'd been arrested. They held her responsible for it, and that she'd somehow ruined his good name by not taking the blame for what he'd done. Evidently to the Kempsleys, things like the truth played second fiddle to protecting their grown son.

Brandon hadn't even gone to prison, despite the quantity of drugs found in his possession. His family had made a deal and he'd gotten off with a fine and community service. But Brandon's dreams of a political career, or his parents' dream for him, were effectively over.

And now, even years after the divorce, they were still making her pay. They made sure every job she'd gotten in the education field had been snatched away from her in the most brutal way possible. No school system would touch her, as Mrs. Johnson would find out if she took a permanent job offer for Charlie any further. The moment she was fully in the Teton County system, the Kempsleys would pounce. They'd put pressure on the principal or school board not to hire her. They'd tell outright lies, if they had to. The result would be the same: unless Charlie wanted to move to a different part of the country, a full-time career in education wasn't available. And right now, that move wasn't possible.

So, she would keep tutoring for the time being. At least it gave her the chance to use her knowledge and skills. So far, the Kempsley family hadn't stopped that, or maybe they just didn't care about something so small. Hopefully, that would stay the case.

Because three opportunities this week to work with

kids, to use her skills, like Mrs. Johnson was offering? Charlie would take it.

Even if one of them was Ethan Bollinger. Mrs. Johnson had assured her that Finn had given his explicit permission for Charlie to tutor his son.

Charlie didn't know what had caused Finn's change of heart. She'd spent the last week *not* thinking about their kiss in the parking lot. And definitely *not* lying awake hours at night reliving it. But at least those thoughts had made the long, sometimes frightening hours go by more quickly.

She would show Finn that she really was good at her chosen almost-career. That she had an unexpected talent with kids and loved helping them overcome their difficulties. She would help Ethan Bollinger with every last ounce of her ability, knowledge, and enthusiasm.

Not just to prove to Finn he was wrong, but because she wanted to help his son. The one that maybe in another life would've been theirs. She pushed that thought away too. No point dwelling on what would never happen.

She could do it. She just needed a chance. And now she was going to get it.

But first she had to get through this shift at the club. She walked in the back door of The Silver Palace, Reddington City's premier—a term used loosely and only in advertisements—gentlemen's club.

No one truly understood chaos until they were in the dressing room backstage of a strip club at ten o'clock on a Saturday night. But Charlie now had a very good understanding of it. Women were running around in various states of undress, talking at every possible volume, tone, and pitch. Some angry, others excited, a few obviously having taken an illegal substance to get them through their shift.

Then there were those with eyes so weary and desperate it broke Charlie's heart.

She'd stopped looking in the mirror, afraid her own eyes might start reflecting that same desperation back at her.

Charlie wasn't a stripper, not that she thought less of the women who danced. She'd just never been able to bring herself to do it. She didn't have the temperament, plus she couldn't dance well anyways. But she bartended here six nights a week.

She may not dance or grind against drunk men for money, but the mesh tank top she was required to wear for her job left very little to the imagination.

She'd been mortified the first night in it, humiliated the second, but on the third, she'd realized that this job was going to provide her the money she needed to survive and make the necessary payments each month. So, she'd left her pride, and her bra, at the door.

Let the men look. As long as she was making the money she needed each month, she no longer gave a shit. Plus, The Silver Palace was in Reddington City, not Oak Creek. Here, she was just Charlie Devereux, bartender in a racy tank top. Not Charlotte Devereux, daughter of Milton Devereux, owner of the town factory and boss of half its residents. That had been her resume in high school.

Nobody from Oak Creek ever came in here. If guys were looking for a strip club, there were at least three closer to town.

Here, she was just another girl hustling to make the money she needed.

"Charlie! You've got a phone call, baby," one of the dancers yelled.

That could only be her mother. Charlie had given her the landline number of the club because her cell phone didn't get any coverage inside the building. It barely got it anywhere. Such was life with the cheapest prepaid service available.

She dashed over to the tiny supply closet that had been set up for the girls to use the phone, closing the door on the din behind her.

"Mama? Is everything okay? Is Dad all right?"

"Hi sweetie, how are you?"

Charlie closed her eyes and prayed for patience. She really didn't have time to chat. Of course, Mama didn't know that.

Mama didn't know a lot of things.

"I'm fine, just busy. What's up?"

"I heard all the noise and I can't believe it gets so loud in a library study room."

Her mom had no idea she worked in a strip club. The last number Charlie had given her had been for a study room, so Mama assumed this was also. She had no idea where the money she and Dad depended on came from.

"It's Saturday night so it's more like gossip central than anything else." That at least wasn't a lie. The women here could run their mouths faster than they could shake their hips. "What's going on?"

The long pause meant something was wrong.

She took a deep breath. "It's okay, Mama. Just tell me. What is it?"

"Your dad took a fall today."

Charlie's heart started pounding. Before she could ask all her questions, Mama continued. "It wasn't bad. Nothing broken. The staff is just going to move him into a more supervised room for a few days, a week or two at the most, just to make sure he has what he needs."

"And you're going to stay with him?" Charlie asked, but

she already knew the answer. Of course Mama was. She would every single night if it didn't cost so much more. Charlie hated that money was what kept her mom in the tiny studio apartment outside of the treatment center, rather than in one of the family suites that would allow them to be together all the time. But there was no way Charlie could come up with the extra money. It was taking every cent she could make just to keep things at the status quo.

Mama's voice was tentative. "I know that costs extra. But he's so agitated right now—"

"Mama, just do it. It will be all right. I've got the money." She definitely *did not* have it.

"Just for two nights, I promise. And you'll come down to see us tomorrow? Milton always loves having you around, even if he can't say it."

Charlie closed her eyes as exhaustion washed over her. If she was going to see her parents tomorrow, she would have to get a room tonight. It was a necessity. She had to shower, fix her hair, put on unwrinkled clothes.

Keep the ruse alive.

And for her parents, she would do it.

"Yeah, of course I'll be there. Wouldn't miss it. I'll see you some time before lunch."

"Okay, sweetie, I'll see you then. I've got to get back to Dad. I love you."

"Love you too. See you tomorrow."

She hung up and leaned her forehead against the wall, doing some quick calculations. Dad in the supervised room would be expensive. But it was temporary. It *all* was. A couple more years at best was all Dad had. She could hang on for that long. Right?

And she could add another night working here, make it seven instead of just six. And talk to her boss, Mack, and see if she could maybe take over cleaning the bar during the day. She could offer a reduced rate as incentive. The crew he had now was unreliable.

She hit her head against the wall softly. It wasn't what she wanted, but it would get her through this month.

At least Mack would work with her in terms of scheduling. He wouldn't care when The Silver Palace got cleaned, so long as it was before the five pm opening.

Because she couldn't bear to think about having to give up the tutoring jobs to get a second full-time job. But she knew it wasn't far off on the horizon if things continued in this direction and Dad needed more pronounced medical care.

Sitting in this closet certainly wasn't going to make her any money. She pushed open the door and made her way back out through the dressing room to the bar.

The noise assaulted her immediately, but she ignored it.

"You look a little pale. Are you okay?" Heather yelled as she made a rum and Coke and slid it toward a man watching the dancer onstage.

"Yeah. My mom called. Family stuff, you know how it is."

The other bartender did. Not Charlie's specific circumstances, but everybody here knew what it was like to have family responsibilities. They might put their bodies on view to make more money, but they did it for a reason. Bills, a mortgage, tuition payments.

Charlie had started working here a little over fourteen months ago, after she'd been fired from yet another educational system position thanks to the Kempsley family. Her first night had been one of the lowest points in her life. Realizing that she would be completely on display for every hour she worked. . .she'd vomited at the end of her shift. But that hadn't stopped her from coming back for her next shift. She made more at The Silver Palace in one night than she had at past bartending jobs in an entire week.

Ironically, she'd gotten through those first difficult months of men leering at her basically naked breasts by thinking about Finn. She and Finn may have had sex in every possible position and location in Oak Creek, but he'd never looked at her with anything but respect.

Even when he'd hated her.

"Everything okay back here?"

Heather shot her a grin. "No worries. Although Rocco was looking for you. He—"

"There's my hottie!"

Charlie barely contained her grimace. Rocco was everything that epitomized the negative side of working here. Wandering hands. Suggestive comments. Eyes that rarely left her chest.

She disliked everything about the man. Except for the tips he left her.

"When you going to start dancing, girl?" Rocco continued. "Maybe in the back room, just you, me, and a few of my friends." The more excited he got, the more pronounced his Eastern European accent became. He licked his lips and bile pooled in her stomach. But at this point, dancing in the back wasn't something she could discount. An hour with Rocco there could make her hundreds.

But the back rooms were for complete nakedness. *Complete.* Sex wasn't allowed, but anything else was pretty much fair game. Charlie would have to expose herself to Rocco in ways she knew she'd never recover from. She didn't judge the women who chose to do it. Some of them found empowerment in it.

Once again, Finn came to her mind. Dancing for Finn

in the back room, exposing herself that way? *That* she could do. She would find a great deal of pleasure in it.

But for Rocco and his friends? That would destroy something in her she could never rebuild. She just couldn't do it.

But she smiled at Rocco anyway. "You just keep thinking about that, honey," she yelled over the music.

Rocco's smile was slimy as he motioned for her to come closer. She barely kept her smile in place as she did. "I'm going to bring some of my friends here. We've been looking for a place for business and I think The Silver Palace will do nicely. Your boss should be very happy he has such good employees like you to help drum up business." He ran his finger up and down her bicep. Nothing she could complain about.

Except that he never looked away from her chest. But then again, why would he?

Charlie couldn't let it matter. Pride was a luxury for people not doing everything they could to survive. She just nodded at Rocco.

She spent the rest of the night smiling, pouring drinks, and stopping some argument between a couple guys from turning into a fight that would disrupt the place. Hustling and making as much money as possible.

As they were closing, she talked to Mack about adding as many shifts as she could, to which he gladly agreed, since Charlie was one of his best and most responsible employees. When she mentioned the cleaning, he was a little more skeptical but relented when she argued the financial advantage. He agreed to try it for a month. He'd even let her start tomorrow.

She left, knowing she had to return in just a couple hours to get it done so she could visit her parents in Denver.

There was no point in getting a hotel room after all. She'd just catch a couple hours sleep in the parking lot before coming back in. She'd wash and fix her hair in the sink the best she could. Mama would probably be too distracted to notice. And it had been years since her precious dad had truly been lucid enough to care.

So yeah, she was going to be tired. The thought of more hours on her feet cleaning the club made her exhausted and she hadn't even done it yet. This wasn't going to be easy.

She had to focus on the positive. Working seven nights a week here plus doing the cleaning would enable her to keep her tutoring jobs. Working in the field she loved would be enough to keep her soul from being crushed under the weight of everything else.

Three days till she got to do what she loved. She would focus on that.

CHAPTER 6

EVERY TUESDAY SOMEONE from Linear Tactical had to get up at the ass crack of dawn and go to Reddington City for a special meeting with state bigwigs. It was actually an honor to be included in discussions about security and best practices, and usually Zac represented the company. Finn didn't want to sit in a meeting if he had another option, no matter how important the other members were.

Ethan was generally Finn's get-out-of-jail-free card when it came to this duty. He couldn't go to Reddington City if he had to get his kid to school. But it was summer and Finn's brother, Blake, or Baby as everyone had called him since birth, had crashed on their couch last night after a marathon viewing of *Phineas and Ferb* with Ethan and a competition to see who could build the highest Lego tower.

So normally Finn would not be heading back to Oak Creek from Reddington City at nine o'clock on a Tuesday morning. He wouldn't be passing The Cactus Motel at that time. It was easily the shadiest in both Teton and Sublette Counties—it was only a matter of time before they started renting rooms out by the hour. And the things that went on there. . .Well, suffice it to say, it wasn't a place anyone booked on Expedia. And it was not on the side of town Finn would normally hang out in.

He'd be able to protect himself if for some reason he decided to, thanks to his close-quarters combat training during his time in the Special Forces. But that didn't mean he was stupid enough to want to push his luck.

So, seeing Charlie Devereux leaving one of the rooms as he drove by nearly caused him to wreck his beloved Jeep.

Utter disbelief flooded his system. He could not think of one single *good* reason why Charlie would be there. Hell, he could hardly think of bad ones. Even if she was meeting a man for some illicit tryst or buying drugs. . .Why would she do it here at a shithole so seedy even a lot of criminals avoided it? No single thing about the Cactus was classy, from the vacancy sign that was only ever half lit, to the trash blowing constantly back and forth across the parking lot, and the overgrown hedges surrounding the front of the one-story building.

Finn couldn't leave without gathering more information.

He continued to drive past so he wouldn't draw attention, then swung his Jeep in a U-turn right smack in the middle of the road. He pulled into the parking lot of the mostly abandoned strip mall across from the motel.

He parked facing the strip mall, then adjusted his rearview mirror so he could see behind him. He was tempted to confront Charlie right now, ask what she could possibly be doing that was worth putting her very life in jeopardy by even being there. He had to tamp the urge down.

He'd only been there ten seconds and had already

spotted two potential threats: a drug addict and/or drunk sleeping in the alley next to the hotel and a man who seemed to be just loitering half a block away. He wouldn't expect Charlie to notice the possible dangers. Most civilians didn't until it was right on them. That was one of the first things they taught at Linear Tactical: situational awareness.

Finn wanted answers, and he would probably be crossing the road to get them right now if Charlie weren't scheduled to tutor Ethan in a few hours. Finn would be able to get his answers then. But he sure as hell wasn't going to leave here without making sure she was safe. Even if she was doing something stupid, no woman should be in this section of town unprotected.

And he wanted to gather intel, know as much as possible when he confronted her. It would be too easy for her to lie or twist the truth.

Why would she be here?

She put a box of something inside her car, then turned and walked back through the room's door she'd kept open by propping a chair against it. A few seconds later she was outside with a suitcase she loaded into her trunk. A laundry basket of clothes was added to the back seat.

What the hell was all that stuff? It couldn't be Charlie's possessions. The entire planet would have to face nuclear annihilation before she would stay at a hotel of this caliber. There were at least half a dozen places between here and Oak Creek she would stay at first. Dozens more in Reddington City.

She brought out a blazer next, holding that over both arms in front of her. She carefully draped it across the back seat.

Finn kept waiting for someone else to come out or something else to happen. Maybe she was moving an acquaintance. Providing assistance. Anything that would explain Charlie's presence here. But on the next trip inside, she pulled the chair away and let the door close, walked back out empty-handed, got in her car, and drove away.

He was tempted to follow her, enough that he even put his Jeep in gear. But he stopped himself. He had to get back home to Ethan, so Baby could go to work. And besides, Charlie had done absolutely nothing suspicious as he watched.

Except for being here in the first place.

All she'd done was carry out a suitcase and some clothes and lay them in her car, like thousands of travelers at hotels every day.

He ran a hand over his head, rubbing the short-cropped hair, attempting to ease some of the tension clamping his skull. He tried to process the ramifications of Charlie in this place but wasn't coming up with much. He'd never been a tactician, like Zac and Aiden. He'd never been one to look at all the angles and come up with a plan. He'd been their eyes. A sharpshooter. Patient, observant, and watchful.

It hadn't been a skill set he'd entered the Army with. He'd been much more impulsive and foolish when he'd been young. It had taken watching Charlie marry someone else to bring out that cold focus. But once it had, it had never gone away.

Eagle.

That had been his radio call sign and nickname, thanks to his ability to be patient and observe. And that's what he would do now. He didn't understand what he'd just seen this morning, but he would find out.

Maybe it was something benign, innocent, like Charlie being so exhausted she couldn't make it back to her house last night so she'd done the responsible thing and stopped before she hurt someone. God knew that would be the right thing to do. Zac had lost his family because a driver had fallen asleep behind the wheel.

Maybe it was just a matter of explaining how truly dangerous it was. He'd never been inside, but it couldn't be much better than the exterior. If for some reason unknown to God and man she hadn't figured that out after her stay there, Finn would tell her.

Who was he kidding? There was no way in hell Charlotte Darlene Devereux did not know this place was a dump at best, crime and bug infested at worst.

The itch in the back of his gut that had saved his life more times than he could count was going haywire now. Charlie was hiding something.

And she was meeting with the most precious thing in his world in just a few hours. Until he knew exactly what was going on with her, Charlie and Ethan wouldn't be spending even a minute out of his sight.

CHAPTER 7

THIRTY MINUTES into the session with Ethan that afternoon, Finn had to face some facts.

First, Charlie was fantastic with Ethan.

She wasn't truly tutoring at all, and he understood now why Mrs. Johnson wanted to bring her on full-time. She was like the freaking kid-whisperer.

He'd been watching them working from a chair with a direct line of sight, monitoring everything going on in the small library conference room. Although it really couldn't be called working. Finn had never heard his son laugh this much at a library. Ethan had brought a book like all the tutors in the past had wanted him to do. The first thing Charlie had asked was if he *wanted* to read it.

Ethan had glanced at Finn. Finn had just shrugged.

"No," Ethan had ventured. "I don't like to read. It's hard."

Instead of listing all the accolades of reading, Charlie had taken Ethan's book, put it on the carpet, and slid it with her foot all the way out of the room. Ethan had watched it go with wide eyes.

"No books?" he asked, looking back and forth between Finn and Charlie.

"Nope," she said. "Not today. Like you said, reading is hard sometimes."

Finn had taken his place outside the door and listened as Charlie got to know his son for the next ten minutes. She'd talked to him not like a teacher or a tutor, but as a person who found another person interesting. And Ethan had responded. His son, normally so silent around strangers, had opened up to Charlie about what he liked to do and play with.

Charlie had gotten some note cards and markers out of her bag, and the next thing Finn knew, she and Ethan were making their own book. One with just three sentences. But instead of trying to make him read it, she'd had him pick five words, and they'd drawn pictures above them. Pictures that would remind Ethan what the words meant.

By the time their session was nearing its end, Ethan had been able to read the sentences with no problems. Then they'd chosen a few others and drawn pictures with those. She was teaching him to associate the sounds of words with pictures and symbols rather than the letters that confused him so much with his dyslexia.

Moreover, she was making it fun. For both, it seemed. Charlie's smile was as big as Ethan's. She authentically loved what she was doing.

He'd been wrong in his judgment. She was talented and passionate in her chosen field. She seemed to have no hidden agenda whatsoever. That was the first fact he had to face, and he was more than happy to, especially since it meant Ethan might be able to get the help he needed.

The second was a little more disturbing.

There was something going on with Charlie that Finn didn't understand at all. The whole crazy incident at The Cactus Motel this morning had him studying her from the moment she'd shown up. He'd admit, he'd been looking for evidence of something bad. Drug use, maybe. Not narcotics, but she wouldn't have been the first rich girl to get caught up in the abuse of prescription drugs.

That would almost explain why she hadn't been able to get back to her house and ended up at the Cactus when she'd been so close. Users couldn't always help where they crashed. And if that was the case, at least she'd had the sense to get somewhere safe—safe being a hugely relative term in this case. The things that could happen to someone like Charlie in a place like the Cactus turned his blood cold.

But she hadn't shown any signs of drug use whatsoever while she'd been with Ethan. No decreased attention span, no problems thinking clearly. No lack of coordination. The opposite, in fact. She'd been engaging Ethan while jotting down notes for the entire hour they'd been together, splitting her focus without ever missing a beat.

And while he could admit she might have changed in the almost eight years since he'd really known her, Charlie had never been the type to use drugs. The woman had way too much internal zest for life to need any sort of chemical help.

God, he'd loved her for it.

And that was totally not where he was going to allow his thoughts to go.

So probably no drugs. He'd still put his ear to the ground for any rumors that the town's ex-princess was shopping for illegal substances, but Finn didn't think that was the case.

But even if she wasn't in trouble with anything illegal, there was other stuff going on with her that he couldn't ignore. Stuff most people wouldn't notice at all.

Like that nice silver BMW 3 Series she'd shown up in again today. Charlotte Devereux in a BMW was nothing new. She'd had one since before her sixteenth birthday, when her father had decreed it one of the highest-rated cars for safety on the planet. She had gotten a new, updated model every couple years. Finn had always been more of a four-wheel drive man himself, but he'd been impressed with the luxury of the BMW at eighteen.

The E92 coupe she was driving now was in good shape. When he and Ethan had met her out in the parking lot, none of the clutter she'd had in her car at The Eagle's Nest last week had been present. The stuff she'd brought out from the Cactus hadn't been in there either.

The BMW was clean and well-kept. It was also ten years old.

A ten-year-old BMW was still a nice vehicle. It just wasn't what a Devereux would drive.

If that was the only odd thing that caught his attention, Finn would've let it go. But it wasn't.

There were also the clothes she was wearing. Again, if he just glanced at the surface, nothing was wrong. Charlie's clothes were neat, clean, and stylish.

And not a single stitch of it was designer. Finn was no expert on designer clothes, but the same was not true for Charlotte. When she was a teenager, she and her mom had taken multiple trips to both the East and West Coasts to go shopping. Admittedly, that had been more Mrs. Devereux's passion than Charlie's, but Charlie had never shied away from wearing the bounty she and her mom found.

So, looking at Charlie now, seeing her wearing a blazer

he happened to know came from Target, since his sister, Wavy, had been admiring it a few weeks ago, once again Finn was once again at a loss. If Charlie wanted to shop at Target, there was nothing wrong with that. She just never really had.

He wouldn't have thought anything about it if he hadn't been looking at the situation as a whole: old car, off-the-rack clothes, seedy motel. What the hell was going on?

"Hey, Dad, we're done." Ethan came running out of the room, smiling.

"How'd it go, sport?" he asked as if he hadn't watched and listened to every single thing.

"I didn't have to read a book." Ethan's face was about to split in two, he was grinning so hard. "We made our own instead with symbols. That was much more fun."

He ruffled his son's hair. "Making your own sounds pretty awesome."

"And now I get to eat pie for lunch. You promised."

At least Ethan wasn't staring at him as if he expected Finn to go back on his word. That had been a pretty common problem when Finn had first gotten custody. Obviously, everyone tiny-Ethan had ever known had broken their word to him.

Finn would never be on that list. It was good to see that Ethan trusted him now without even thinking about it.

"You want to head on over to the Frontier? I'll be there in just a minute after I talk to Ms. Devereux."

"You can call her Charlie, Dad."

Finn smothered a laugh. "Okay, I will. Tell Wavy I'll be there in just a minute, and don't bother Trey if he has a lot to cook. He has other things to do besides sit around and talk to you."

His son flew out of the library as fast as his legs could

carry him. Finn grimaced. He was going to hear about that from Mr. Mazille, the librarian, who was at least 130 years old and had worked there since Finn was born.

Charlie was packing the rest of her items into her *faux leather* tote bag as Finn entered.

The smile she gave him, so bright, open, and honest, took his breath away.

This was the Charlie he remembered. Excited and full of life and passion. This was the sort of vibrancy she'd always exuded.

And he hadn't realized until right now it had been missing the last couple times he'd seen her. He'd been so caught up in his own anger, maybe even rightfully so, that he hadn't realized how subdued Charlie had been.

"Finn, I think it went really well. I know you were listening in, and maybe some of my methods seemed a little odd, like throwing the book out of the room—"

He held his hand up to stop her. "Look, I learned very early in my Army career not to question methods if they get results. Hell, even if you were only doing it for the shock factor, it seemed to work."

She shrugged. "Sometimes it's better to just leave behind the status quo. Start with the unexpected. Part of Ethan's problem now is not just his dyslexia or any other learning challenges, it's his negative views of reading and his own abilities."

He rubbed the back of his neck. "Yes, as he's getting older he realizes he's different from the other kids."

"I'll talk to Mrs. Johnson and write up my suggestions, but truly, I don't think there's any reason why, with a few out-of-the-box coping mechanisms and some hard work, he can't be reading at his normal grade level by the end of the next school year."

Finn closed his eyes, relief flooding his system. He wasn't sure he'd ever heard such good news.

Charlie stood and slipped the strap of her tote bag over her shoulder. "It doesn't have to be me who works with him," she added softly. "I know you were uncomfortable with me as his tutor. Honestly, anybody schooled in this methodology could work with Ethan successfully."

"You don't want to work with him?"

She shifted from one foot to the other, her gaze straying toward the table. "I'm just saying I understand if you want that. But," she cleared her throat, "if you wouldn't mind letting Mrs. Johnson know that it isn't a professional issue you have with me, that would be helpful. Um, that sort of keeps me from getting other tutoring jobs."

And just like that all the light and passion he'd seen on her face a few minutes ago was gone. It was replaced by something he'd never seen on Charlotte Devereux's features before, especially not in a situation like this.

Defeat.

Even after everything, he couldn't stand the thought.

"No," he said. "I didn't mean to insinuate I had any professional problems with you before. I would've talked to her immediately if I'd known it was keeping you from getting jobs."

"Thanks." She still wasn't looking him in the eye.

"But I would like you to continue working with Ethan if you have time in your schedule. I've never seen him respond so well. Usually it's like pulling teeth."

Now she looked up. "Really? That'd be great because I have some ideas. He loves building and creating with his hands." She rolled her eyes. "Sound like anyone you know?"

He gave her a half smile. "That's what I'm afraid of. I was never the best student either."

"You're plenty smart. You were just never interested in academics. Ethan is too. As soon as we're able to give him coping strategies to make reading easier, he'll be fine. He may still be like you and not want to have anything to do with school, but not because it's too difficult."

"You have no idea how relieved I am to hear that. Ethan has. . .struggled. He had difficulties early in his life."

He didn't want to go into the situation surrounding Ethan's birth and first few years. Charlie had made it clear years ago he wasn't good enough for her; that would just confirm it.

When he didn't say more, she shifted her tote on her shoulder. "Well, I definitely think he's got a bright future ahead of him. So, you can call Mrs. Johnson and we can schedule some sessions. I would suggest two to three times a week until school starts. Give us as big of a jump as we can get. I'll see you later."

He grabbed her arm before she could move any farther. Before he could think better of it. "Have lunch with us. My treat."

God knew she looked like she could use a full meal.

He studied her closer, another piece of the puzzle joining the others. She looked like she needed a *dozen* full meals. She'd always been tiny, but curvy. Now she was tiny and almost. . . fragile.

"Finn." She was preparing to say no; he could tell by her tone.

"You don't have to eat pie for lunch if you don't want to. That's completely optional. You've got to eat, so it might as well be on my dime. I'm sure Wavy would like to see you."

She studied his face for a long moment. He didn't know what she was looking for. Hell, he didn't know what *he* was with this invitation.

This was probably a bad idea.

Probably? Being anywhere around her was a bad idea. So why was he trying to talk her into it?

"Okay," she breathed.

He wasn't sure if it was relief or dread that filled him up.

CHAPTER 8

THIS WAS SUCH A BAD IDEA.

She couldn't think of a way to refuse without being rude. And who was she kidding? She'd rather be with him than anywhere else in the world anyway.

Even if those green eyes of his were too damn perceptive.

Since she'd already cleaned the club, she didn't have to be anywhere until her shift later. And Finn was right. She had to eat.

Normally she made do with a loaf of bread and peanut butter for one or two meals a day. The latter gave her some protein, and she bought fresh fruits and vegetables when she could.

All the while reminding herself, again, that this wasn't forever.

But seriously, the thought of a huge burger and fries, and a slice of that pie that Ethan would be eating as his entire meal? Heaven.

So, she'd said okay, despite her better judgment.

They walked the short distance to the diner —after Mr. Mazille caught them first to discuss the importance of instilling respect for the library in Ethan. Finn held the door open for her and his hand fell to the small of her back, like it was just muscle memory for them.

She knew the exact moment he realized it as he snatched his hand away.

And still they found themselves heading toward the corner booth. The one where they'd always sat in high school. Ethan was already at the bar talking to Trey and his Aunt Wavy, a waitress here. Several people said hello to Finn, some recognizing her, others not.

Wavy came over to talk to them as soon as they were seated. "Hey, big bro." She turned to Charlie. "And hey to you too, Charlie. Good to see you. Ethan won't shut up about his teacher who threw the book out of the room. I think you're his hero."

Charlie winced. "I didn't actually *throw* it. I just slid it out the door."

Wavy laughed. "Well, in Ethan's eyes, anybody who gets rid of books is a keeper."

"They weren't actually. They just made their own," Finn said. "It was pretty brilliant. Ethan was reading without getting all caught up in the fact that he was."

"Are you a teacher or something?" Wavy asked. "Honestly, I lost track of you after. . ." They all looked awkwardly at one another as Wavy trailed off.

"After I begged her, in front of the entire town, not to marry Brandon Kempsley and she did anyway?" Finn raised an eyebrow. "Is that what you mean, Wavy?"

Wavy punched her brother in the shoulder. "What I was going to say was after she got married and moved away, jackass."

"Yeah, I got my master's in special education, with a particular focus on reading disabilities." Charlie ignored the part about Brandon and her wedding. Because what could she say? It was nothing but true, even if Finn didn't know her reasoning behind it.

"So, are you working for Teton County?" Wavy asked. "Sounds like you're pretty good at your job."

"No, nothing full-time right now. I'm just doing tutoring a few hours a week."

Although she was facing Wavy, she could feel Finn's eyes on her as he weighed her statement. She didn't dare look at him.

"Oh man." Wavy sighed. "It must be so nice to just work a few hours a week and still have enough money to live."

Hysterical laughter bubbled up inside her. Between the tutoring session and this meal, this was the longest she'd sat down in over a week.

"I heard you and Brandon divorced and he moved away," Wavy continued.

"Yeah. We. . .separated a little over four years ago." She totally did not want to go into this, so she changed the subject. "You still painting, Wavy?"

Both Finn and his sister looked surprised at the question.

"Oh, I'm sorry," she backpedaled. "Was I not supposed to ask about that?"

Finn shook his head. "No, I'm just surprised you remember."

She remembered everything. He had no idea how the thought of him, of what their life could have been, had kept her going for so many years. Wavy would've been her sister-in-law. Of course she recalled the younger woman painted. But Charlie just shrugged.

"Yeah, I still love it," Waverly said. "I've got my own place now and turned the garage into a sort of studio. But the Frontier remains my primary means of income, since, you know, gotta pay the bills."

Charlie nodded. "I understand that."

Wavy didn't argue, but her look said she didn't think Charlie could. And why shouldn't Wavy feel that way? As far as anybody knew, Charlie had grown up with money and then married more. She smiled weakly and shrugged again.

She expected some sort of scoff from Finn too. He wouldn't be as silent and polite about it as his sister. But he remained quiet, studying her with those eagle eyes from across the booth.

Wavy took their order. Charlie got the burger she'd been fantasizing about. Finn just told her to have Trey surprise him. Wavy rolled her eyes. Obviously, this wasn't anything new.

Wavy left and she and Finn stared at each other across the table.

"We spent a lot of hours here," he finally said.

She smiled. "Actually, for most of that time, I think I was sitting next to you, rather than across from you."

She'd give anything to be able to do that now. To have his big body corner hers in the booth. To constantly have his arm around her, when it wasn't misbehaving up her thigh.

Finn wasn't smiling. He obviously wasn't remembering the same way she was, or if so, it didn't resurrect the same sort of feelings. She looked away from those emerald eyes.

He still hated her.

"This was a mistake," she murmured. Delicious

hamburger or not, she didn't know if she could sit here with all the weight bearing down on them. She began to slide out of the booth.

His hand shot out and touched her wrist before she could. She'd forgotten how fast he could move when he wanted to.

"You and I being within a fifty-foot radius of one another may very well be a mistake," he said. "But you are not leaving without eating."

He sat there, staring at her with one black eyebrow raised, as if daring her to argue. Before she could even decide if she was going to or not, another man, just as big and muscular as Finn but with lighter hair, slid in next to her.

"Good timing, Aiden," Finn said. "I think she was just about to make a run for it."

Aiden grinned and held out his hand for her to shake. "In my book that just shows you have good taste, if you're trying to escape from Bollinger. I'm Aiden Teague. I have the dubious honor of being one of his partners at Linear Tactical."

"Charlie Devereux. Linear Tactical? I don't think I know what that is." Aiden didn't let go of her hand.

Finn leaned back in his seat. "It's the business Zac, Aiden, and a few of our Army buddies, and myself started when we got out. We do different types of survival intelligence training for anybody who wants to learn. Self-defense, wilderness survival, situational awareness, weapons instruction. That sort of stuff." He narrowed his eyes at Aiden. "You can stop groping her now."

Aiden's thumb continued to rub along the top of her hand. "I've lived in this one-horse town for nearly four years now and know I would recall meeting you if we had before."

"Charlie is Ethan's tutor," Finn said before she could respond. "The one I was telling you about."

Awareness dawned in Aiden's striking hazel eyes. His hand slid gently off hers. "I see."

And evidently what he saw, or had heard from Finn, wasn't good. Or it at least put her in the not-worthy-of-being-flirted-with category.

"But Charlie and Ethan met today," Finn continued. "And it went very well. Charlie is going to meet with him a few times each week until school starts."

"Great." Aiden's smile was in no way flirtatious now, just friendly. "I love that kid and want to see him do well."

"I think he'll do great with the right tools," she said.

Wavy brought their food over and took Aiden's order.

"I got a call from Major Pinnock today," Aiden said as he stole one of Finn's fries, part of the fish and chips plate Trey had chosen for him. "He's got some more details on that issue he was discussing with us."

"Have things escalated?" Finn asked.

She bit into her hamburger and couldn't stop the moan that fell from her lips. God, it had been so long since she had eaten something this good. Almost everything she put into her body for the past two years had been purchased either because of its low cost or nutritional value. Taste had not been a factor.

Both men turned to stare at her.

"Good burger?" Finn's voice was a little strained.

"Sorry," she muttered. Most people were not going to understand how she found a burger almost orgasmic. "Do you guys need me to sit somewhere else so you don't have to talk in code?"

"It's not code." Finn stabbed at Aiden's hand with his fork as he tried to steal another french fry. "On rare occasions Linear Tactical helps out law enforcement. Evidently somebody is trying to sell state secrets from a nearby military base and they want our assistance."

And knowing Finn and his best friend, Zac, they loved it, the potential danger, being the heroes. It was why Finn had gone into the Army to start with. Aiden was probably just as crazy. She wasn't surprised to hear that they had started some sort of superhero school.

She tuned them out as they discussed details. She focused instead on every bite of her burger, not wanting to miss one moment of this meal. Who knew when she'd get another like it?

It would probably be excessive to lick the plate when she was done. She needed to remember that. And more importantly, could she fit a piece of pie in her belly?

It was nice, eating here like a normal person rather than in her car or at the back room in the club, having two handsome men talk shop in low voices while she half listened.

She took the last bite of the burger and dipped a fry in ketchup. It might be nice, but it wasn't real. She would do her best to remember that.

But Finn had agreed to let her work with Ethan some more. She glanced over her shoulder to where the little boy was sitting at the bar, talking to his aunt and the cook. She had so many ideas about how to help him. She'd spent her entire master's thesis developing a method of shapes and codes to help children who suffered from dyslexia and other reading difficulties. Ethan's love of shapes and blocks already made him a perfect candidate.

Her time with him would help balance out all the soulsucking of everything else. The jobs. The knowledge that her father didn't have long to live. That the man she'd been in love with her whole life—even when she'd been married to someone else—hated her, or at best barely tolerated her.

She wasn't going to fool herself into thinking there would be more lunches like this.

It was just one more thing she would learn to live without.

Finn stood as Aiden scooted out of the booth and Charlie excused herself to go to the bathroom. They both watched her walk across the diner.

"Christ, Finn. I hope you're taking that woman out to get more food sometime soon. Better than what they have here, if that's the sound she makes biting into something she likes."

The impression of a zipper was molded onto certain parts of his body after that sound had escaped Charlie's lips. He dropped back down into the booth with a thud. "Yeah, no kidding."

"I'm going to assume you've only heard fifty percent of what I said." Aiden chuckled.

Finn tore his gaze away from Charlie's retreating form. "Fifty may be a little generous."

"So that's Charlotte, the tutor you weren't going to let anywhere near your son."

Finn shrugged. "I talked to his teacher and she convinced me to give Charlie a chance."

"She goes by Charlie?"

Finn couldn't help but smile. "Yeah. I gave her the nickname in high school to try to piss her off. But she loved it. And hell, she's always been more of a Charlie than a Charlotte." That actually wasn't true. She'd been a perfect blend of both: the rich, pampered Charlotte and the feisty, gutsy Charlie who never backed down from a dare.

Who was she now?

That was it, wasn't it? Finn couldn't seem to find the old Charlotte *or* Charlie in the woman he was facing today. But damn it, he couldn't let this be his problem. Not again.

Charlie, Charlotte, both could take care of herself. She'd never needed him.

He looked up at Aiden. "Yeah, so tell me what Pinnock said again. I'm really listening this time." They hadn't wanted to go into much detail in front of Charlie.

"Henry was able to set up a way in for me. Got me on Cline's radar, the guy shopping around info on the holes in NORAD's air defense. Henry is calling the mission Project Sparrow."

"You're going undercover?"

Aiden shrugged. "I'm not as well known around here as you and Zac. Anybody who knows the two of you would know Teton County's golden boys are never going to end up on the wrong side of the law. But me? I'm new. A bit more of an unknown factor."

"You do know you're not a cop, right? You've got no jurisdiction, no real backup. You can't arrest anyone. You'll be completely on your own."

Aiden nodded. "I'm just gathering information."

Which had always been Aiden's forte. In the Army, he'd always been the man sent in to gather intel. He could speak at least five languages; Finn had lost count of the actual number. And even more, he had the uncanny ability to fit in to situations, to be the person the target needed him to be. He could become invisible and indispensable at the same time.

He could've made a killing in Hollywood, the way he played so many different roles.

"Just be careful."

Aiden rolled his eyes. "Yes, Mom."

Finn's attention was drawn back to Charlie as she made her way out of the restroom. Multiple people stopped her along the way to say hello.

Then they all looked over at him, as if afraid he might feel betrayed. Charlie saw it too and winced. It was a small town with a long memory. No one was going to be quick to forget that the two of them had once been one of the town's most passionate couples. And that she'd married someone else without much warning and despite Finn's best attempt to convince her otherwise.

Let Aiden go play undercover superhero.

It would take all sorts of miracles for Finn to get out of his own situation unscathed.

CHAPTER 9

THE MUSIC WAS STILL as loud, the hands were still as gropey, and the looks at her breasts were still as leery, but two weeks later Charlie found she could get through her shift at The Silver Palace with a smile.

Okay, maybe not a smile, but at least without a grimace.

Things were finally, *finally* looking up. Yes, she was still exhausted. Yes, she was still working almost a hundred hours a week between all her various jobs. But she had been able to make this month's payment for Dad's treatment center, even with the added costs from his fall and Mama staying with him what ended up being three nights rather than two.

Charlie had gotten into a pattern, so cleaning was something she could do almost remotely. All she had to do was show up and her body took over. The vacuum didn't care if she was eighty percent asleep as she used it. And Mack had been pleased with her work, or at least at the amount of money he was saving, so he'd offered her more hours.

Most importantly, she'd had seven different tutoring

jobs in the last two weeks—four with Ethan and three with other families. It was going so well it almost made her giddy. Already she could see a true change in Ethan. His attitude toward reading and his own abilities had completely shifted. The kid was so smart. At first, she'd helped him develop the different codes and patterns to use to replace sight words for reading. Now his brain could visualize an image rather than the letters that were so confusing to him.

Once he'd understood the concept, Ethan had run with it. The last time they'd met two days ago, he'd written an entire short book by himself with his different codes and patterns.

Maybe nobody else could read it, but the important thing was, Ethan could. In essence it was a sort of hieroglyphics, patterns and shapes on paper forming a method of written communication easier for his brain to understand.

Admittedly, they were still a long way off from him being able to read regular books at grade level, but it was a start. And it was an educational method—at least the part about writing their own books—that Charlie had developed for her master's thesis. She'd studied the tie between educational ownership/confidence and reading ability, the concept that a child was more likely to want to read something they'd written and developed themselves. Once they had, their confidence would improve, and therefore their reading ability would also.

What she'd explored in theory in her master's thesis was now being proven correct in practice.

It was the most wonderful feeling in the world.

"You've got really pretty titties. You should be a dancer." A drunken voice pulled her out of her thoughts.

All Charlie had to do was not kill anybody and everything would be all right. A frat boy was resting his chin on his arms at the bar. She hoped the bouncer checked his ID at the door because he barely looked twenty-one. "Well, sweetheart, somebody has to serve the drinks. What can I get you?"

The kid's gaze didn't move from her breasts. "DVR."

Double vodka Red Bull. Great. Do stupid things faster.

She made the beverage before moving to the station printer, which was spitting out another drink order from a waitress. It was a Tuesday night and shouldn't be this busy, but April, the third bartender, hadn't shown up for her shift again. Heather had, but two of her three kids were sick, and she'd spent half the night on the phone with the babysitter.

Busy was good, it meant more tips, but so busy you couldn't get orders out meant watching those tips disappear. It was frustrating for everyone on all levels.

"Charlie, I'm going to have to leave," Heather said around ten. "Both my kids are throwing up and the babysitter refuses to stay. I've called everyone I know, including my miserable ex. Nobody is available."

They were pouring drinks as they talked. Charlie knew Heather wasn't faking. Like her, Heather would never leave when it was so busy. There was too much potential for making tips.

"Mack is going to kill me. I told him I could come in, and now he's going to get a ton of complaints."

"It's not your fault. April is the one who didn't show up for her shift. I'm sure she's already fired." Which wasn't going to help them now.

Heather looked over at Charlie, tears in her eyes. "You're never going to be able to handle this on your own. Plus, Rocco has a VIP group in the back. Nobody's supposed to go in there, but it will need to be cleaned at the end of the night. They prepaid for everything."

Charlie slid a beer to a guy at the end of the bar without even looking at him. "I know you wouldn't leave me if you had any other choice. Not to mention it's not some national crisis if people need to wait a few extra minutes for some drinks. Your kids are more important. They need their mom."

It was clear Heather was thankful Charlie understood. And she did. But an hour later, Charlie was wishing *she* was the one vomiting so she wouldn't have to deal with all the angry customers, waitresses, and dancers. Everyone was pissed, and it was all directed at Charlie.

She only had two goddamn hands.

"Excuse me, I was supposed to talk to someone named Charlie about possibly tending bar here. Mack said Tuesday was a good night to come by." The voice of the tall, slender woman at the end of the bar was so quiet Charlie almost didn't hear her when she walked by. She totally didn't have time for this.

"Normally it would be, but not tonight. Sorry." Charlie spared a glance from the tray of drinks she was preparing.

Something desperate flew through the woman's big gray eyes before she blinked it away. "I understand. Thanks for your time," the woman said just as quietly as she had the first time. She turned away.

Charlie rubbed an exhausted hand across her forehead. Damn it, she understood that look. Hell, if she was going to turn someone away who had it in their eyes.

"Hey!" she called out to the woman, who turned back with something akin to fear in her eyes. "You ever bartended before?"

The woman shook her head no.

Great. Damn Mack for not vetting potential employees before sending them to her.

"Can you start tonight?" Charlie asked. "Like right now?"

The woman nodded. Charlie reached into a cabinet underneath the register and pulled out one of the obnoxious Silver Palace mesh tank tops. She threw it at the woman.

"Put this on. We'll keep you on simple stuff tonight." She could at least pour beer and make easy cocktails. "What's your name?"

"Jordan Reiss."

Somebody behind Charlie started clamoring for another drink, but she held up a finger for them to wait. She recognized the name right away.

"I thought you were in prison."

Something passed through those gray eyes again. "I'm out as of last week. Does this mean I'm not hired?"

Jordan had gone to prison for manslaughter when she was eighteen. She'd fallen asleep behind the wheel and killed a woman and her baby. Not just any though, Becky and Micah Mackay, family of Zac, Oak Creek legend and Finn's best friend.

Six years later Jordan was just now getting paroled. Everybody in a three-county radius knew who she was. And they knew her sentencing had been so harsh—even though she'd had no prior arrests, nor had she ever been in any trouble with the law before—because of her father, Michael Reiss.

The man who had swindled half of Oak Creek out of their retirement accounts, then skipped town.

"I'm not going to steal from you, if that's what you're worried about," Jordan said. "I just need a job. I'm sorry for anything my dad did to you or your family. I had no part in that."

It was obviously a line she was used to repeating.

She might be the only woman from Oak Creek more hated than Charlie.

"Your dad didn't get anything from my family. We had our own financial advisors." Not that they'd done much good. Look at Charlie now.

Understanding dawned in Jordan's eyes. "You're Charlotte Devereux."

"Charlie. Go get changed. We've got work to do."

CHAPTER 10

CHARLIE HONESTLY DIDN'T KNOW how she would've made it through her shift without Jordan. At best, it would've ended with everyone unhappy. At worst, Charlie would've taken Jordan's place in prison.

The younger woman didn't say a lot, and obviously didn't know much about bartending, but she was a hard worker and Charlie would be glad to have her on any shift. She easily recognized the look on Jordan's face when the woman counted her tips at the end of the night.

The closing of eyes in relief and the silent prayer of gratitude. The knowledge that she was, in fact, going to be able to survive.

Charlie had been there.

Charlie didn't know what exactly was going on with Jordan—and honestly had so much to deal with in her own life that she really couldn't bring herself to care—but she was glad the woman at least now had a way of providing for herself.

Jordan helped with the closing chores and promised to

be back the next night. The waitresses were all gone, and the dancers were filing out one by one when Charlie remembered Rocco's VIP room still needed to be cleaned. She'd muttered a curse under her breath, grabbed a tray and headed there.

The Silver Palace's back area was immense, almost as large as the front section of the club. The rooms were all interconnected and each had multiple doors. There was a main conference-style room—although why there was a need to do legitimate business at a gentlemen's club, Charlie would never understand—and then other individual rooms used for private dancing. They were a pain in the ass to clean, but their interconnectivity made the back scenario safer for dancers.

The only way to be completely private back here was to buy out all the rooms. That rarely happened because of the price. But evidently that hadn't been a concern for Rocco and his "business" friends.

Charlie sighed and rubbed the back of her neck as she walked into the main room. Glasses and bottles were everywhere, since, like Heather had told her, they'd prepaid for everything and hadn't wanted service from any bartenders all evening. Good thing, since Charlie wouldn't have been able to give the VIPs much attention anyway.

She was stacking empty glassware on her tray when she saw a man's suit jacket hanging on the back of a chair. She reached over and picked it up. She would put it by the bar, because surely someone would come back in the next couple days to get it.

A piece of paper fell out of the pocket. She was putting it back when the series of symbols and numbers caught her attention, making her smile. They looked like the code she was developing with Ethan.

In Ethan language, this particular code said: *Blue baby eat just when my old dog sleep.*

The sentence didn't make any sense, of course. Each child she worked with assigned their own words to symbols. She just remembered Ethan's because she'd spent the most time with him. *Blue baby eat just when my old dog sleep.* All those words were part of the Dolch list, a list of words people who suffered from dyslexia were most likely to struggle with. Hopefully with this new method, that wouldn't be true for long—

"What the fuck are you doing?"

The open door behind her and the angry question caught her by surprise. She stuffed the paper back in the pocket and dropped the jacket over the chair again.

She turned to face the voice, dread pooling in her belly when three men walked out of the private room. One was Rocco; the others she didn't recognize at all. At least one more stayed farther back in the darkness of the other room. She couldn't make out any of his features.

"Rocco told us there would be no interruptions," said a man big enough to crush her with his bare hands. He looked angry. All of them did.

And they had guns. One—the biggest hulk—had gotten his out of the holster and was holding it in his hand. At least he wasn't pointing it at her.

Yet.

Charlie whirled back to the table and began stacking glassware again. These men were dangerous. She had no doubt about it. She'd walked in on some sort of business, all right, but not the legal kind.

And they were pissed she was here.

Not looking at them was probably her best bet. "I'm sorry. I thought these rooms were already empty and just needed to be cleaned. I'll leave now." She made a beeline for the door.

She'd almost made it when the big man spoke again. "Wait."

Shit.

She stopped but didn't turn around. Honestly, whatever business these guys were doing, she didn't care. Probably drugs. She didn't condone it, but she had her own problems. Even if they were selling back here, she wasn't going to say anything since telling the police would get this place shut down. She needed this job. She just wanted to get out of here and leave them to whatever they were doing.

But promising her silence would do nothing but get her killed.

Think, Charlie.

All the men were watching her carefully, even the shorter one staying farther in the dark. She tried not to let her gaze rest on any of them, choosing instead to look at the floor.

Promising to forget anything she saw here wasn't going to help her, but maybe making them think she was too stupid to understand anything she saw might work.

Plus, besides a crap-ton of empty bottles and some weird figures on a piece of paper that didn't mean anything to her outside of tutoring, what had she seen? What did she know? Nothing.

"He-eyyyyy." She drew out the vowel like she was talking to a group of friends. "I really didn't mean to interrupt. I thought everyone was gone. But you guys just take your time, I have plenty of other work to do. I'll just finish cleaning after you're gone." Praying, she turned back toward the door again.

"Did we say you could leave?"

Shit. Shit.

She closed her eyes and took a breath, then opened them and turned back around, still keeping her gaze no higher than their waists. "Your bottles are empty. Did you need some more? I mean, as long as there's a little extra tip in it for me, I don't mind how long you guys stay." She kept the bright smile and simpleton tone.

She dared to glance at their faces. The men were all looking at each other now, obviously trying to gauge what sort of a threat she was, if any. The big man took a step back, obviously having been called by the man still in the dark room. Then he stepped out.

"What were you doing with this jacket?"

She laughed, beyond thankful when it came out sounding light rather than hysterical. "I thought someone had left it. I was going to put it behind the bar. I was sort of hoping for a reward for keeping it nice and clean, you know?" She wrinkled her nose and gave them a pout.

Money-hungry, not-real-bright bartender. Money-hungry, not-real-bright bartender. It may be the role that saved her life.

The much bigger guy with the gun looked over at the smaller one in the shadows. Charlie couldn't tell if he was buying her story or not.

She didn't want to die here.

She was saved by Jade—Charlie's least favorite dancer, but who cared?—coming out of the back room. She was grinning slyly, high, drunk, or both.

Charlie didn't even want to know what Jade had been doing with or for the men. She suspected it was much more than merely dancing, especially given the huge wad of cash in her hand. Charlie just wanted to use the woman as an excuse to get out of here.

"Hey, Jade!" She kept her voice as bright as possible as she waved enthusiastically to the other woman, whose real name she didn't even know. "It's been so crazy busy tonight, hasn't it? My feet are killing me. Can't believe it's just a Tuesday."

Jade nodded as she walked across the room, looking a little confused, probably because she and Charlie had never spoken this much to each other in the fourteen months Charlie had been working here.

"Um. Yeah, busy," the other woman finally said.

As Jade came by on her way to the door, Charlie turned and linked their arms. Jade gave her another weird look but thankfully didn't pull away. "Yeah, I've still got so much work to do. Heather's kids were vomiting so she had to leave, and April didn't show up for her shift, *again*. Probably broke up with that no-good boyfriend of hers. You know how they're always on-again, off-again."

Charlie blabbered on as they walked out the door, waiting in fear for the men to call her back. But they didn't. Only when the door closed behind them did she dare stop talking. It was all she could do to keep from collapsing.

"You okay?" Jade asked. "You're acting a little weird."

"Are *you*?" Her eyes flew over Jade, looking for any sign of abuse on her.

But Jade just held up her money and smiled. "More than. Like you said, it was crazy busy tonight." She turned and made her way toward the dressing room.

Charlie wanted to run, just sprint out the door and go straight to the police. But what would she tell them? That there had been men in a strip club and they'd been upset she'd barged in on their private room after they'd paid to have the entire place to themselves? That she suspected foul play even though there was not one bit of evidence of it? Yeah, they had guns. But this was Wyoming. A lot of people did.

And damn it. She needed this job. She hadn't really seen anything, so she didn't need to report anything. If the men came through the front of the building to exit, she just needed to convince them of that too.

Money-hungry, not-real-bright bartender.

She just needed to act like everything was normal. If she didn't freak out, they would just leave, and this would all blow over.

Every minute that passed when the men didn't call her back into the room, she relaxed a little more. The only thing she had to make sure of was that she wasn't left alone with them. Not having any witnesses around might tempt them beyond measure.

She scrubbed behind the bar, cleaned all the cabinets. Stuff she normally never would've done at the end of a backbreaking shift, but she was afraid to leave. *Just act normal.*

A few minutes later, Paul, one of the club's bouncers, wandered over to the bar. Charlie didn't know him very well, any of the bouncers honestly. She couldn't remember a time he'd actually come over and tried to talk to her. As a matter of fact, the only person he'd ever seemed tight with was Jade.

"It's getting late. Is that group in the back finished?" They sometimes had some that paid to stay past closing, so it wasn't unheard of.

Charlie kept wiping down the cabinet she was cleaning. "I hope so. I wasn't the one who took the actual booking, so I'm honestly not sure."

"But you went back and talked to them, right? What's going on? What were they doing?"

Why on this night had he decided to be so chatty? And to ask what they were doing?

Money-hungry, not-real-bright bartender.

She rolled her eyes. "I totally wasn't paying any attention to them. I just ran back there to grab empty glasses, so I could run them through the dishwasher. Jade was just finishing dancing so hopefully they're almost done. I just want to get my tips and go, you know?"

Paul looked her over for a second, then nodded. She went back to her faux cleaning and he returned to looming by the entrance.

But when she looked over at him a few minutes later, he wasn't there. He was quietly entering the back rooms. Was he kicking them out? That wouldn't be right. Bouncers never talked directly to customers, and they definitely wouldn't to VIPs. A bartender, or Mack himself, if he was here, would inform the group it was time to leave.

Was Paul reporting to the guys in the back? Damn it, did she need to run? Because as much as she wanted this job, nothing was worth her life.

Or was she just being completely paranoid?

The door was cracked. She walked over so she could eavesdrop. She'd rather be paranoid than dead.

". . . just wants to take her tips and go home. I don't think anything drastic is necessary. She's worked at the bar for a long time, but you can tell, she's just like the rest of the girls. Not so smart. Just looking to make money."

It was Rocco talking.

"I don't like loose ends, Rocco," the voice—someone else, not the big guy—responded. "She had my jacket. Knows our faces."

"But Paul said she didn't say anything suspicious. She

just thinks we're a group of friends or business acquaintances, like any that comes back here."

Charlie held her breath, waiting for a response. Should she run now while no one was around? If she did, that would certainly convince them she was a threat.

And where would she go?

Finn. He would be her only option. But how could she do that? How could she lay this potential danger at his doorstep? What about Ethan? They might hurt the boy too.

"Fine." The annoyance in the small man's tone was clear. "We do nothing about the bartender. . ."

Charlie didn't wait to hear the rest. She moved from the door, crossing back to the bar as quickly as possible. Paul was already coming out by the time she made it there.

"They almost done?" she asked.

"Yes. I'll be escorting them out the back door."

Thank God. Thank God. Thank God. "Okay, I'll be in there to clean once they're gone."

She ducked into the dishwasher room, leaning against the wall and taking deep breaths. She stayed in there a full fifteen minutes until she was sure they were gone. She'd just leave the cleaning for tomorrow when she came back to do daytime janitor duties. She wanted to get out of here while there were still other people around.

She had the keys to the building since she was often the last one out, and of course, the first in. Being here alone had never bothered her—she usually enjoyed it. But not tonight. She did not want to be alone in The Silver Palace tonight.

She exited the building with the last two dancers and Paul, who had returned after escorting his VIP criminal buddies out. She locked the back door behind her, the other two women chatting about their upcoming shift the next night, then glanced around to make sure no one suspicious was in the parking lot. Nothing.

As a matter of fact, a police cruiser was pulling in. Charlie breathed a sigh of relief and waved to the dancers as they called out their goodbyes. She glanced at Paul to see if he was concerned, but he wasn't even paying attention to the cop car. So evidently whatever was happening in the back couldn't be too bad.

Maybe Charlie was just paranoid.

It wasn't unusual for the police to do a drive-by here around closing time, just to make sure everyone was safe, although it tended to be closer to when the customers were leaving. But she'd never been so relieved to see the police in her life. She gave the officer a wave and then walked to her car.

She was just getting in when the officer pulled next to her and rolled down his window.

"Everything okay here?" he asked.

"Yes, Officer. Just had some late customers so I'm finishing my shift."

He nodded. "Late customers, that's got to be frustrating when you're trying to wrap up a long day, or night, as it is."

She gave him a tight smile. "Yeah, I guess some people don't have much respect for other people's time."

"Oh yeah? These late customers, you have any problems with them? They cause you trouble or anything like that?" The officer was sitting far enough back in his car that she couldn't get a clear look at him. Why was he asking her this? The police had never stopped to talk in the past when they'd made their late-night sweep.

Why was he talking to her tonight? It was just like Paul.

Suddenly she knew. It was *exactly* like Paul. The man was double-checking to make sure she didn't really know or suspect anything. Who better to confess a problem to than a police officer who just happened to be at the right place at the right time?

"Because you know if you ever saw anything suspicious," the policeman continued, "you could always let our office know. I would be more than happy to look into anything for you."

Money-hungry, not-real-bright bartender.

"Oh well, there were a couple guys who kept grabbing my ass tonight." She giggled, a sound obviously forced even to her ears, but the officer didn't know better. "But they left me a good tip, so I guess it's okay. But besides that, just another day at the office."

The officer didn't say anything for a long moment, so she smiled at him again. "Thanks for driving by and making sure we all get out to our cars safely. That's sweet of you."

He nodded. "Just part of the job. Have a good night."

Charlie wanted to have a breakdown right then, but she had to get out of here. Whoever this group was, they had enough money and power to keep at least one officer on their payroll.

She started her car and drove as calmly as she could out of the parking lot. Was she safe? After getting both Paul and the policeman to confirm she didn't have any suspicions, would they leave her alone?

She hadn't planned to stay at the Cactus tonight, even though she had a tutoring appointment tomorrow with Ethan and could really use a shower. But now she would have to. There was no way she'd be able to sleep otherwise.

But hours later, even with all her exhaustion and a locked motel door with a chair wedged under the knob between her and the outside world, she was wide awake.

CHAPTER 11

"I DON'T KNOW, Dad. I really want the Captain America kit, but the *Millennium Falcon* is the best ship in the world. It made the Kessel Run in less than twelve parsecs."

Ethan had earned a Lego kit as his reward for doing so well in his tutoring. Who knew picking one would be such a monumental decision?

"I'll only buy you the *Millennium Falcon* if you can repeat the most important rule back to me," Finn said.

"Han shot first." Ethan rolled his little eyes. "Everybody knows that."

Finn ruffled his son's hair. "Everybody *doesn't* know that. That's the problem with the world today."

Ethan's voice got serious. "I don't want you to be upset about this, Dad, but I'm leaning toward the superhero set." Ethan glanced up at him and patted his arm. "But don't worry, there's always Christmas."

"I'll try to keep my disappointment in check."

Finn was excited that he could take his son to tutoring

without it being a huge battle. Now when Ethan looked at a book, he didn't break out in hives. Yes, his best friend was still a four-year-old, and he liked hanging out with her more than anything, but Finn would tackle one thing at a time.

Ethan's sessions with Charlie had continued to get better. The things they were doing with the symbols and numbers Finn honestly didn't understand at all, but he was willing to take a leap of faith. Mostly they were still "writing" their own books, but he'd seen how Charlie had slipped in others. She'd shown how the symbols and codes could be transferred from what they wrote to other books.

Ethan hadn't liked it at first, but Charlie was patient and kept showing him how the methods he'd learned translated to all sorts of written words. Basically, Ethan was replacing words, particularly the ones that gave him the most trouble, with numbers and symbols. It was a different way to memorize sight words.

Charlie had been quick to explain to Finn that she wasn't really teaching Ethan reading skills, but coping skills. She explained it as if she were afraid Finn might attack her methodology.

Coping skills he understood far better than he'd probably understand any academic mumbo-jumbo. And hell, he didn't care what she called it if her methods got results.

He still hadn't figured out exactly what was going on with Charlie herself. He'd been careful to keep away from The Cactus Motel. He told himself it was none of his business what she was doing there so long as her actions didn't negatively affect his son, which was true. It was none of his business that every time they had an appointment, she had darker circles under her eyes and continued to be way too thin, which was also true.

He'd tried to get her to join them for another meal but

hadn't pushed when she'd said no. Because he didn't care.

That, whether he liked it or not, was false.

He spotted Charlie's BMW in the parking lot of the library and realized a moment later that she was asleep inside the car. Why did that concern him so much? He'd taken a nap in his Jeep from time to time. Everybody had.

"Hey, sport, why don't you go inside, work on some of the stuff Charlie gave you, okay? We'll be right in. And please don't run. I don't want another two-hour lecture from Mr. Mazille."

Ethan grinned and took off running. Finn sighed. Lecture number 382 coming his way.

He walked over to Charlie's car, waiting to see if she would wake up. Cat-napping people could usually feel eyes on them. But Charlie didn't stir. As he walked closer, he realized she hadn't even laid the seat back, like someone normally would to rest in their car. Her head had just fallen to the side, as if she hadn't planned to sleep at all, had just been overwhelmed by it.

Deep shadows rested under her eyes. Her skin was pale, and tension bracketed her mouth even in sleep. He looked down the rest of her body.

Damn it, she'd lost more weight in the two weeks since they'd gone to the Frontier. Maybe a pound or two, but like she'd always said, on a five-foot-three frame made a difference.

The thought of drug use tagged his brain once again. But how could she be using and still be so alert and fantastic with Ethan?

Was she sick?

That would answer a lot of questions. If she had the flu or something, vomiting, couldn't keep food in her system? That would explain the exhaustion too.

Of course, she'd never shown any signs of that during tutoring either, nor of being anything less than one hundred percent focused and attentive.

He glanced in the back of her car. It wasn't as clean as the last time he'd seen it, but it wasn't nearly as messy as that night at The Eagle's Nest three weeks ago. There were some boxes or something on the floor of the back seat, but they were covered by a neatly folded blanket. The only thing truly visible was a plastic grocery bag, with a loaf of bread and a jar of peanut butter peeking out. A couple apples had rolled out and onto the seat.

Finn moved his attention back up to Charlie. He almost hated to wake her up. She had one hand tucked against her cheek, the other in a fist down by her leg. But when he looked closer, he realized her fist was holding a can of pepper spray.

He shook his head. Who was cautious enough to nap with that in their hand, but incautious enough to get a room at The Cactus Motel? Didn't make any sense.

He'd be the first to admit he had never one hundred percent understood Charlie. Hell, it had been part of the overall appeal, knowing he'd never completely figure her out. But now, the more he learned about her, the less he understood. There was some big piece of this puzzle he did not have.

Those blue eyes popped open, and she bolted straight up. Finn had been in enough combat situations to know abject fear when he saw it. This was way more than just waking and trying to get her bearings.

He took a step back from the car, holding his arms out in front of him in a gesture of harmlessness. "Charlie, it's Finn."

His heart cracked a little at the look on her face, like she couldn't really piece together what was happening. Her chest was heaving in and out as if she couldn't get enough air.

He'd never seen her like this, and he'd woken up with her more times than he could count. "You're okay, sweetheart." He kept his voice soothing, even though he had to be loud enough for her to hear him through the door. "You just fell asleep in your car."

"F-Finn?"

He moved to the door as he heard it unlock, opening it and squatting beside her. She was still caught up in whatever panic had gripped her mind. "It's okay, princess. You're safe."

"I-I..."

She let go of the can of pepper spray and gripped the steering wheel with both hands, her breath still sawing in and out of her chest. The pale skin of her face was pulled tight over her cheekbones.

Any other woman might burst into tears, but not Charlie. He could see her trying to pull herself together, trying to keep whatever bad things were happening to her under wraps.

Trying and failing.

He couldn't stand to see her like this.

"Come here." He went down on one knee and yanked her against his chest, curling both arms around her tiny frame.

His heart cracked a little more when she just melted into him without resistance, falling half out of the car. He pulled her tighter as her slender arms wrapped around his shoulders and she buried her face in his neck.

He held her that way for long minutes, not saying anything, just rubbing gentle circles along her back. Eventually, as he'd never had any doubt she would, she began to straighten, finding her strength, pulling away from him.

He let her go, ignoring the part of him that told him to call his mom to come get Ethan and drag Charlie back to his house—to his *bed*—and not let her go until she told him exactly what the hell was going on with her.

After he made love to her a couple dozen times.

And fed her until she no longer made orgasmic sounds at a bite of a diner hamburger, just at the feel of him biting into *her*.

His fists clenched at his side as she moved back into the car. "You want to tell me what's going on?" he asked.

She didn't look at him, staring out the windshield. She waited so long to answer that just for a second, he thought she might actually tell him what was happening to her.

"I woke up in the middle of a bad dream, I guess."

Of course, that was her answer. It was just a derivative of the answer she'd given him last time he'd asked her to explain what was happening, why her life seemed so out of control. He'd asked her that—said those exact words: *You want to tell me what's going on?*—the day she was marrying someone else instead of him when they'd spent the last five years talking about how they would spend forever together.

Her answer then had been "This is just the way things have to be."

So basically, *fuck off and leave me alone.*

Same answer then. Same now. Finn should've learned that lesson the first time.

"Okay, well, Ethan's waiting inside. So, whenever you're ready." He stood.

Those crystal blue eyes tracked him. "Finn, I . . ."

He stopped and waited. Was she going to tell him? Tell him why she was driving a car that was ten years old? Why she dragged tension and exhaustion everywhere she went, even though she tried to hide it? Tell him why her Target blazer, the nicest piece of clothing she had, was not only off-the-rack, but ill-fitting?

Too big, as if she'd lost weight since she'd bought it.

Would she tell him why the wrists attached to her hands gripping the steering wheel were thin and fragile? God knew Finn could've broken them at any point given his training, but now he'd have to be careful not to break them accidentally.

Would she tell him *why*? Would she ever give him the piece he was missing? Maybe he could help her, or hell, maybe she didn't even need it. Charlie was no damsel in distress. She could and would go toe to toe with anyone.

Would she trust him and let him in?

Because he knew for a fact if she did—despite how utterly stupid it might make him—he would close the gap between them. It wouldn't be the same as before, but it would be a start.

He crouched back down so they were eye to eye. "Tell me, Charlotte."

"I . . . I . . . ." Her eyes raced to points all over. His eyes, his mouth, his chest, over his shoulder, back to his eyes.

He wanted to help her. Expressing her problems had never been Charlie's forte. But he couldn't do this for her. He couldn't just slam through her walls; she had to choose to let him help. To trust him.

God, he wanted her to.

"It was just a nightmare," she finally whispered. "I'll be fine."

He stood and nodded. "I'll see you inside."

She'd made her choice.

CHAPTER 12

"THE THINGS we do for our country, man."

Finn chuckled at Aiden's comment as he got out of his car in the parking lot of The Silver Palace two days later. His brother, Baby, exited from the passenger side.

Henry Nicholson had contacted them yesterday and informed them that some of the criminals they were after had been here at this strip club earlier in the week. Aiden was still setting up his undercover persona and hopefully his appearance here would help solidify that. Finn, with Baby as a wingman, was here just to find out any information he could.

Not that Finn expected very much. He may be single, but he was past the age where places like these interested him. Of course, maybe it would help get Charlie off his mind. Maybe hanging around at a strip club with a bunch of mostly naked women would help him forget about her face.

And about the fact that it was *her* body he'd choose to see naked. He'd pick her over a hundred naked strangers. So maybe he wasn't thrilled to be here, but he had a job to do and he was going to do it.

Baby, on the other hand, was in his element. Finn could hardly keep from rolling his eyes at his brother's barely harnessed excitement at visiting a club he'd never been to. They'd driven separately from Aiden since they wouldn't have the same agenda once they got inside. Aiden would need to do whatever was best to get him further inside Stellman's circle. Finn would be gathering intel, while Baby did what he was best known for: being his charming twenty-five-year-old self.

"You up for this?" Aiden asked, one eyebrow raised.

Finn wasn't sure if he meant the club, undercover work, or both.

"Yeah, I'm good." And he was. So what if he hadn't been able to get Charlie's face out of his mind since seeing her two days ago. After refusing to tell him what was going on at her car, she had come into the library a few minutes later and had a perfectly successful session with Ethan. Maybe she hadn't looked Finn in the eye. Maybe he'd spent the entire session in the hall studying her, but instead of making sure she was doing her job with his son, he'd been trying to figure out what could be going on with her whenever she wasn't around.

He'd even run a brief background check on her. She still leased the condo on the far east side of town, the same she'd lived in not long after they had graduated high school and she'd gone to college. Finn had joined the Army, and Charlie had gone to the Reddington City campus of Wyoming State.

Hell, they'd picked that place out together when they'd been twenty. Her parents had provided the money for it, but Finn had wanted to make sure Charlie had a nice place since he was gone so much. He'd wanted her to have a safe place until he had enough money saved up to ask her to marry him. Then she would go with him wherever the Army sent them. That, of course, had never happened. He wasn't sure how he felt about the fact that she was still living there now, the place they'd always planned to live together.

But it didn't matter, because now, just like then, she didn't want Finn involved in her life.

And yet he'd *still* watched her through the whole tutoring session, trying to figure out what was eating at her. Letting her go afterward, with those goddamn rings under her eyes even more pronounced and her body tensed as if ready for some blow, had been the hardest thing Finn had done since the last time he'd had to let her go looking that way—to walk down the aisle.

The door to the club opened and blaring music poured out. Finn shook off his thoughts as Baby slapped him on his shoulder.

Finn forced a grin onto his face. Some things you could change, others you couldn't. There was no use dwelling on the latter. He was going to have to learn to live with whatever he couldn't rise above.

But tonight was not about Charlotte. It was about stopping some very bad men from bringing their very bad drugs into the country.

While watching mostly-naked women dance.

Aiden was right, not a bad job to have. Ethan was at his grandma's house all weekend, so Finn could devote his time and energy to the situation here.

He smiled at Aiden and Baby, holding out his fist. "For God and country."

Aiden tapped Finn's knuckles with his own, as did Baby.

His brother winked. "And lots of boobies."

"Remind me to never take you anywhere where I'm the one trying to be undercover." The second waitress in thirty minutes had come over to deliver his brother a beer.

One he hadn't ordered.

The first had sat on Baby's lap to talk and this last one had obviously thought Baby was dying because she'd immediately started delivering five minutes of mouth-to-mouth resuscitation.

One side of Baby's mouth turned up in a grin. "They're just friends. Sweet girls I knew in high school. I never come here, so I didn't know this was where they worked. And besides, it's not like any of your Linear guys are going to come be wingman for you."

Baby definitely had a point. Zac had no interest in a strip club; he was too busy falling all over himself for Annie, the sweet doctor who had moved back into town recently. Dorian's PTSD wouldn't allow him much time in a loud and crowded place like this. Gavin would do it. Hell, the thought of his straitlaced friend at a strip club brought a smile to Finn's face. But Baby was the best choice. He had a way of getting people to open up to him without them even realizing they were doing it.

They could've used his skills on their Special Forces team, but Baby had never been interested in joining. He'd never wanted to leave Oak Creek. He was happy as a mechanic.

Hell, the way the women fawned all over him, who could blame him?

They had a table near the back, far from Aiden, which enabled them to see anybody who might be going in and out of the back rooms. Back rooms that Baby had already been invited to by two different dancers. One had been kind enough to add that Finn could come along too.

Besides a nuclear holocaust, there was very little Finn could think of that he wanted less than to go back into one of these rooms. Especially with his brother.

"I'll probably get Jasmine"—Baby pointed to the petite Asian woman who'd kissed him earlier and was currently giving a lap dance at a table closer to the stage—"and go in the back. She and I have known each other for a long time, and she likes to talk. I'll see what information I can get out of her."

"You've got to be subtle. It can't get back to these guys that people have been asking about them. That will scare them off."

Baby just rolled those green eyes so much like Finn's own. "I may not be a super soldier, but I'm not an idiot. And seriously, Jasmine likes to talk *a lot*. She's a good place to start."

"Mom would be so proud of your willingness to take one for the team."

His brother smirked. "Should I take some pictures so she can post her proud moments on Facebook? I understand motor-boating is what all the cool moms boast about."

Finn laughed. "You're such an ass."

He turned back toward the stage but didn't give much attention to the young woman holding her body at an extreme angle against the pole. Instead he tried to scan the crowd, looking for groups who might be doing any sort of business. Without being near them, it was difficult to decipher what the pockets of men, and a few women, were discussing.

He shifted in his chair to see the bar, which was just as packed as the rest of the club. Over the heads of men sitting there, he could clearly see one tall brunette bartender.

"Oh shit, is that Jordan Reiss?"

Baby's head turned to look. "Damn. Sure is. I heard she asked all around Oak Creek trying to get a job and no one would hire her. I mean, not that I blame them after what her dad did, and she is a convicted felon. But still . . ."

"I guess she got a job here."

Finn was turning away—Jordan's employment here may be interesting, but it wasn't going to help with their undercover situation—when a man got up from the bar, giving Finn an unfettered view of the other bartender.

"Oh my freaking sweet baby Jesus God." Baby said it, but Finn was thinking it.

Charlie.

Finn stared. He couldn't have torn his eyes away if the building was burning down around him.

She was wearing the same revealing mesh tank top as the other bartenders, which, granted, was more than a lot of the women were wearing. Unlike Jordan, Charlie didn't seem uncomfortable in the outfit. It didn't take a genius to figure out that was because she had worked here long enough for it not to faze her.

"Hey, bro." Baby smacked him on the shoulder. "Are you about to pull out some weapon and go all Rambo on everybody in here? Or are we about to get in some huge rumble because of the guys looking at Charlie? Because if so, I think I'd like to call in some backup."

Baby's words were light, but there was an uncharacteristic thread of seriousness in them. Finn realized he was standing. He forced himself to sit back down.

"No, I'm not going to kill anybody."

"But kicking somebody's ass might be an option? Don't

forget how that Navy SEAL went to jail for getting into a fight with a regular guy."

"That was a movie, dumbass. And Nicolas Cage's character was a Ranger, not a SEAL." Finn appreciated his brother's attempt to diffuse the situation. And Baby was right, ten years ago Finn would've fought every man who so much as glanced at Charlie in that outfit.

And yes, part of him still wanted to walk over there and peel off his shirt and cover her with it. But again, it wasn't like she was sobbing or scared. She was just making money like every other woman in here.

That was what bothered him.

If Charlie wanted to take all her clothes off, that was completely up to her. Finn wasn't so narrow-minded that if a woman wanted to do that, dance, whatever she was comfortable with, he would judge her for it. Charlie was a beautiful woman with curves that literally took his breath away, for damn sure, so if she wanted to use them, more power to her.

But even though she wasn't uncomfortable in her job and tending bar, it obviously didn't bring her the sort of fulfillment her tutoring work did.

So, she was here because she needed the *money*.

Why the hell did the crown princess of Oak Creek need money? And if she needed it, why didn't she work full-time for the Teton County Educational Department?

To hell with whether she wanted to share what was going on. He'd wanted to be invited in, not to break down her walls. But he was not leaving without some answers to some very specific questions.

Tonight, he wasn't waiting for an invitation. Tonight, he was a fucking wrecking ball.

CHAPTER 13

CHARLIE'S SMILE was plastered on her face, but it very definitely did not reach her eyes.

Not that any of the guys here were looking at her eyes.

And she hadn't slept more than two hours since she'd left after Wednesday night's shift, afraid for her life. Including the twenty minutes she'd caught in the library parking lot before waking up in a panic and almost spilling her guts to Finn.

She hadn't had contact with any of the VIPs in the back, or that police officer asking so many questions. They hadn't returned either of the two nights since then, not even Rocco. But she'd been too terrified to sleep the night she had the room at the Cactus. Sleeping in her car the nights since hadn't been restful at all.

Here at the club she could convince herself that it was all something she'd made up in her mind, that she'd made the entire situation more ominous than it really was.

But in her car in a dark parking lot after she'd left, on her own, terrified if she shut her eyes she'd wake up to someone determined to kill her, there was no way rest would come.

She had no idea how she was going to make it through her shift tonight. It was only ten thirty; she still had another five hours on her feet. Her head was pounding, and her stomach was queasy.

She would have to get a room at the Cactus again tonight. She had to sleep. A complete physical shutdown was not far off if she didn't give herself a break soon. Not enough sleep, not enough food. Too much . . .everything bad.

She couldn't even bear to think about Finn and whatever had happened between them in the library parking lot. All she knew was that she'd hurt him, *again*. Disappointed him, *again*. At this point he had to be used to it.

She'd wanted to tell him. All of it. Her parents. Her divorce. Her financial situation and jobs. Even Rocco's people.

But the words wouldn't come. She just couldn't push them past her lips. And even if she could, how completely unfair was it to dump that all on him? They had no relationship. They weren't even friends.

Still, she'd halfway expected him to argue when she wouldn't tell him what was wrong. But evidently, he'd finally decided it wasn't worth the effort. *She* wasn't worth the effort.

She slid a beer down to Jordan to give to a customer. Charlie pushed her thoughts of Finn away. She had enough to worry about just staying on her feet tonight. She would have to leave the broken-heart stuff for another day. God knew it would still be there.

Jordan took a few steps closer to Charlie. She didn't blame the younger woman. The first couple weeks in this job in this outfit were nerve-racking. The wandering eyes and hands, the pace, the sheer volume. So far, Jordan had been handling it like a trooper.

Or maybe like someone who didn't have any other option.

Jordan slid a mug under the beer tap, leaning close to Charlie so she wouldn't have to yell. "Uh, I know you know more about my history than I do about yours because, well, because pretty much every mistake I've ever made has been literally broadcasted over the news."

Charlie winced. The younger woman hadn't had it easy. But where was she going with this? "Doesn't matter here. All I care about is that you're doing your job."

"Right, okay. Well, you know I. . .I killed Zac Mackay's wife and baby."

Charlie put her hand on the other woman's on the tap. "Yes. Knew that before you started working here."

"I think Zac might possibly have forgiven me, but a lot of other people from Oak Creek haven't."

Charlie didn't want to rush Jordan, but orders were starting to pile up. She gave the slender woman a gentle smile. "Why don't we talk about this after our shift, so nobody has a panic attack from not getting their drinks immediately?"

Jordan nodded. "Sure. Sure. I don't really want to talk about it actually. Just, if someone still pissed at me comes in here and makes a scene, I wanted to prepare you."

"Something make you think that's going to happen?"

Jordan grimaced. "Yeah. Maybe. Guy sitting in the back has been staring over here for the past twenty minutes, looking pretty pissed. I just realized it's Zac's best friend, Finn."

Jordan continued, but Charlie couldn't focus on what

the woman was saying. All she could do was lock eyes with Finn from across the room.

Jordan served the beer she'd poured, then came back to Charlie. "I don't think he'd hurt me or anything. I just wanted you to be aware that a storm was brewing."

Oh, a storm was brewing all right.

"Finn's anger isn't directed at you." She finally forced the words out. "He's here for me."

Someone sat down in the empty chair at the bar, blocking Finn from her view. But even not able to see him, she knew he was coming for her. That look on his handsome face meant she was not getting out of here without giving him answers.

So, she did what she'd never done before in her life: she ran.

She couldn't see if Finn was walking toward the bar, but even if he wasn't right at this moment, he would soon. She couldn't face him. Not now. Not here. Not when she was so exhausted, and her breasts were all but completely visible.

She grabbed both Jordan and Heather and pulled them to the corner of the bar, out of Finn's line of sight.

"I've got to go."

Heather's brows immediately gathered in concern. "Are you sick? You've been dragging all night."

"Something like that." She *was*. Maybe not the contagious kind, but her stomach *was* rolling like she might vomit at any moment. "I'm sorry. I hate to leave you guys in a lurch, but I can't stay."

"Go." Heather put one hand on her shoulder while shushing a customer demanding a drink with the other. "God knows you've covered for me enough times. I'll let Mack know you were sick and you'll be back when you can."

She felt like a coward, but it didn't matter. She couldn't face Finn. She just nodded and walked toward the far end of the bar. Jordan caught up with her.

"I'll stall Finn for as long as I can if he comes this way. *When* he does because I think we both know he's going to."

Charlie nodded, resisting the urge to look over her shoulder. "Thank you, Jordan."

For one of the first times in her entire life, Charlie was glad she barely cleared five feet in height. She kept out of the line of sight of Finn's table and made her way to the changing room in back. She grabbed her sweater and purse from her locker and slid out the employee door without saying another word to anyone.

She half expected Finn to be sitting against her car when she got there, but he wasn't. She gave up all pretense of not hurrying, ran over, and unlocked it. She was pulling out of the parking lot when she glanced in her rearview mirror.

Finn was coming out the door.

She pressed down on the gas, which was the wrong move. The small squeal of her tires drew his attention. He made a dash for his Jeep. Heart racing, she tore out of the parking lot and immediately drove toward the on-ramp for Hwy 190, headed toward downtown Reddington City. She took the first exit, knowing there was no way he could follow without her noticing once they were on city streets.

She drove for thirty minutes before her heart stopped racing enough that she could loosen her death grip on the steering wheel. It was another thirty after that before she truly began to believe Finn hadn't been able to follow her.

She began to berate herself. What had she done with this little car chase besides prolong the inevitable? He knew where she worked now. Knew where to find her. Time was on his side, not hers.

Now that the adrenaline was well and truly gone, her body was completely crashing. She rubbed her knuckles against the pain in her stomach—the peanut butter sandwich she'd eaten at five this afternoon had long since burned through her system. She was so tired now she literally couldn't keep her eyes open.

She didn't have the money budgeted for another night at the Cactus this week, but it couldn't be helped. A shudder ran through her body, and she rubbed her aching head again. She had to rest somewhere she felt marginally safe. Give her body time to repair itself and her mind time to figure out how to deal with Finn.

She didn't want to stay at the Cactus with their threadbare sheets, stained carpets, and hot water that never got past lukewarm. She didn't want to have to carry all her stuff in from the car because there was only a fifty-fifty chance it wouldn't get broken into.

She didn't want to live like this.

Another shudder ran through her, and to her dismay she could feel tears trying to leak from the corners of her eyes. She swiped at them.

"Suck it up, Charlie. This is the way it is."

She hadn't cried. Not after her marriage or divorce. Not after she realized her family was broke. Not after the Kempsleys had kept her from the profession she loved.

She damn well wasn't going to cry now over a dirty motel room.

But that wasn't what was urging on her tears. It was Finn and the thought of him seeing her like this.

She rubbed her eyes and took a minute to massage her forehead, ignoring the ache there that was spreading through her body. She would go to the Cactus. Finn might be back at The Silver Palace tomorrow, but the seedy motel was the last place he'd look for her in the meantime.

She would be ready for him by then, her defenses in place.

She was feeling significantly worse by the time she made it back to the motel on the far eastern side of town, almost halfway between Reddington City and Oak Creek. She checked in at the front desk and paid in cash. The man in his fifties working it, perpetual cigarette hanging out of his mouth, had long since stopped propositioning her. She'd been coming here every week long enough for him to know she'd just shut him down.

"You okay?" the guy muttered as he handed over her change.

"Yeah. Why?"

He shrugged and looked back down at the television he'd set up behind the counter. "Just look a little sick. Don't throw up on the carpet or it'll cost you an extra deep cleaning fee."

Nothing in this damn hotel had ever been deep cleaned, extra charge or not.

"I won't."

He slid the key card partway to her. "Room forty-nine."

"Damn it, why in the back?" Not much about this place was safe, but the five rooms facing the alley were even worse.

"Don't want your vomiting to be disturbing any other guests. Take it or leave it."

She had to focus on his face to keep the world from spinning around her. Shit. She *was* getting sick. "Fine."

He slid the key the rest of the way and she took it, breathing carefully in and out of her nose to keep herself steady. She was almost there. Five minutes and she could lock herself in her room and collapse on the bed.

She walked out to her car and, after a couple tries, managed to get the key in and started. Everything was spinning like she was drunk. She just had to get across the parking lot and around the other side of the building. Surely, she could do that.

She drove slowly and managed to park in a spot by her door. One of the overhead safety lamps was flickering and the other wasn't working at all, but she got the room door open and dragged the cheap plastic chair over to hold it open.

She could carry everything inside in three trips. Just one foot in front of the other.

She wrestled her suitcase and bag of food from the car and slowly made her way back toward the door that seemed to be moving in and out in a dizzying pattern. She finally got to it, relieved to lay her cheek against its cool paint.

Until she felt a knife press against the side of her neck and someone grip her hair and yank it back.

"I hear you make good money. I think you're going to need to give that to me."

CHAPTER 14

CHARLIE SHOULD DO SOMETHING. She had learned specific moves just in case something like this ever happened, but her feverish brain couldn't figure out what action to take.

"Didn't think you'd be here until later, honestly." The voice was hot in her ear.

Fight. She was supposed to fight. But all she could focus on was the drip of liquid running down the side of her neck. Was she sweating? Then the burn of pain set in.

No, it was blood.

"I don't have much money." She hated how shaky her voice sounded. "I had to leave work early, so I don't have any."

That was the truth. Maybe if she gave this guy the seventeen dollars she had in her wallet he would leave.

He laughed, his putrid breath nauseating her stomach so much more, and pressed the knife harder against her neck. "I guess I'll have to take payment in other ways."

Her exhausted sick brain finally kicked in. She hit his

hand with the knife, pushing it away from her neck enough that she could drop her weight to the ground. It enabled her to move without getting cut further, but she found herself with his fist still wrapped in her hair.

He laughed again. "Ground will work too."

She yanked her head away, ignoring the pain that shredded through her, and flipped over. Oh God, it was that druggie guy she sometimes saw in the alley. She hadn't thought he was this dangerous. He wasn't very big and was completely strung out. On most days she would be able to take him. But she could already feel everything graying around her.

She had to hang on. Had to get out of here.

All she could see as he crawled over her was the space where one of Druggie's front teeth was missing. He had the knife in his hand again. "Been a long time since I had a woman. Wasn't what I was after tonight, but I guess that's okay."

She pushed at his chest with all her strength, but it wasn't nearly enough. She willed herself to fight harder, to find some inner core of determination, but it was all she could do to just to hold on to consciousness.

And then the man went flying off her. She immediately scrambled to the side and started crawling toward the door. If his dealer or other druggie enemy was coming after him, she wasn't going to wait around to see how it turned out.

She got to her feet, albeit unsteadily, and focused on the door. It was all she could manage, just focusing on one thing at a time.

Door. Car. Escape.

A hand grabbed her shoulder and she ripped around in terror.

"Charlie, it's okay, baby. It's me."

"Finn?" The relief was almost more weakening than the fear. Her legs collapsed again.

"I've got you." Those strong arms wrapped around her. She couldn't do anything except lean into his strength. She couldn't see him very well in the dim light, but she didn't need to. She just wanted to stay here, breathe in his scent, borrow some of that strength he took for granted.

God, she just needed a moment to lean.

The druggie who had attacked her was moaning on the ground.

"Let's get you out of here." He reached over and touched her neck. "He cut you, but it doesn't look too bad. Are you all right?"

"I knocked the knife away before he could do any real damage. How'd you find me?"

She wished she hadn't asked the question when he stepped back from her, taking away that strength she needed so badly. It was all she could do not to reach for him. Not to cry out at the loss.

"Oh, I think there's quite a bit you and I need to discuss. Finding you here is just the tip of the iceberg. Now let's get out of here in case any of this guy's pals decide to come looking for him. I'll call the sheriff and get him to deal with this situation."

"Finn. . ."

"So help me God, Charlie, if you argue with me about leaving this place, I will take you over my knee and—"

She raised an eyebrow, feigning a casualness she didn't feel. "We both know how that would turn out if tradition holds."

He almost smiled. He hid it, but she could tell. Good. If he was exasperated with her, maybe he wouldn't realize how close to complete collapse she was.

But her traitorous body decided to pick that moment to stop working. Everything spun. She didn't even realize she was falling until he caught her.

"Goddammit, Charlie. Why didn't you tell me you were hurt? We need to get you to a hospital."

The world spun even more as he swept her up into his arms. Like she weighed nothing. Like he had the strength to carry her for a million miles. Which he probably did.

She wanted to remember this. She wanted to hold on to this moment. She never thought she'd be here again.

But she couldn't even get her arms to function enough to wrap around his neck. All she could do was collapse against his shoulder.

It should scare her to be this helpless, but if there was one thing she knew about Finn Bollinger, it was that he wouldn't let her fall.

"I'm not hurt. Just that little cut."

She felt Finn's fingers graze her cheek. "Jesus, you're burning up. Let's go." A moment later he was tucking her gently into the passenger side of his Jeep.

"No hospitals." The words came out as a whisper, but she didn't care. She couldn't afford it.

He shook his head. "Are you going to tell me why?"

"Not if I don't have to."

He reached over and fastened the seat belt around her. "Still so stubborn," he muttered.

She wanted to tell him he sounded just like Ethan whenever she mentioned starting a longer and harder book. But she couldn't get the words to form. She could only stare at his darkly handsome face.

"You're going to be okay, princess." He shook his head ruefully, then reached over and kissed her on the forehead.

"I'm here. Go to sleep now, nothing's going to happen to you."

And as if her body had just been waiting for him to say it, she did.

CHAPTER 15

CHARLIE DIDN'T WAKE up when Finn got her suitcase and loaded it into the back of the Jeep.

She didn't wake up when he made a phone call to Sheriff Nelson, and then Dorian, and explained about the attack.

She didn't wake up when he called Zac and asked if his girlfriend, an emergency room doctor, was off work and might be willing to make a house call.

She didn't wake up when he carried her out of the Jeep and into his bedroom.

It was a good thing Annie was in the room checking on Charlie now, otherwise Finn would've been taking her to the hospital.

"Nobody should sleep that long and hard unless they've been drugged or something," Finn said to Zac as they sat in the kitchen waiting for Annie to finish and come report Charlie's medical status.

"Especially not Charlie," Zac agreed. "Remember how

you used to say she would do well in Special Forces because of how long she could go without sleep?"

Sleep deprivation had been part of their survival training. Definitely not Finn's favorite. He would rather be physically beaten than forced to stay awake for days at a time.

He walked to the fridge and pulled out a beer, offering one to Zac.

"It's not just the sleep." Finn brought the cold bottle to his lips. "It's the fever and the fact that she weighs all of ten pounds. Jesus, Zac, what if she has cancer?"

"Let's not borrow trouble until we have to. Annie will tell us if further tests are needed or anything like that. How did you run into Charlie anyway? I thought you were going to some strip club to help Major Pinnock."

Finn took a long sip of his beer. "Charlie was working there."

Zac's eyes grew big. "Dancing?"

"Bartending."

"At The Silver Palace?" Zac shook his head. "I thought she was some sort of education guru. Didn't you tell me she was working wonders tutoring Ethan?"

"Honestly, I have no idea what's going on with Charlie." Finn explained about seeing her at The Cactus Motel last week, then finding her there again tonight. "She still owns that condo on the east side. You can spare me the lecture, but I ran her through the Linear system last week."

Zac just lifted his beer in a silent salute. "I ran Annie when she first came back to town, so no judgment here."

Finn shrugged. "Yeah, well, you were trying to help Annie. I'm not exactly sure what my motives were. But I only got the details about her condo. At least I didn't move into complete stalkerhood."

"Still plenty of time for that." Zac grinned.

"I won't have to. Charlie is not leaving this house until I get some answers. That's if she ever wakes up."

"She woke up for a few minutes to answer some of my questions." Annie entered the kitchen, putting her makeshift house call bag on the table.

Finn's grip on the bottle tightened. "She all right? God, Annie, I think it might be cancer. Is it?"

Annie gave him a gentle smile, then took a sip of her boyfriend's beer as his arm came around her waist, anchoring her against him. "There's definitely no reason to think Charlie has cancer or that anything is permanently wrong with her."

"Then why wouldn't she wake up? Why did she have a fever? Why has she lost so much weight?"

"She's tired, Finn. That's why she's sleeping."

He slammed a hand down on the kitchen island. "There's something a damn sight more wrong with her than just being tired."

Zac's eyebrows rose. Finn didn't blame him. Annie was here on her own free time and as a favor. "Watch it there, Eagle."

"It's okay," Annie told Zac. "He's just concerned. Dealing with a patient's loved ones is a part of my job."

Finn ran his hand over his face, not even acknowledging the *loved one* statement. "No, Zac's right, Annie. I'm sorry. But you are also. I am concerned. This isn't like Charlie. There are so many things that don't add up."

"I specifically asked if she had serious health issues because if she did—anemia, an autoimmune disorder, or, like you said, cancer—I needed to know. She said she didn't, Finn, and I believe her."

"Then why is she so tired? So skinny?"

"She said she's been working a lot. Multiple jobs. And

not eating right. She gave me permission to talk to you about her medically, so you wouldn't be too worried."

Zac shook his head, staring at Finn. "Why would the princess of Oak Creek be working multiple jobs?"

Finn threw up his hands. "And why would one of them be at The Silver Palace for God's sake? It would be one thing if she wanted to work in education full-time. After seeing her with Ethan I could totally understand why. But *there*? And as a bartender? I mean, if she wanted to dance, I might not like it, but at least it would be understandable. Creative outlet or some such shit. But a *bartender*?"

Finn drained the rest of his beer while neither Annie nor Zac said anything, because what really could be said? None of this made any sense.

"She has a fever from a virus," Annie said quietly. "Her immune system has taken a hit due to her exhaustion and diet. I gave her some ibuprofen and helped her into one of your T-shirts. I'll be surprised if the fever isn't gone tomorrow."

"What does she need?" he finally asked. "What can I do to take care of her?"

Because at the end of the day, that was all that mattered. There was no way Finn could exist knowing Charlie was on the verge of some sort of collapse.

Annie walked over and put her hand on Finn's arm. Her brown eyes were calm and friendly, like her smile. She was a gentle soul, so quiet and reserved. The opposite of Charlie. Annie fought if the need called for it—she'd proved that well enough when she'd been attacked last month—but it wasn't a natural part of her personality.

Charlie, on the other hand, was a warrior. *Though she be but little, she is fierce.*

God, Charlie would have a field day if she knew he was quoting Shakespeare for her.

Annie smiled. "I bandaged the wound on her neck. It didn't need stitches, and confirmed she was up-to-date on her tetanus shot. I wrote her a script for antibiotics since who knows where that knife has been, so you'll need to get that filled. As for everything else, it's my professional opinion she needs rest. Let her sleep as long as she will, which may be a lot more hours."

"Is that bad for her?"

"Not at all. You can ask Zac. There are plenty of times after a double shift at the hospital that I'm dead to the world for twelve or fourteen."

Zac shrugged. "True. It's a little scary, but it's what her body needs."

"What about eating?" Finn asked.

"Her body will direct her to her most important needs. Right now, it needs sleep more than food. If that changes, she'll wake up. Then, if you can talk her into it, keep her off her feet for a couple days. Feed her nutritious, high-calorie foods. And try not to kill each other. Just because Charlie had a momentary setback doesn't mean she's not going to wake up swinging." Annie reached up and kissed him on the cheek.

"The first two are no problem. The third . . .nobody can ever promise that Charlie and I won't kill each other." He shrugged, then pulled Annie in for a hug. "Thank you for coming. She didn't want to go to a hospital, and I didn't know what else to do."

Annie walked back over to Zac, who stood so they could leave. "Charlie was never mean to me in high school. She never made fun of my stuttering like a lot of people did. I mean, I still would've helped her even if she had, but I just wanted you to know."

That didn't surprise him at all. "Charlie may be privileged, even a snob, but she's never been cruel."

"Only to you, brother," Zac said as he led Annie toward the door. "Only to you."

Finn let his friends out, then checked with the sheriff to see if there was word about the addict who'd attacked Charlie. Sheriff Nelson hadn't found the man yet, but the Cactus's front desk clerk felt sure it was the homeless guy known as "Sam." There was an APB out on him.

After the call and cleaning up the kitchen, Finn couldn't stop any longer from checking on her, cursing himself the entire way up. He had to see her. To touch her.

Charlie this weak and defenseless scared him to death.

He'd known her nearly half his life and she'd always brimmed with an internal power much stronger than her smaller stature suggested. A force to be reckoned with.

Fierce.

Something wasn't right in the world when Charlotte Devereux was curled up in a helpless, shivering ball in the middle of his bed.

But even through his worry, he couldn't stop his small smile at how she'd moved into the middle. She had always been a bed hog. They'd never lived together and hadn't gotten to sleep all night in one together often, but whenever they had, she'd thrashed around like she was running an obstacle course. He'd basically had to bear hug her the entire night to keep her still.

He stared at the tiny mound of blankets that was Charlie. He should leave, go sleep on the couch. But instead he changed into a pair of sweatpants and got in beside her.

CHAPTER 16

CHARLIE WOKE UP, aware of a feeling she hadn't known in fourteen months, since the day she'd sublet her condo and technically became homeless.

Safety.

The biggest part of that came from the man who was all but wrapped around her. Finn's leg was thrown over both of hers, his arm crossed over her torso, the weight of his chest on her shoulder pinning her to the bed. She should feel trapped, restrained. But she felt secure.

She'd already known he was in bed with her. She had woken up at some point, starving, and he had been there. A few seconds later, he'd helped her sit up and drink one of those nutrition shake things and given her some antibiotics Annie had prescribed.

She had gone to the bathroom, again with his help. She'd been too weak to even be embarrassed about it. Back in bed she had waited for questions, for some sort of inquisition, but it hadn't come. He'd just pulled her back against him. She hadn't thought she'd be able to sleep. She hadn't wanted to. If this was going to be the only time she got to lay in Finn's arms, she wanted to stay awake and enjoy it.

Obviously, her body had disagreed, considering she was waking up to a bright sun outside.

So, she would enjoy it now. She shifted a little to see him more fully. It was so ridiculous that someone as strong and powerful as Finn could be so beautiful. Her fingers itched to stroke his jaw, to touch those cheekbones that looked like they were carved from granite. To feel the rough prickle of his stubble against her fingertips.

She wanted to rub her thumb against that tiny place above his nose where his brows met and ease the stress lines that had formed there over the years, visible even in sleep.

She wanted to kiss that face, every single inch of it, repeatedly. One kiss for every day she had lost. For every day she hadn't been with him.

God, she wanted to do so much more than kiss him. Or kiss so much more of his body than just his face. Having him so close brought parts of her own alive that had lain dormant for too long, in her struggle to just survive.

She wanted to push his heavy weight off and climb on top of him, then lick and nip her way down his chest and see if he still made that seductive groan.

She wanted to drag the sweatpants down those sexy hips with her teeth. If the hardness pushed up against her hip right now was any indication, they'd both be groaning after that.

"You no longer sleep like you're caught in some sort of wrestling match." His voice startled her out of her seductive daydream. She should've known he wouldn't stay asleep once she moved.

What could she tell him about her nocturnal changes? That sleeping in her car five or six days a week over the last year had taught her how to keep still? Or that she'd learned it long before then, during her marriage, when the thought of touching her husband while she slept was so abhorrent?

"I guess I finally grew up."

Those green eyes of his still didn't open, but at least he didn't move away from her, although she knew the withdrawal was coming.

Tensing, she waited for it.

Damn it. When had she become this person? When had she become someone who lay passive and silent, waiting for something bad to happen to her when the good thing she so desperately wanted was literally lying on top of her?

She. Wanted. Finn.

He might still push her away, and honestly, she couldn't blame him if he did. But she wasn't going to be a coward. She'd been many things in her life, but never a coward.

"We should get up, so you can eat," Finn said. "Annie said you need as many calories in you as possible."

He hadn't moved, but she could feel him inching away from her.

"There's something I think I need more than food right at this particular moment." She meant it to come out sexy, but to her ears it sounded a little desperate, which wasn't entirely inaccurate.

Now those green eyes opened. "Sleep? Annie also said to let you as much as you could."

Not a coward, she reminded herself. "You. I need you."

Heat burned through his eyes for just a second before chivalry doused it. His leg slid off hers. "Let's just go have breakfast. You were sick last night, running a fever—"

"I'm not now."

"—and so exhausted that you didn't even wake up when I carried you from the Jeep to the bed."

She brought her hand up to touch that jaw. Feel that stubble. She rubbed her thighs together to ease some of the ache there. "I'm not exhausted now."

He didn't pull away, but he didn't ease into her touch either. "Charlie . . .I'm just not sure this is what you really want."

She raised an eyebrow. "Since when have I not known what I want?"

He rolled the rest of the way off her, onto his back, then threw an arm over his eyes. "Jesus, last night you damn near scared me to death. And I'm not talking about the attack by that drug addict. I'm talking about *you*. The state you were in. I've never seen you look so . . .little."

Something clenched deep in her heart. Finn had always respected her strength. He'd never treated her as less than his equal. Even when they'd fought—which, given both their strong personalities, had been a lot—they'd always respected each other's opinions and strength. And now he thought hers was gone.

It wasn't.

She sat up and threw one of her legs over his hips, so she was straddling him and trailed her fingers along the arm covering his eyes. "I *was* little, Finn. You're right. Last night, I was weak, scared, and little. And you were there for me, just like you've always been when I needed you. Strong, courageous, and big."

His arm moved, and she could see in his eyes the demons he was fighting. There were a lot of years between them. A lot of pain. A lot of lies.

She reached down and grasped his bottom lip between

her teeth, biting gently. He hissed, and his hips pressed up against hers.

She let go of his lip and whispered, "I'm not little now. Not weak. I know what I want—what I *need*—and that's you. I owe you an explanation, I know that. But first give me this. Give me you, strong, courageous, and big with me. Around me. *Inside me.*"

His growl was her only warning.

Her shirt was ripped over her head and he had her flipped around and tucked under him almost before she could finish the last word. She'd forgotten how fast he could move.

"Damn you, woman, you have always known how to push my buttons." He fisted her hair tight, pulling her head to the side, giving him access to her neck on the unmarked side.

Now she was the one hissing as his mouth nipped and sucked along her throat until he reached that tender place where her neck met her shoulder, biting gently. His hand slid to her distended nipple, fingers pinching just short of pain, sending a bolt of lust through her whole body.

She ran her hands along his shoulders and biceps. His body was still perfect. Not bulky, but powerful. She hadn't been exaggerating before: strong and courageous and big.

She relished the moan that seemed torn from his throat as she reached between their bodies, down those hard abs. He held his breath as her fingers slid under the band of his sweatpants and stroked the length of him. His face collapsed against her neck, his breath uneven.

She smiled. "Hmmm, this button still seems to work too."

He lifted his head, staring down at her with hooded eyes. "Keep it up and this is going to be the shortest love-making session you and I have ever had. You still make me crazy, princess. That hasn't changed, for sure."

Short and crazy was more than fine with her. He had no idea how long it had been. If she told him, he wouldn't believe her. Over four years. Way over. She and Brandon had stopped having sex long before they'd divorced.

She let go of him and brought both hands up to cradle his head, so she could look right into his eyes. She wanted him to know how sure she was of this. "I *want* crazy. I want you inside me right now."

She wanted him to chase away all the distance, fear, and lost time between them.

His lips fell hard on hers for a moment before he moved off the bed with a groan and went into the bathroom. He came back out a moment later, condom in hand and gloriously naked.

She couldn't even think of words.

Now it was his turn to grin. "Hell, princess, if I had known seeing me naked was all it took to strike you dumb, I would've been walking around in my birthday suit for a while now."

"Shut up and get in the bed, Bollinger." She sat up on one elbow, barely refraining from licking her lips as she stared at him.

She squealed as she found herself dragged to the edge of the bed until her legs were hanging over the side. All the air whooshed from her lungs as he lowered himself onto a knee on the floor and grabbed her underwear, sliding it down her hips.

If he noticed the material wasn't nearly as expensive or lacy as what she used to wear, he didn't mention it. The way he was staring at her body, she didn't think he noticed at all.

"I've decided fast and crazy isn't the way I want to go," he whispered, staring at her.

His lips started a path up her knees to her inner thigh,

but just as they were getting close to where she desperately wanted them, he started back down the other side. When he repeated the pattern again, her hips began a restless slide against the edge of the bed. It had been *so long*.

"Finn . . ."

She started to sit up, to argue her case, but one of his strong arms stretched, his hand skimming a delicious path along her stomach until it rested between her breasts and pushed her back down.

"Stay," he murmured against her upper thigh. His hand slid back down and spread her legs wider. And finally —*finally*—his mouth moved onto her core.

It was too much, her body was already too sensitive. After just a few gasping moments, she was torn between wanting to hold his head tighter to her and trying to move away from that vastly talented, too-gentle tongue. He took the choice from her, those strong hands holding her in place as he softly sucked, circled, and laved her right to the edge of sanity.

"Finn. *Finn*. Please, come up here." She needed more. Less. *Everything*. That desperate orgasm was looming in front of her just out of reach and she couldn't figure out how to—

"*Please*, Finn." Her voice was a wail she hardly recognized, her head thrashing back and forth.

He knew what she needed. He stopped the gentle touch and flicked his tongue firmly against her clit, finally giving her the pressure she needed exactly where she needed it.

Her back arched off the bed as wave after wave of pleasure drenched her. Finn's tongue continued to lave her as she came down from the explosion of sensations.

Coherent thought might not ever be possible again.

With the beautiful taste of Charlie still on his tongue, the sound of her orgasm ringing in his ears, he stood. He scooped her up in his arms and slid her back on the bed, loving the flushed, dazed, look on her face. All that blonde hair sprawled out everywhere. He'd never thought he'd see this again. Part of him wanted to just soak it in. He crawled in beside her.

She pushed on his chest until he was lying on his back. "My turn."

He shook his head. He wasn't going to last one minute if Charlie got her hot little mouth on him. "Next time."

They stared at each other for just a second. Would there be a next time? Charlie just gave him a little nod.

He made quick work of the condom, then grasped her hips and pulled her until she was straddling him once again. Their eyes met, fire burning between them, as she slowly sank down onto his erection.

He kept his eyes locked on those bright blue ones, as if it wasn't taking every bit of his restraint not to thrust home. Holy hell, she was tight. He gripped her hips, easing her forward and back, hissing as she slid down farther, still agonizingly slowly.

"Help me," she panted.

"My pleasure." There wasn't anything on this earth he'd rather do more.

He slipped one hand into her hair, pulling her down for a kiss. He slid the other between their bodies and began to circle her clit, knowing it wouldn't be enough, just like it hadn't been when he'd used his mouth. A desperate whine fell from her lips and her hips began to jerk, seeking more as he toyed with her.

God, would he ever grow tired of that sound? Of the feel of her body wanting what he could give her? It didn't matter how many years had passed, this heat was still the same.

Unable to hold out any longer, he gave her the firm touch she wanted, rocking her body forward until she'd sheathed him completely. His breath hissed out, his hands gripping her hips, as he reveled in the feel of being inside her once more.

Then he began to move.

Rolling Charlie so she was on her side, he hiked one leg over his hips, giving him a deeper angle. He thrust hard and caught her cry in his mouth. He stopped, afraid he'd gone too far—damn, she really was tiny—but then she rolled her hips forward in feminine welcome.

"Charlie," he groaned. "You feel so damn good."

He thrust into her repeatedly. Deep. Hard. Slow.

He watched as her eyes glazed over. Her body moved in a primal rhythm, past talking now, just holding on to him. The way he liked it.

He picked up the pace, his hand sliding under her thigh and lifting it, opening her to him further. Her cries echoed in his ears, a sound he'd never forgotten. Would never forget. He continued to thrust until she came apart around him, her cries turning to keens. Only then did he let himself go, his blood thundering in his own ears as he shouted her name.

Being with Charlie was like coming home.

CHAPTER 17

THEY LAY IN SILENCE, collapsed in each other's arms, trying to catch their breath. They were silent when Finn picked her up and carried her into the shower. They were silent as they stood together, arms wrapped around each other, under the spray.

They were silent even as what started as the innocent washing of each other's bodies turned into him pinning Charlie against the stall wall. The only sound was their desperate breathing and skin slapping against skin in their attempt to get closer.

The silence was unusual for them, but not awkward. So much needed to be said, but neither wanted to break their closeness to say it.

So . . .silence.

But that was a fantasy world. It wouldn't protect him from Charlie, from a past that had left him broken and bleeding. No matter how much her body called to him, how perfect they were together, how much he wanted to lay her on the bed *again* and never let her out of it, some things never changed.

The worlds of Finn Bollinger and Charlotte Devereux did not mix.

She was the one who finally broke the silence. Sitting on his bed, back in one of his T-shirts—Finn painfully aware she had nothing on underneath it—she whispered, "I know you have questions."

He didn't want to respond. If he stayed silent, if he walked over to her and peeled that shirt from her body and told her to get on her hands and knees on the bed, she would do it. They would lose themselves again—as the silence turned into pants and groans and cries—as his body drove into hers. He was so damn tempted.

But even if he did it, they would still end up right back here.

He did have questions.

So, he broke the silence too. "I'll make you something to eat while we talk. Annie said you need to eat as much high-calorie, nutritious food as you can."

She nodded and suddenly getting answers was more important than getting inside her. Not something Finn would've ever thought would be true. "Can you make it to the kitchen?"

Her glare made him chuckle, which got him the look of death. She was so damned independent.

He still followed half a step behind her as she walked just in case she was weaker than both of them thought. She didn't stumble, but he didn't like how slowly she had to take it. He probably should've taken that into consideration when he was utilizing all her energy upstairs the last couple hours.

He pulled out a chair for her at the kitchen table, then

moved to the refrigerator. He opened it without really seeing the items inside. There was one question he had to have answered first, before anything else. Something he probably should've asked before their lovemaking.

He didn't turn to her. "I want you to tell me the truth about this one thing. Hell, I want you to tell me the truth about all of it, but this one question, Charlie . . .If there was ever anything between us at all, you have to promise me you'll be honest about this."

"Okay," she whispered.

He took a breath and faced her. "Are you ill? Like really sick, cancer or something? Is that why you were so weak last night?"

Surprise lit her eyes. "Finn, no. I promise. There's nothing wrong with me like that."

A relief so profound it took his breath away washed over him. She wasn't dying. Everything else was secondary.

"I'm sorry that's what you thought," she whispered. "That I scared you that way."

"What the hell else was I supposed to think? You've been asleep in my bed for over eighteen hours. You're basically skin and bones." He punctuated the sentence by bringing her a nutrition shake. The same kind he'd used when he first got custody of Ethan, full of the calories the small boy had needed. Just seeing those bottles gave him a sick feeling in his gut, and knowing Charlie needed them now did not help it go away.

"I guess I've been working a lot and haven't really been taking care of myself the way I should." She opened the bottle and took a drink. He waited for her to continue but she didn't.

Charlie wasn't going to offer information easily. Finn would have to drag it out of her.

This wasn't his first interrogation. He rested his weight on his arms on the table, not caring if that meant he towered over her. "Okay, why don't we start with that: your jobs. I think I'm aware of two of them. Educating tomorrow's future by day and serving drinks at a strip club by night. Are there any more I should know about?"

He said it in sarcasm, but when she looked away . . . "Oh my God, you have *another* job?"

"Sort of. I clean the bar during the day."

"Like, as the janitor?" She nodded as she took another sip. If his hair were long enough, he would've pulled it. He took a deep breath and straightened, walking back to the fridge.

Stay calm, Bollinger. Escalating things into a yelling match wasn't going to help anyone.

"What would you like to eat?" he asked in the most relaxed voice he could find. "I've got stuff for a full breakfast, or if you prefer, I can make pasta. Or steak and potatoes."

"Breakfast food would be fine. I can help."

He glared at her over his shoulder, pointing at her chair. "So help me God, Charlie, if you get up right now and try to do any work, I'm going to lose my shit. Your only job right now is to answer questions."

The word job had him cringing. *Three?* What the hell? He turned back to the fridge and got out bacon and eggs and the items he needed for a small batch of pancakes. Maybe it wasn't the most nutritious meal, but at least it had calories.

He laid the bacon in the pan, trying to get his thoughts together. He had so many questions, he wasn't sure where to start.

"Why are you working at The Silver Palace?"

"The money is good, much better than at a regular bar. The cleaning part is more convenient than lucrative."

He turned the flame on under the pan and began mixing the pancake ingredients on the kitchen island, so he could face her. These were the wrong questions. Obviously, she was there for money. The real question was, why would Milton Devereux's daughter need money? Why would he let her work somewhere like that?

Those were the right questions. Or at least in the right direction.

"Where are your parents?"

Surprise lit her blue eyes. Bingo. This all had to do with her parents.

"How did you—I mean, what makes you think anything has to do with them? I'm an adult."

"I may not have always gotten along with your mom and dad, but one thing I know for sure, your father would not allow this," he flung a hand at her, "if he knew about it."

She began peeling the packaging off her empty bottle. "Dad is sick. Prion disease. It's a rare condition that attacks the brain. He's at a care facility in Denver. Mama moved with him."

Okay. Now they were getting somewhere. He set out another pan to heat for the pancakes and flipped the bacon. But there were still a lot of things that didn't make sense.

"But why would that mean you need to work three jobs? I know your father had to have insurance. Or hell, even if not, he had the money to pay for being in this facility."

She shook her head. "We got hit really hard in the stock market crash a few years ago. It also happened right when oil prices skyrocketed and devastated the factory in Oak Creek. Dad sold the business but didn't get a fair price. We lost almost everything. There's just no money."

He poured the first batch into the pan and tried to work out the timeline in his head. This all must've happened after she married Kempsley, but before Finn had gotten out of the Army. She must not have gotten very much out of her divorce settlement.

Given the fact that she had married Kempsley for money, the irony that she was working three jobs now just to survive wasn't lost on him. Nor was the fact that had *he* and Charlie still been together, he would've given every cent he had to help her dad. To help her.

"Your dad can't be happy that you're having to work this hard."

"He's not very lucid a lot of the time. He's lasted a lot longer because of an experimental drug treatment he was a part of. But his condition has led to advanced dementia, so most of the time when I see him he doesn't even recognize me."

That sucked. Charlie had always been close with her parents. "I'm sorry, sweetheart." And he was. About it all. He wasn't so much of a bastard that he would wish this on her.

"It's not forever. That's what I tell myself. Despite . . .everything, I know Dad doesn't have much longer. So, I just keep working. It's the least I can do after everything they did for me."

Finn's own father had died over a decade ago, but there was nothing he wouldn't do for his mother. Especially if she was in the end stages of her life. So, he understood what Charlie was saying.

But she had to find a better balance. Mr. Devereux would not want her working herself into this state, even to prolong his life.

Finn made the eggs, took the rest of the food off the

burners, and plated their food before carrying it over to the table.

They began to eat. He knew the question he had to ask, but he didn't want to. He wouldn't on any day, but he particularly didn't want to while she was sitting across from him, hair tousled and cheeks still flushed from their lovemaking.

"What about Brandon? I know you guys are divorced, but the Kempsley family has a ton of money. Could he help you out? Even if it was a loan or something?"

It was like watching an iron curtain slam down over her features. "No, the Kempsleys aren't an option. Period." She stared down at her plate, shoveling more food into her mouth.

Not an amicable divorce then. He was man enough to admit that the idea didn't make him sad. At one point he might've been tempted to lord her mistake over her, try to get her to admit what she had lost, ask her if giving up their relationship had been worth what she'd gained. But that would just be petty.

Finn wasn't above being petty when the occasion called for it, but that wasn't what he wanted. Even if she admitted she'd made the worst mistake of her life by marrying Kempsley, what would it get him? Seeing Charlie this way— almost broken, exhausted, hopeless—didn't bring him any joy. Even at his most angry he'd never wanted to see her like this.

"What about working full-time in education? I know you're wonderful with Ethan and Mrs. Johnson said you're one of the most talented education specialists she's ever seen."

Charlie peered up from her plate, a bit of life now shining in her eyes. "I love the work I do. And Ethan, God

Finn, he's such a great kid. I would love to do that full-time." Watching that light fade from her eyes was almost physically painful. "But I can't. And it's not enough anyway."

"You can't right now. But like you said, this won't be forever."

Her smile was tight. "Right. Not forever."

Finn wasn't sure exactly what she was thinking, but probably working three jobs made anything feel like forever.

"You know, Linear Tactical is doing really well. Better than any of us thought it would do only four years in."

Her face lit up again. "That's fantastic, Finn. And I'm not surprised. The best of all possible worlds, huh?" She took a small bite of her eggs. "Doing the soldier stuff you love. Working with Zac and your buddies. Making money. I'm so happy for you."

And she was, he realized. She wasn't saying it for any other reason than because she was excited for him.

"I wasn't trying to rub it in your face. I just wanted to let you know that I have some money saved up and—"

"Finn, stop."

"—I mean, I don't know how much the medical expenses are every month, but I could help out."

She reached across the table and grabbed his hand. "I'm not taking your money, Bollinger. But you have no idea how much it means to me that you would offer. After everything."

He gave her a half smile. "Hey, getting humiliated in front of the entire town builds a man's character."

Finn expected some smart-aleck reply but was gutted when her beautiful blue eyes filled with tears.

Shock ricocheted through him. Charlie Devereux didn't cry. Ever.

"*Hey*. Hey, I was just kidding." He squeezed the hand that had not let go of his.

"I'm so sorry I hurt you," she whispered, the tears falling down her cheek. "You can believe whatever bad things you want about me, but please believe that I am so sorry I hurt you. I just . . .I had to choose."

Had to choose between a soldier's paycheck with Finn or the luxurious lifestyle Brandon Kempsley could provide.

But the agony in her eyes now, the *tears*, made that all seem so distant. Finn couldn't stand it. He went to her side, scooped her up, and sat down in her chair with her in his lap.

"I survived. And you survived. It's okay."

She just buried her face in his neck and held on.

He couldn't help but feel he was missing something again. His nickname was Eagle because he observed and attacked, so why did he feel so blind around this woman?

He held her for a few minutes as she finally relaxed against him. She was tired again, needed rest. Ethan wasn't coming home until tomorrow, so Finn planned to take her back up to his bed, so she could sleep.

"I need to go to work," she said against his neck.

He wrapped his arms more tightly around her. "Not tonight. I got in touch with Jordan, explained to her that you were mugged. She's going to tell your boss. Sheriff Nelson was planning to give him a call too, just to let him know nobody was faking."

Finn had made those calls before understanding exactly what was going on with Charlie. Now that he knew, he was doubly glad he'd contacted her workplace. He still didn't like her being at The Silver Palace, but he respected her willingness to work hard.

He could almost hear her adding up figures in her head now.

He spoke through his teeth with forced restraint. "You will damn well let me lend you the few hundred dollars you missed out on in tips last night and tonight. Hell, princess, I have that just in mad money in the Bible upstairs."

She leaned back and smiled at him. "I thought only women had mad money."

He winked at her. "I like to have it for any emotion I may be feeling. In this case though, I will be angry if you don't take it. I promise it's not a hardship. Okay?"

She nodded, and he silently let out a breath of relief. "Okay."

"And I won't even give you a hard time about working three jobs." Although he would be keeping an eye on her. "But your parents wouldn't like it if they knew the state you were in. *Are* in. You're going to have to do better at taking care of yourself. I know you don't have a lot of time to eat or sleep, but make time, all right?"

She looked like she wanted to say something else, to make some sort of argument, but finally just nodded and melted back against him.

"Take me back to bed, Finn. I just want one more night of pretending like there's no yesterday and no tomorrow."

So did he. Leaving the dishes where they were, he walked up the steps with her wrapped in his arms.

Even though he knew it meant sleep would be a long time in coming.

CHAPTER 18

"I'M IN."

It was seven o'clock the next morning and Finn sipped coffee at his kitchen table as Aiden entered through the side door, looking like hell.

"In what?" Finn asked. "My house, or a shitload of trouble? Because you look like a hot mess."

Aiden stumbled the rest of the way in and collapsed into one of the kitchen chairs, scrubbing both hands over his face. "Coffee. Please for the love of Mike, coffee."

He chuckled and got up to pour it for his friend. "So, by 'in' I'm assuming you mean the network trying to buy the NORAD info."

"Yeah. As a weapons smuggler. Ends up my military background and Linear Tactical form the perfect backstory."

He handed his tired friend the coffee. "How so?"

"All I had to do was play a disgruntled partner. That Linear has all these contacts overseas and we're not using them to our financial advantage."

That probably wasn't far from the truth. All of them had several contacts from their years in the Middle East and Europe. If they were looking to bring illegal substances or weapons into or out of the United States, suppliers or buyers wouldn't be hard to find.

"I'm glad Saturday night wasn't a total wash since I completely bailed on you."

Aiden took a sip of his coffee, closing his eyes in relief as the brew entered his system. "Actually you not being there was probably for the best, given I'm supposedly trafficking weapons right under your nose."

He nodded. "So, they bought your story?"

Aiden nodded and took a sip. "I'll admit I talked a lot of shit about you guys. And we should probably try to keep this cover in place long-term. It could come in handy for other stuff."

Linear's primary objective was to teach survival intelligence. But from time to time they stepped out of the training field and back into the heart of trouble, helping corporations and individuals with dangerous situations: kidnap and ransom, extortion, detention.

A cover story that a member of Linear wasn't afraid to dip into illegal activities could definitely be to their advantage.

"I agree," Finn said. "But be careful. That could bring trouble back on you."

Aiden took another sip. "Like having to stay out till the crack of dawn two nights in a row at two different strip clubs? That sort of trouble?"

He chuckled. "That wasn't exactly what I meant, but yeah."

A knock came at his front door.

Aiden turned toward it. "That's Henry. He was in the area, so I told him to stop by."

Finn shook the other man's hand, then led him in and offered him a cup of coffee. Henry looked marginally better than Aiden, but not much.

"Cline bought your cover," Henry said to Aiden as he took a sip. "I found a transmission late last night that included you as a potential buyer."

Aiden grimaced. "Good. Because I'm ass-deep in this now. From what I've been able to find out, Cline is not stupid. He's setting up an auction for the Operation Sparrow stuff, trying to pull together as many potential buyers as he can that might be interested in flight pattern info."

Henry nodded and sat down in the kitchen chair Finn gestured to. "That's why you got in so relatively easily. Selling the info is a one-time shot for Cline, so he wants to make as much as he can."

"Smart on his part," Finn said.

Henry circled the rim of his mug with his finger. "I just wish there was something more I could do. I'm a DoD civilian now, not active duty anymore. But just sitting around, gathering intel doesn't make me happy."

"What branch were you in?"

"Air Force. Combat controller. Until I blew out my knee."

Both Finn and Aiden nodded respectfully. Air Force combat controllers were held in high regard among the Special Forces community. They generally acted as a one-man attachment to special operations teams where air traffic was involved, working in remote and often hostile locations. Lone warriors—both part of a team and yet separate from it.

"You caught Cline in the act. That's the most important thing," Finn told him. "Aiden will make sure he goes down."

Aiden took another sip of his coffee. "Believe that. I know it's tough doing nothing when everything you've ever been trained to do tells you otherwise. But I promise we will take them down. Not just Cline, the buyers too."

"Did you find out anything this weekend?" Henry asked.

"They're meeting at different clubs each week, or sometimes even private residences." Aiden rubbed a hand over his eyes. "Cline gives them a little teaser of what he'll be offering. There's a lot of foreigners around, Russians, South Americans. But there are also some good old home-grown criminals like me."

"And what about the mysterious Mr. Stellman?" Finn asked. "Any word on who he is, how to nail him?"

"I haven't been asking a lot of questions, not wanting to draw undue attention. But once drinks are flowing most of those bastards gossip like old women. I don't know who Stellman is, but I know they're all damn scared of him. He's the one coordinating this whole thing for Cline."

Henry took another sip. "My intel confirms Stellman isn't interested in the airspace intel, just in being the broker."

Aiden shifted back in his seat, smothering a yawn. "Honestly, I think there's more going on than just the info with Operation Sparrow, but I have no proof. It's just a gut feeling."

That was enough for Finn. "I'll take your gut feeling over most hard evidence any day. Shamrock has gotten us out of many a dire situation."

Aiden laughed at his Army nickname, which he'd gotten not only because of his Irish name, but because good luck seemed to follow him around. Every single one of their Special Forces team had been shot, stabbed, or damn near blown to kingdom come. Except Aiden. The man never seemed to get a scratch on him.

"All luck runs out sometime, brother. Let's just hope this isn't it. Word is, when Stellman has something to sell, he only shows up at one place and stays out of sight. Once the deal is finished, he makes sure there are no civilian witnesses left to identify him. Evidently, the criminals he works with know not to double-cross him, but civilians he just eliminates."

"Damn, Aiden." Finn's eyebrows drew together. "Be careful you're not in over your head."

Henry's face mirrored Finn's concern.

"Believe me, with no real backup or support? I know it." Aiden nodded. "I just want to figure out where and when the sale is going down. So, for my foreseeable future I'm going to need lots of ones and fives. I'm too old for this shit, you guys."

"I'll be sure to provide you any information I can," Henry said. "You're not completely without backup or support."

They all glanced up when they heard water running upstairs. Finn's house was large—really, way too big for just him and Ethan—and the piping was old. Quiet wasn't an option here.

"Ethan?" Aiden asked.

"No, he's with my mom. It's Charlie."

He'd left her asleep in his bed when he'd come downstairs. The two of them had spent the last sixteen hours in a sort of surreal mixture of sleeping, eating, and lovemaking.

But now it was time for real life to restart. They couldn't lock themselves away from reality any longer. Ethan would be coming home in a couple hours and Charlie had her own condo to go to.

"Zac mentioned Charlie got mugged and you brought her here," Aiden said.

Henry looked surprised. "She's here right now?"

"Yeah, she needed somewhere to crash." Finn turned to Henry. "Do you know her?"

Henry shook his head. "Just heard of her."

Finn refrained from rolling his eyes. He shouldn't be surprised. You couldn't get far around here without knowing about Charlie and their history.

"Is she okay?" Aiden asked. "I heard a knife was involved."

"Yeah, that was just a nick. The bigger problem was exhaustion. Evidently she's been working three jobs for a while."

At least now he knew why she'd been at The Cactus Motel. It had to be easier to stay there a couple nights a week than to drive all the way to her condo in Oak Creek.

Aiden scratched his jaw. "Is she going to be sticking around your place permanently?"

"Hell no, she's got to leave in the next few minutes. There's no way I want her here when Ethan gets home."

Not that Ethan didn't like Charlie or would be upset to find her here. It was just time to get back to real life, a life Finn had conveniently pushed aside during the last thirty-six hours of mind-blowing sex.

"It was nice of you to give her a place to crash." Aiden folded his arms across his chest. "A lot of ex-boyfriends wouldn't even do that. Or might try to take advantage of her."

Aiden hadn't been accusing him, but he couldn't control

his wince. *Shit.* Is that what had happened? She'd been so adamant otherwise, but in her weakened state . . .

He wiped a hand over his face. "I—I . . ."

"Bollinger didn't take advantage of me," a feminine voice said from the doorway. "But I very definitely took advantage of him."

Three handsome faces, all with that military air, swung around to look at Charlie as she walked through the kitchen doorway. She kept a smile on her face even though Finn's comment about making sure she wasn't here when Ethan got home cut at her heart.

What had she expected? That this was the start of a relationship with him?

She'd thrown herself at him in bed and he'd reciprocated. Hot sex, that was all it was. She'd lost the right to hope for anything more eight years ago.

She smiled at the guys. "I'm sure Finn's too much of an officer and a gentleman to say I was the one doing all of the advantage-taking, but it's still true."

Finn looked like he might actually blush. "I was never an officer," he muttered.

Aiden smirked over at him. "Or a gentleman, if you're honest."

"No offense," she said to Aiden, "but it looks like you weren't too much of one yourself last night." She raised an eyebrow at him. "Weren't you at The Silver Palace on Saturday night, too? Sounds like you Linear Tactical guys stay pretty busy."

She wouldn't have figured Finn to be much of a strip club guy. But how well could she say she really knew him anyway? He walked over to the kitchen counter and poured her a cup of coffee. "Still milk and sugar?"

She had learned to drink her coffee with nothing in it to cut down on cost, but hell, if he was offering . . . "Yes, thank you."

"And oatmeal. You still need to eat."

She rolled her eyes. "Yes, Mother."

He was right, she did. God knew they had burned as many calories as she had gotten into her system yesterday. One glance at Finn told her he was thinking the same thing.

The man she didn't know held out his hand. "Henry Nicholson."

She shook it. "Charlotte Devereux. Nice to meet you."

Finn handed her the coffee. "Believe it or not, Aiden and I aren't regular strip club attendees. He's working undercover. Henry is the brains behind it all."

She wiggled her eyebrows at Aiden. "Undercover at a strip club, not a bad gig."

He raised his coffee mug at her in a salute. "I've definitely had worse."

"Same thing you guys were talking about at the Frontier that day at lunch?"

Finn sat beside her. At least he was willing to do that. "Yes, Aiden's going undercover to stop the sale of some government secrets. Henry's the one that discovered it in the first place."

"It's a hodgepodge of criminals and they've been known to meet at clubs," Aiden said.

She nodded. "We get some shady people at The Silver Palace. Last Wednesday night a group reserved the back rooms. They had guns and freaked me out pretty bad."

Henry leaned closer from across the table. "Do you remember anyone who was there?"

She took another sip of her coffee for fortitude. "Big guy with a gun. Little guy who I think was in charge but hid in the dark. There may have been others in the dark room too. Jade, one of our dancers, was back there, probably doing a lot more than just dancing. But that's her business, not mine. The only person I recognized was a guy named Rocco. He's a regular at The Silver Palace."

"Rocco Christensen?" Aiden asked, then glanced at Henry, who gave a little nod.

She shrugged. "I don't know his last name. I just know he's around all the time and brought his friends into the VIP room last week. They weren't happy when I came in to clean up before they were done."

She didn't mention her paranoia about Paul and the police officer talking to her that night. Now that she'd had rest and food, she could recognize they hadn't done anything overtly suspicious.

"I'll look into Rocco more closely," Aiden said.

Henry stood. "Me too. I've got to get going, but I'll be in touch with any info I find."

Finn stood and pointed at her as he walked Henry to the door. "And you stay far away from them if they show back up. Way far."

He came back in and made the three of them oatmeal—giving her a dirty look again when she offered to help—and he and Aiden moved the conversation to funny stories from their time in the Army. She had finished her oatmeal and was laughing as they argued about who held the record for the longest hike carrying a backpack with fifty pounds of gear.

"One time I had to carry Finn *and* his backpack for two miles, so I win anyway," Aiden said as he finished his last bite of oatmeal.

"Why? Did you lose a bet?" she asked.

Their laughter died and the look between the two became solemn. "Our boy here had just taken one for the team," Aiden said softly. "Needed a little help getting out of enemy territory."

Charlie's eyes flew to Finn's. If Aiden had carried him out of enemy territory, then he'd been in pretty desperate shape.

"How bad?" The question came out strangled.

"Not bad."

"Bad."

Both answered at the same time, Finn downplaying his injuries, Aiden probably telling the truth.

She turned to Aiden. "How long ago?"

"Eight years. He was pretty reckless back then."

Her eyes fell on Finn. Right after she'd married Brandon. He'd been hurting, confused, and reckless. And he'd almost died because of it.

Because of *her*.

He reached over and grabbed her hand. "Hey, I lived. Takes more than a group of isolated Afghani extremists to put me down."

Finn was the strongest man she'd ever known. In every possible way.

She couldn't stay at the table, not without spilling her guts and begging for his forgiveness and trying to explain away all the mistakes she'd made. It was too late for that.

She picked up the empty bowls and walked them over to the sink, looking out the window at the morning sun rising higher into the sky. It was time to go. In more ways than one.

"Can you give me a ride back to my car?" she asked. "I'll get out of your hair. I know you've got stuff to do."

"Why don't I just take you to your condo," Finn said. "I'll get one of the guys to run by the Cactus and bring your car to you."

There was no way he could take her to the condo. "No, I need to go into work. It's already past midnight for this Cinderella. Playtime is over."

He brought the coffee cups to the sink and stood beside her. "You've got to promise me you'll stay away from the Cactus. That place is not safe."

She had no desire to go back there, but she might not have a choice. She reached up and brushed his cheek with her hand. "I promise I'm going to take better care of myself." And she was. She couldn't take a chance on getting that rundown again. She felt so much better now after multiple good meals and lots of sleep. Or at least lots of time lying on a bed.

Finn looked skeptical.

"I promise," she said again, careful not to be too specific.

Aiden offered to give her a ride since Ethan was due home soon. She grabbed her suitcase and was ready to go a few minutes later. Aiden took the suitcase and went out to the car.

She was on her way out, too, when Finn grabbed her waist and spun her around. Her arms wrapped around his neck and she pulled his lips down to hers. "Thank you," she said against his mouth. "For everything."

"You and I need to talk about what happened here. The sex. We both know that."

Just like they both knew talking wasn't going to change anything about their past. "Do we? What can be said besides rehashing what we've already lived through? I have no place in your life, Finn. I know that."

And she'd give anything for it not to be true.

He had this beautiful big house here in the woods, one she would've chosen if she'd been around to choose. He had this beautiful full life and she wasn't part of it. No talk was going to change—

He kissed her.

He kissed her in a way didn't change any facts about their past, but it gave her hope about their future.

CHAPTER 19

THREE WEEKS later Charlie was back working the open-to-close shift at The Silver Palace. The hours were still long and wince-worthy, except now not only did her feet hurt, but certain distinct other parts of her body ached too.

At least pleasant memories accompanied those.

Pleasant. If ever there was too tame a word, that was it. But what was the appropriate word for panty-melting, whisker-burns-on-her-inner-thighs great sex?

She hadn't planned on any sexcapades yesterday. She'd been very professional and proper as she'd tutored Ethan in the small library conference room. The kid had come so far. His ability to remember the symbols and numbers they were substituting for words was amazing. They'd basically come up with their own code. It wouldn't make sense to anyone else, but it didn't have to. It did to Ethan, and that's what mattered. She fully expected him to be applying the system to other books and reading at grade level by Christmas.

But having Finn sit in the large chair—which was

supposed to be used for *reading*, damn it—during the tutoring session, studying her with those green eyes . . . Not the way he had during the first session, like he wanted to make sure she didn't do anything unprofessional.

This time he watched with his eyes hooded, his elbow leaning on the arm of the chair, chin resting on his fingers, one tapping his cheek. To anyone else, he'd just look like he was waiting for a meeting to be over.

To Charlie, it was clear he was remembering every *unprofessional* thing they'd done in the past three weeks.

In very clear detail.

And he was imagining quite a few more he'd like to do to her now.

He didn't do or say anything that would jeopardize the tutoring session. And little Ethan was completely unaware of the tension crackling between his dad and Charlie.

She, on the other hand, was afraid she might spontaneously combust.

Finn had remained completely respectful and professional afterward when he'd insisted on buying her lunch. But she couldn't even concentrate on the delicious food because of the way those green eyes kept pinning her from across the table. Finn's eyes hadn't left hers when he'd asked Ethan if he wanted to hang out at the Frontier for a bit while he drove Charlie somewhere.

They were in his Jeep thirty seconds later, heading out of town. They hadn't even made it to the city limits before she was reaching over to unzip his jeans. His groan echoed through the car as she reached inside.

She stroked him, teasing his length. "You were very naughty in the library."

She unbuckled her seat belt and leaned down to lick across the exposed length of him. One of his hands tangled in her hair and his hips jerked up. His strangled curse filled the car.

"I didn't do or say *anything*." His voice was raspy. "I made sure of it."

She took more of him into her mouth, trailing her tongue as far as she could reach, then back up to the tip, before sucking him harder. "But I knew what you were thinking. You were remembering me in your bed, on my hands and knees holding on to the headboard."

His groan reverberated though the vehicle. Maybe he'd been remembering something else, but it didn't matter. There were a lot of options.

"Jesus, Charlie." His fist tightened in her hair. "I can't drive with your little mouth making me crazy in more ways than one."

She had always loved it when he got a little rough. Lost control. She smiled around him, using her hands to drive him crazier still. "Then you better hurry up and get us to one of our old, trusty hideouts." God knew they'd had enough in high school.

He had. Five minutes and multiple groans from him later, as she took him deeper into her mouth, he all but swerved the Jeep into an old picnic area that people had stopped coming to after a bridge collapsed and made it difficult to access. That had been ten years ago.

She didn't have much time to look around before Finn yanked her from her seat and dragged her out his door, his pants still pulled down over his hips. His mouth crashed into hers for just a few seconds—hard, brutal, beautiful—as he worked open the buttons of her blouse, then closed his fingers around her breast, teasing her nipples into hard points through her bra. She was panting by the time he pulled the lacy material down, exposing her nipples.

Keening as he lifted her by the waist, so he could reach them with his mouth.

She couldn't stop her cry of protest when he put her back down on the ground a minute later. Until he turned her and bent her over the driver's seat.

The leather was warm and stiff against her damp nipples and she couldn't help but rub against it for the friction. His hands skimmed roughly up the back of her thighs, bringing the soft cotton of her skirt up with them. He grasped the top of her panties with one hand, pulling them down as he leaned over and whispered hotly in her ear.

"You better hold on to that emergency brake, baby. I don't have any gentle left in me."

She grabbed it with both hands, but it was so long and hard, so phallic in her hands, she couldn't help giving him a sassy look over her shoulder as she curled her fingers around it and stroked it, just like she would his cock if she'd had it in her hands.

Those green eyes narrowed into slits. "That's going to get you so fucked," he promised, voice deeper than she'd ever heard it.

Hers wasn't any less husky. "I hope so."

And it had. Oh, how it had, from a moment later when he thrust in to the hilt until not long after, when she was truly hanging on to the brake as he slammed into her over and over. All she could do was sob his name as the world shattered around her.

By the time they'd made it back to the Frontier forty-five minutes later, she was sure everybody in the entire town knew what they'd been doing. Wavy certainly had, though Finn's sister hadn't said anything as they walked back into the diner.

But when Mia Stevenson, pediatric nurse and town

gossip, saw them come back into the Frontier parking lot, Finn stealing one last kiss, Charlie knew they were in trouble. It wouldn't be long until everyone knew about them.

They'd been sneaking around having sex every moment they could find alone for the last three weeks. But she and Finn still hadn't talked like he'd said he wanted to that morning at his house. And she hadn't pushed it. Because that meant solidifying. She'd rather not talk and still be able to spend time with him than know exactly where she stood —apart.

So, each time they got together, fear wrapped around her heart in an icy grip for those first few minutes.

Had he come to his senses this time?

Decided he'd had enough?

Realized he wasn't ever going to be able to forgive her?

Was this the time he wouldn't pull her into his arms, but instead put her in her place—tell her he was done?

Waiting for the other shoe to drop weighed on her. But she would carry the weight, even knowing this all had to end. When it did, it would no doubt leave her a bloody mess, but she still rushed to meet him every chance she got.

She didn't even try to fool herself into thinking she was going to stop. She wasn't sure she was going to have the strength to walk away once he was done with her. She damn well didn't have it when he wanted her. All she could do was hold on to each moment and collect them in her heart for when she didn't have him anymore.

The other thing she was collecting was all the secrets she was keeping from him. He still didn't know she was homeless. She just couldn't bear to tell him. He would want her to move in with him and she couldn't do that. It wasn't the right choice for him or her. Or a good example for Ethan.

The money he'd given her—closer to a thousand than a couple hundred—had given her a little bit of a cushion, enough that she was making sure she got two full meals every day. Protein. Vegetables. And a bunch of carbs, since her body was blowing through them. She hadn't gained any weight, but at least she hadn't lost any either.

And she'd been sleeping. The two nights at his house had helped chase away the fear that Rocco's business friends might still be after her. They weren't. That had been just her own exhausted paranoia.

The Cactus . . .well, that couldn't be helped. Finn didn't want her there, but if he knew the alternative—sleeping in her car—he'd understand.

No, he wouldn't. He definitely wouldn't. So, she just did her best to make sure it never came up. So long as she didn't look too tired, he didn't pry. She still slept in her car some, but not nearly as often.

If he knew she'd sublet her condo and had no actual address, he would kill her. He'd want to know why she hadn't told him from the very beginning, or let him help. Even when she explained—this was her responsibility, not his—he still wasn't going to understand.

She delivered another drink to a customer. Thank God it was almost closing time. Delicious aches or not, she still had a lot of work to do. Paul hadn't shown up for the third shift in a row. Mack had officially declared him fired, since he hadn't been able to get in touch with him and the guy had just left them in a lurch. Charlie hadn't liked him, even when the scary-people-in-the-back-room incident turned out to be nothing, so it was no skin off her back. But it meant they were short-staffed. More work for everyone.

Jordan approached her after the last drink had been served and all the customers were gone. They were both closing when Jordan cleared her throat, tucking a strand of her dark brown hair behind her ear.

"You know I spent the last six years in prison."

Charlie shook her head and kept wiping down the bar. "*You* know that you don't have to start every conversation you have with me with that information, right?"

Jordan looked down and rubbed her neck. "Yeah, I know. It's a bad habit I've gotten into, framing everything around my incarceration."

Jordan really was a smart young woman. Well-spoken, despite the time she'd been in jail. She should be in college somewhere, not working here. But some thing things didn't turn out the way you planned.

"Let's just agree that I know, I don't care, the past is the past, and you never have to mention it to me again, deal?"

"Deal."

"So, what did you need?"

Jordan grabbed a rack of cleaned glasses and began returning them to their place. She cleared her throat again. "I wanted to see if maybe you and I could work out some sort of a trade-off. I think maybe we could help each other."

"How so?"

Jordan's face reddened as she put away the glasses with much more care than necessary. "Look, I'm not trying to hurt your feelings or your pride or anything. I have the utmost respect for you and—"

"Jordan. Spit it out." Charlie went over to stand right next to the other woman. Jordan may have five inches on her, but the way she was hunched over, it was almost unnoticeable.

"I wanted to know if you wanted to do a trade. Driving here every day from Oak Creek is a long way and my car isn't the best, and gas costs a ton. You and I are basically working every shift we can here . . ."

"So, you need a ride." Shit. This was going to get complicated.

Jordan stopped stacking the glasses. "Yes. And in return, I thought you could live with me at my house. Actually, it was my mother's before she died, and it's completely paid off, which is why I have it." Her words began to speed up. "You're probably like most people and think I don't deserve to have a house after what my father did to everyone and then me—"

Charlie touched her arm. "Past is the past, remember? And I definitely don't hold you responsible for your father's sins."

Jordan blew out a puff of air, her shoulders hunching even more, like a balloon deflating. "You're in the minority."

"Look, Jordan—"

"I know you sleep in your car some nights, Charlie. That you don't have anywhere to live."

She nearly dropped the glass she was holding. "What? How did you know—?"

"Let's chalk it up to me having six year's practice watching other people and figuring them out. I've seen you wash up in the bathroom here after closing more than once. I've seen what you eat, and it's never anything like leftovers from the night before. When you arrive for your shift, you sometimes wear the same clothes from the night before when you left."

"Shit." Now a flush was creeping across her own cheeks.

"This isn't charity. It's not because I feel sorry for you or anything. I don't have money to get a new car. You don't seem to have enough to afford a place to live. We both have what the other needs."

Jordan licked her lips with a nervous sort of hope. The woman was telling the truth. She wasn't making this offer out of pity, but because it was a good fit for them.

"Okay, yes," Charlie finally said. She'd be an idiot not to. Especially since it would also help someone who was becoming a friend.

She'd almost forgotten what those were like.

"Great." Jordan bumped her shoulder against Charlie's. "And, I overheard Mia Stevenson talking about seeing you and Finn kissing in a parking lot yesterday."

She just made a *hmmm* noise in her throat, not sure where Jordan was going with it.

"So, I guess I should tell you that my house is only a couple miles from his place."

She couldn't stop her smile. Now it was truly an offer she couldn't refuse.

CHAPTER 20

FINN STARED at himself in the bathroom mirror.

"You think more is the answer? What are you, a glutton for punishment? You're not in high school anymore, for fuck's sake. You know better."

He did know better.

But he still put on just a tiny bit more aftershave.

Finn couldn't help but laugh at himself, glad none of his friends were around to see him as he got ready to go out with Charlie. He didn't even want to think about what his new nickname would be become. Forget Eagle. They would change it to *Axe* or *Bod*.

"Dad, come on." Ethan banged on the bathroom door. "Quit messing around. We're going to be late."

Finn opened the door and look down at his son. "Might I remind you, little dude, that I had to drag you away from playing with Jess and Sky? If you didn't want us to be late, you probably should've taken that into consideration."

Ethan still spent all his free time with the little girl. But maybe continuing to gain confidence with his reading would help. Make him feel more at ease with kids his age. Until then, Finn wasn't going to fight him on it. One battle at a time.

"But I'm not the one in the bathroom now, painting my nails and curling my hair." Ethan grinned up at him.

Finn rolled his eyes and flicked his son gently on the forehead. God, there had been a time when he'd never thought they would get to this point, where they could laugh and joke. When he'd first gotten custody, the kid had been so silent and withdrawn Finn had been afraid he was permanently damaged. Now he was saying stuff that was perfectly sarcastic and funny.

"Yeah." Finn put on his best falsetto. "But do I look pretty?"

Ethan cackled out loud and Finn hauled him in for a hug. He was taking the boy into the Frontier for lunch before his tutoring appointment. Then Grandma would be picking him up for another sleepover—a last hurrah before school started next week.

And a chance to take Charlie to dinner, where they were going to talk and not have sex.

Or, hopefully, talk and *then* have sex.

She had to work tonight, he knew, and he'd have her back in time to get there. Might even find himself hanging out at The Silver Palace and escorting a certain bartender home. To his bed or hers, he wasn't particular.

But first they had to talk about what was happening between them. They didn't have to figure everything out. Hell, they didn't have to figure *anything* out, but things couldn't go on the way they had been.

Charlie thought he detested her for marrying Kempsley, that whatever was happening between the two of them was some sort of revenge sex for her leaving Finn eight years ago.

It had taken him a while to realize what that wary look in her eyes meant—she was preparing for an emotional blow. From him. For him to cut her loose and tell her he was finished.

Or that he planned to keep any sort of relationship with her hidden from everyone else. He'd seen her near panic when Mia had caught them kissing.

She expected him to tell her that she meant nothing to him. That he was just using her for sordid, raunchy sex, but that all he felt for her beyond that was loathing.

And maybe at one point that would've been true. But not now. Life was too short to hold on to grudges. The Army had taught him that. Too many deaths, too many good men and women gone without warning, when they thought they had so much time left.

Life held no guarantees.

Charlie had married Kempsley for his money. Maybe that made her selfish and self-serving. But it wasn't an unforgivable sin. God forbid everybody be judged the rest of their lives for the decisions they made in their early twenties.

So that was the talk he wanted to have with her. That maybe he wasn't exactly sure what the future was going to look like, but he didn't want to keep staring at the past.

Forgiveness was a tricky thing. It wasn't like a switch you flipped, and bam, one day someone just decided to forgive someone else. It was a constant process. Every time a situation presented itself where his instinct was to lash out at Charlie or let the bitterness build up, he would have to choose to let it go, choose to forgive until, finally, it stopped popping up so often. And maybe some day not at all.

It was conditioning. Special Forces had taught him the

importance of it, physically and mentally. And it applied now.

So, no more lunch quickies where he couldn't keep his hands and mouth off her. At least not today. Not until they talked, and she understood that he didn't already have one foot out the door. He wasn't going anywhere.

But tomorrow? Tomorrow and every day after their conversation was fair game for any sort of quickie he could talk her into.

He and Ethan chatted all the way into town. Ethan was still in a deep debate over which Lego kit he wanted. He was also excited about the new codes he'd come up with for the much longer chapter book he and Charlie were working on. It was a shit ton of memorization, all these different symbols for words, but Ethan didn't mind. Memorization of codes was something he understood and could conquer.

They pulled up at the Frontier, Ethan yelling out his order to Trey and Wavy as they walked in the door, before sitting down to talk to Trey. Finn took a seat at the bar too.

"What are you grinning about, big bro?" Wavy asked as she got him some water. "Please don't tell me I have babysitting duty again while you go, ahem, *gallivanting* around town."

"No, actually, I'm planning to take Charlie on a very proper date tonight. And Mom has already agreed to watch the rugrat."

"People are going to talk, you know that, right? I mean, they sort of already are, since Mia saw you two a few days ago."

Finn just lifted a hand, palm up. "Since when do people *not* gossip in Oak Creek?"

Wavy rubbed at an eyebrow. "Nobody wants to see her

hurt you again, that's all. Nobody really trusts her, and I'm not sure you should either."

He was about to argue the point with his sister and explain that Charlie wasn't the bad guy in this situation when Sheriff Nelson walked through the door. Finn turned to greet him like everyone else. Instead of the wave he'd expected in return, the sheriff moved directly toward him.

The look in the older man's eyes had Finn's blood turning cold.

"Got a moment I can talk to you outside, Finn?" The sheriff's words did not reassure him in any way.

He looked at Wavy.

"I've got Ethan," she whispered.

He followed the sheriff outside. "What's going on?"

Sheriff Nelson took his hat off and rubbed a hand over his dark, shaved head. "I've heard you're friendly again with Charlotte Devereux."

"She's tutoring Ethan. And yeah, we're sort of seeing each other, I guess. Why?"

"Do you have any contact info for her family? I know the Devereuxes sold their business and house and moved years ago, but no one seems to know where they are presently."

This did not sound good. "Why, Sheriff?"

"There was a fire at Charlotte's condo early this morning. In the paperwork the condo office had, you were listed as her emergency contact. I didn't think that sounded right, but . . ."

"I might have been once, but I can't believe she'd still have me listed. She said her dad is in some sort of medical facility in Denver, but I'm not sure where. Is Charlie okay? Is she in the hospital? I need to go to her right away." He was already turning toward his Jeep. They could figure out where her parents were later.

"Son." The sheriff put his hand on Finn's shoulder to stop him. "By the time the firefighters got there, the blaze was out of control. There was one casualty. Female. I'm sorry."

Finn felt like all the oxygen had been sucked out of the entire planet. This could not be happening. "Ch-Charlie?"

"The body was burned pretty extensively, so an immediate positive ID wasn't possible. But it's her name listed on the unit paperwork. Unless you know somewhere else she's moved to?"

Sheriff Nelson's voice sounded a million miles away. "No. Nowhere else. That's Charlie's place."

CHAPTER 21

THREE HOURS LATER, Finn let himself into his house, completely numb.

The first thing he'd done was try Charlie's phone. It'd gone immediately to voicemail. The way it had the next one hundred times he'd called her.

Just in case.

Next, he'd texted Wavy to ask their mom to get Ethan. He couldn't go back inside. He couldn't see any of them right now. Not when his own world was crumbling at his feet.

Then he'd asked Sheriff Nelson to take him to the morgue. He would've begged if necessary, but it hadn't been. Even if the body was burned beyond recognition, he had to see it for himself. He couldn't possibly believe it until he did.

The sheriff had wanted to drive him, but Finn had refused. What if this was all a mistake and Charlie called and needed him somewhere? He would have to be able to get to her.

He still couldn't accept that this was happening. How

could Charlie possibly be gone?

The sheriff directed him to sit in a hard plastic chair in the hallway outside the morgue while he went inside to arrange things. Finn looked up and down the empty hallway. He had lived in Oak Creek his whole life and never been here, even when his dad had died. He'd never even thought about where the morgue was.

He was in some sort of fog.

The door at the end of the hall opened and Zac hurried in, breathing hard like he'd been running. He stopped as he got to Finn.

He and Zac had known each other their entire lives. This man was closer to him than even his own family. Zac didn't say anything, just put his hand on Finn's shoulder.

Two minutes later Aiden walked through the door, followed by Gavin. They both gave him solemn nods, but neither said anything either. When Dorian, another partner, entered the hallway not long after, it was the same.

These were his brothers. They had stood with each other before as soldiers when death had come for one of their own. They would stand shoulder to shoulder now.

After the sheriff and coroner showed Finn the body, he came back out into the hallway.

He shook his head at his friends, every emotion he had buried in ice. "The sheriff was right. There's no way to visually identify her. They're working on dental records."

But he had to admit the size of the charred body roughly matched Charlie's small frame.

"I should feel something, shouldn't I?" he asked Zac in that barren hallway. Zac had lost his wife, knew death firsthand. "Knowledge in my gut that that's not her? Or that it is?"

Zac shook his head. "It doesn't always work that way,

brother, you know that."

"Right."

The guys had wanted to drive him home, but he'd refused. At least one of them still followed, probably Gavin, and no doubt Dorian would be running around in his beloved wilderness, keeping an eye on Finn's house from a distance.

They didn't need to worry that he was going to have some sort of breakdown. That required emotion. He couldn't feel anything.

Sheriff Nelson was now trying to find Charlie's parents. He'd promised to call as soon as he'd reached them. Finn didn't know why he'd insisted on that, or why he was going to insist on being with the sheriff when he talked to them. Charlie's parents had never liked him. But if the sheriff was going to tell them their daughter was dead, Finn was going with him.

He tried Charlie's phone again, just in case. And to hear her voice.

This is Charlie. Leave a message.

He didn't. He hung up and called again.

This is Charlie. Leave a message.

He set his phone on the table and sank down onto his couch, unable to bear the thought that might be the last time he ever heard her voice. He could feel the ice begin to crack and knew the pain wasn't far behind.

There was a light tap on his door, but he didn't get up. Instead he tried to pull the ice back around him. It had to be better than the pain. His front door creaked open.

"Finn, are you here? I saw your Jeep outside. Did I get our tutoring appointment time wrong? I went to the library, but no one was there."

Charlie's voice. For just a second, he thought his brain

had taken her voice and transposed it to his doorway. Then he realized.

Charlie was at his door.

"Oh, my God."

Less than three seconds later he had her yanked inside the door, pinned against the wall, his mouth on hers.

"Charlie. Charlie." He couldn't stop saying her name, even as he devoured her mouth. He wasn't sure if it was a prayer of wonder, thankfulness, or both. His hands cupped her cheeks, her jaw, moved down her shoulders to her arms, touching her all over as if to convince his mind she was really there.

"Finn, what's wrong?" Her eyes were frantic as he finally eased back. Now her hands were wandering over his face and jaw and shoulders. "What? What happened? I went into the library when we were supposed to meet but you guys weren't there. Are you okay?"

"Where is your phone?" He couldn't be angry, not when relief was still flooding every part of his system.

"I left it at . . .home."

He noticed the slight hesitation at the word. He needed answers, but first he had to make a call before the sheriff found Charlie's parents and told them she might be dead.

"Hang on a second and let me stop the world from ending."

"What?"

He still hadn't moved his body completely away from hers. Panic simmered just underneath the relief. He couldn't stop touching her. He started to take off her shirt with one hand as he reached for his phone with the other. He called Zac, who picked up after the first ring.

"You doing all right—"

Finn cut him off. "Charlie just showed up at my house.

Notify Nelson and let him know he's got the wrong girl. I'll call you later."

He wasn't even sure he got the last word out before he disconnected and tossed the phone aside.

All he knew was he had to be inside Charlie *right now*.

She was wearing that same skirt from last week. Which was a good thing, because Finn didn't think he had the patience to get any other clothes off of her. He backed her up hard against the wall, reached under her skirt and pulled her underwear all the way down her legs.

"Finn . . ."

He could feel her wetness against his fingers, could hear her breathing just as hard as he was. He knew she wasn't trying to stop him with her words, just trying to understand what was going on. But he couldn't stop, couldn't take the time to explain things to her. He barely got himself out of his jeans before he slid his hands under her ass and lifted her against the wall.

Her legs slid around his hips and with one thrust he slammed home. Her grunt was full of equal measures pleasure and pain, but he couldn't stop. He slid in and out of her brutally, angling her weight so he could get as deep inside her as possible.

He'd thought she was gone.

He would know all the details of what the hell had happened, but right now he would know nothing but the tightness of her surrounding him, milking him like a fist.

Her eyes started to close. "No." The rasp of his voice was harsh. "Keep your eyes open. Look at me." His forehead fell against hers, his eyes pinning those crystalline blue ones just as his hips pinned her lower body.

He had to see those eyes. He'd thought he would never see them again.

But soon neither of them could keep theirs open. He buried his face in her neck as their sweat ran together. Her fingernails scored his back under his shirt as he thrust into her, his pace frantic. Manic.

But for the first time in his life—especially with Charlie—his orgasm seemed elusive. Physically, everything was perfect . . .her tight, wet heat gripping him. But oh God. Oh God, he'd thought she was gone.

He didn't want to stop, didn't want to separate from her. But he was afraid nothing would wipe away the thought that he'd lost her. No amount of sex. No number of orgasms.

"Finn, look at me."

He opened his eyes and brought his face up, so he could see her, keeping her body pinned tightly against the wall. He was still thrusting in and out of her as her small hands gripped his cheeks, her thumbs rubbing over his brow.

"I'm here, okay? Whatever it is, I'm here."

And then, even though he'd been pounding her against a wall, still moving hard inside her with no other foreplay or touch, she smiled. It was the most beautiful thing he'd ever seen.

"I'm here," she whispered again.

And that was what his mind needed to release the demons that had consumed it. *She was here.* He began thrusting earnestly again, holding more of her weight, careful now not to hurt her. Within moments, his orgasm was bearing down on him.

He hooked her leg higher with his arm, hitting that place inside her that would have her chasing her own, holding on until she caught up with him. Only when she was yelling his name, her hands digging into his shoulders, clutching him to her, did he finally let himself go.

And as he did he whispered her name.

CHAPTER 22

"I'M NOT sure what just happened, but I don't know if I'm going to be able to walk," Charlie said a few minutes later.

Finn wasn't quite sure either. They were sitting on the couch where he'd carried her after nearly breaking down the wall by his door. He grabbed a washcloth in the bathroom and cleaned them both up, staring at their bodies when he realized a condom hadn't even crossed his mind.

But that conversation would have to get in line behind all the others they needed to have.

"Do you want to explain to me what just happened?" She opened her eyes after he sat down next to her. "I'm all for being jumped at the door, but that seemed a little intense."

There wasn't any way to put this off. "Sheriff Nelson is looking for you. Your condo burned down."

Charlie sat straight up. *"What?"*

"Burned to the ground." Finn swallowed hard. "A woman inside died."

"Oh, my God."

He realized she was still trying to process the initial news. "I'm sorry, Charlie. Did you have a friend staying with you or something?"

She got up and began pacing. "Honestly, I don't even remember the name of the woman I sublet the condo to. I would have to look it up. She was a college student."

What? "I don't understand. You don't live there?"

She rubbed a hand through her hair. "No. It was too expensive to keep up once I had to pay for everything with Mama and Dad. I haven't lived there for eighteen months." She turned and looked at him, eyes getting big as she finally processed what was happening. "You thought it was me. The dead woman."

He threw a hand up in the air. "What the hell else was I supposed to think? You weren't answering your phone, and as far as I knew that was still your home. Don't you think you probably ought to give me your new address, for crying out loud? What if I had come by your condo looking for you?"

Her gaze didn't quite meet his. "Sure. Yeah, my address. I'll write it down for you."

She was avoiding again. Maybe not lying, but not telling the whole truth. Damn it, he was not going to let her get away with it. Not today. Not after what he had been through.

"What is your address, Charlie? It's not a hard question. I don't need you to write it down, I've lived in this town my whole life, I'll know where it is."

"Finn . . ."

"What is the damn address, Charlie?"

"I'm living with Jordan." Her eyes narrowed, and she took a step back, going on the offensive. "Do you have a problem with that?"

He ignored her attempt to deflect and change the subject. "How long have you lived with her?"

He could see the wheels turning in her head, trying to find a way to spin this. And suddenly it all made sense: her lack of sleep, her weight loss, catching her at the Cactus.

"Are you lying again now?" he asked. "If I go out to your car and open the trunk, am I going to find everything you own inside that BMW? Goddammit, Charlie," he slammed his palm down on his coffee table, "are you *homeless*?"

She didn't look at him, and that told everything. He couldn't believe this. Now *he* got up and began pacing.

"No," she finally answered. "You won't find all my stuff in the car. I'm telling the truth, I moved in with Jordan."

"When?" he asked, his words no less deadly for their low volume.

"This morning, after our shift last night."

"And before that?"

"You were right." She wrapped both arms around her chest, hugging herself. "I was mostly staying in my car, or a couple nights a week at the Cactus."

Finn wasn't even sure how to respond. Rage, fear, disbelief all warred inside his brain.

He wasn't just angry at her, he was pissed at himself. He'd *known* something was wrong. All the pieces had been right in front of him and he'd just refused to put them together. Hell, he'd seen all the stuff in her car. He'd watched her wear the same outfit over and over. He'd seen her lose weight right in front of his eyes.

"Jesus, Charlie, why didn't you tell someone? If not me, then someone else?"

Her shoulders hunched, and she didn't look at him. "I made my choice eight years ago. When I turned my back on you, I turned my back on this town. Everybody knew it."

He scrubbed a hand over his eyes. "Fine, nobody liked what happened between us. But none of them would've let you live in your *car*, for God's sake."

Her frown turned mutinous. "It was my problem to handle."

"You're too damn stubborn for your own good." He threw up his hands.

She just shrugged. "Too proud and too stupid also if you're keeping an accurate record of all my wrongdoings." She sank back down on the couch.

He wanted to hold on to his anger, wanted to rant and rave about the danger she'd put herself in, but he had to face the simple fact. If she had stayed in that condo, she would've died in that fire. Homeless for a few months didn't seem so bad in comparison.

But no matter what, it was proof that she still didn't trust him. She hadn't really ever trusted him. Not eight years ago. Not now.

He sighed and sat back down beside her. "Are you really living with Jordan? Because you can damn well bet I'm going to be coming over there. A lot. It's only a couple miles from here."

She curled up beside him up. He couldn't stop himself from pulling her entire body onto his lap. Her arms wrapped around his neck. "I promise. She and I worked out a deal that is kind of perfect for both of us. So, no more sleeping in my car or at the Cactus."

"Do you know how much danger you were in?"

Charlie wiggled herself around, so she was facing him, straddling his hips. "You mean the worst sort, like a druggie attacking me?"

"Yes, that's exactly what I mean."

"Do you recall the rest of that story, where I was

rescued by a handsome soldier who then took me to his bed and kept me in a state of sexual delirium for the next two days?" She ground herself against him, her smile pure evil femininity.

He couldn't hold on to the anger. He was so happy to have her here, alive, safe with him. But two could play at that game. He reached under her skirt, where she was still naked, and drew light circles around her clit.

"Yes, it's all very dangerous. The sort of stuff that can lead to this." He leaned her back on one arm and moved his head down to suck hard on her nipple through her thin top. He alternated between the two until she was grinding against his fingers.

He gave her a just a few more seconds, driving her closer to losing control, before he stopped suddenly, grabbed her by the waist and stood, moving her away. She cried out in protest.

"Hey!"

"See? Told you it was dangerous. Now we've got to see the sheriff and prove you're alive. Maybe if you're good we can pick back up where we left off."

Those blue eyes narrowed dangerously. "Be careful, Bollinger. Turnabout is fair play."

He reached over and kissed her. "I'm counting on it."

Being alive was a lot more work than Charlie had planned. Sheriff Nelson was glad to see her, although they were all saddened about the death of Cynthia Reynolds, the woman Charlie had sublet her condo to.

"Don't you own it anymore?" Finn had asked.

"No, I had to sell it during my parents' financial crisis.

But I couldn't bear to let it go completely, so I leased it back, even when I wasn't living here."

She didn't tell Finn the reason the thought of letting it go had been so painful was because of him. That had been the place they'd always thought they would start their life together.

"Brandon knew how much I loved it, so at first he paid for it, but when we divorced, I took over the payments." She shrugged. "When I needed more for Dad's care, subletting seemed like the easiest solution. Both Cynthia and I were trying to save money, so we didn't go through official channels. She just paid me every month, and my name is still on all the lease papers."

It wasn't surprising, given the circumstances, that everyone thought the dead woman had been Charlie. She spent the rest of the afternoon working through details: finding Cynthia's information for the sheriff so he could contact her family, then talking to the condo managers, insurance representatives, and even a fire inspector.

That one threw her a little. Evidently, although it wasn't impossible the fire had been an accident since it was a gas leak that had caught a spark, they were still considering foul play.

Charlie hadn't known Cynthia well enough to know if anyone wanted to hurt her, but the police would be looking into it.

Her date with Finn had been postponed. That made her both sad and happy. Sad because honestly, she would take every second Finn would give her . . .not to mention she'd never turn down a full meal for the rest of her life.

But also because. . .he wanted to have *the talk*. About how what was between them was nothing permanent. That it was sex, maybe even fantastic sex, but that was all. About how he was never going to be able to fully forgive her or trust her again, forget ever loving her.

He wouldn't say it like that, of course. Honestly, he probably didn't even think of it like that. Instead the words *casual* and *friendly* and *light* would be part of the conversation. And smiles. Just wanting to make sure she understood, you know? So no one got hurt.

She could see and hear it perfectly coming from Finn's sexy lips. And she would smile and nod in return and pray he couldn't see her heart shattering.

And in a few weeks when he was done with her, when someone in town warned him about getting burned by the same flame twice and he took that advice to heart that time, she would just have to let him go. And never let him see how she ached for so much more. How she yearned for *everything* with him.

Knowing she'd had that everything once and let it go . . . it was the most unbearable of weights. Crushing. But what she'd told him about being homeless applied to this also: it was her problem to handle.

She'd avoided the talk tonight, since she'd had to go straight to work by the time she was done with everything concerning the fire. Work was at least easier, now that she had somewhere to go after, somewhere safe to really get a good night's sleep.

The next morning, Finn showed up unannounced at Jordan's house. They had rescheduled her session with Ethan, and Finn said he was just offering her a ride into town. But Charlie knew he was making sure this living arrangement was legitimate.

As they climbed into the Jeep, Ethan smiling in the back seat, Finn raised an eyebrow when she accused him of not trusting her. "Me not trust you to give me all the details? How could that ever happen?"

That was an argument she would never win, so she let it go.

Later, Finn insisted on taking her to the Frontier after the tutoring session.

"Come on, Charlie. Everybody has to eat," Ethan argued, standing next to Finn, looking so much like his dad her heart clinched. "And it's key lime pie day!"

To the little boy, that obviously settled all arguments.

"Then I guess I must," she said.

The words were barely out of her mouth before Ethan was asking Finn if he could go ahead. And of course, Mr. Mazille caught Ethan running again on his way out.

"You know we really shouldn't be seen together any more than we have been," she said as they exited the library and walked toward the diner. "Rumors are already starting to fly."

Finn just shrugged. "I'm not afraid of them. People around here are going to talk regardless. They'll move on to the next thing when they realize there's nothing to see here."

He smiled and she somehow managed to return it. *Nothing to see here.* Maybe she didn't even have as much time left with him as she'd thought.

She tried to remind herself that any time was more than she'd ever thought she would get, but as he put his hand on the small of her back and led her into the Frontier, she couldn't quite convince herself.

"Are you okay?" he asked after they'd settled in and ordered. "You're a little quiet."

She managed a smile again. "Yeah. Just everything, you know. The fire, settling in at Jordan's place."

And the fact that everyone inside was, in fact, staring at them. Word about the fire had spread, and people were more curious about the two of them sitting together than ever.

"Tell me what's wrong, princess."

Nothing. Everything. Just waiting on you to decide when you're going to shred my heart into pieces.

"I don't—"

The door of the diner burst open and Riley Wilde came running in. Charlie would've thought the ER nurse was there to announce some citywide emergency if it weren't for the huge grin splitting her face.

"Boy Riley is here. It's time for the back-to-school special!" she yelled.

Charlie had no idea what the younger woman was talking about.

"Where?" Wavy asked.

"The quarry. Jumping from Pikes Peak." Riley was fairly humming with excitement. "Broadcasting live."

"How? Helicopter?" Charlie was surprised to hear the question come from Finn. "Pikes Peak isn't accessible by any trails."

If possible, Riley's grin got bigger. "Free climb. Going up will be just as big a danger as coming down. Don't worry, a safety team is in place, as always. One hour, people! Picnic and party after."

She ran out the door as fast as she had run in.

"Last call!" Wavy yelled.

Charlie turned to Finn. "Can you please explain what is going on? Did Riley just come in here, refer to herself as a boy in the third person, and announce she was about to jump off Pikes Peak, which is basically tantamount to suicide?"

Finn began shoveling his food in his mouth. "No," he said between bites. "She wasn't talking about herself. She was talking about Riley Harrison."

"I don't know who that is. Should I?"

"He's a local celebrity. Hell, he's a celebrity everywhere. A YouTube extreme sport sensation. We all call him Boy Riley since we already had one Riley addicted to extreme sports in the town. He does a lot of traveling all over, different stunts and stuff, but he's back here a few times a year. Mostly, I think, for Girl Riley."

"Nobody cares that he might be about to kill himself by climbing and jumping off Pikes Peak?" She looked around. Everyone was rapidly eating and paying, obviously about to head out for the show. "I mean, is the Frontier actually going to close right in the middle of the day?"

Finn laughed. "Everything is, except the hospital. Watching Boy Riley is sort of a phenomenon and a tradition over the last few years. Town-wide picnic."

"It just sounds dangerous and a little reckless. I'm not sure I want to witness that."

"I'm ready, Dad!" Ethan yelled from the bar. "I'll just have to eat key lime pie next week."

"You're going to let Ethan go?" she asked.

Finn reached over and chucked her on the chin. "Come on, Charlie. Dangerous and reckless used to be your middle name. Don't you want to see what is worth missing key lime pie day for?"

"I—I . . ." What was her problem exactly? She had no idea.

Now Finn's fingers trailed down her cheek. "It's been too long for you, princess. That might make me most sad of all."

"Too long for what?"

"Since you remembered what it was like to just sit back and enjoy a day of fun."

Charlie jerked back to start arguing but stopped at Finn's raised brow.

"You want to tell me that's not true? When was the last time you did nothing?"

"I do nothing all the time." She lowered her volume. "I spent a great deal of time doing nothing but hanging out naked in bed with you last weekend."

He smiled and took his last bite. "And I enjoyed that very much. But even then, you weren't relaxed. Your brain is always running a million miles an hour. You're always working angles, figuring out how to rob Peter to pay Paul. Deciding if what you're doing is the most efficient use of your time or if you should be doing something else instead. Always bracing yourself for whatever life throws at you next. Even with me. Maybe *especially* when you're with me."

She stared at him. All of what he'd said was true. But she never thought he'd noticed.

He reached over and took her hand, bringing her fingers to his lips. "Come do nothing with me. No worrying about the future or the past, just enjoying the sunshine and water, each other, and some crazy kid attempting a stunt we might have been stupid enough to try at one time. Just be, Charlie. For one afternoon, just *be*."

She nodded. What else could she do?

He grinned. "Good. We'll have to stop by your house because you'll have to *just be* in a bikini."

CHAPTER 23

LITERALLY HALF THE town was here for the event. The quarry, which wasn't one at all, but a large lake, was surrounded by cliffs on three sides. Two were relatively low and could be reached by trails. One even had a small rope ladder leading up from the water. During the summer, Oak Creek residents could be found swimming and jumping and, ahem, doing other things if Charlie's high school memories served correctly.

As she laid out on the blanket Finn had set up, letting her skin soak in the sun's rays, she realized how right he had been. For months, *years* if she was honest, she'd just been waiting for the next bad thing. She peeked up at Finn, who was with Ethan in the water. Everyone was playing now, and eating, and enjoying a part of life you could only find in a small town.

Boy Riley had finished his stunt, filmed everything, and gotten over fifty thousand hits on his website in the first two hours, from what she'd heard. Everyone was laughing, talking, and congratulating him. Charlie rolled onto her stomach and propped her chin on her hands to see them better. His arm hadn't left Girl Riley's waist since the moment he'd exited the water.

Movement at the far side of the clearing caught her attention. Someone was standing there, watching everything going on—the laughing, the playing—but not coming any closer. It took Charlie a minute to realize it was Jordan. She'd seen the other woman at the house when she'd run inside to change, had invited her to come, although she'd adamantly refused.

It took guts for her to be here now. Charlie didn't want her to feel alone. She was about to sit up to get the other woman's attention when freezing droplets of water on her back had her screeching and falling back on the blanket.

Finn laughed. "You should come in the water."

She sat up and faced him. "I was just going to invite . . ." She looked over to where Jordan had been standing but couldn't see her anymore. Maybe she'd found someone else to hang out with. Probably best. "Never mind. But I think those drops were plenty for me. Where is Ethan?"

"I lost him to Jess and Sky." Finn pointed to a little girl, maybe three years old. She and Ethan were building things out of small pieces of wood they could find on the shore of the lake. A puppy was dashing back and forth between them.

"Looks like they're having fun. It's nice he would play with someone younger than him."

Finn sighed. "I used to think that too until I realized he doesn't want to play with anyone *except* Jess. Ethan doesn't have any friends his own age. No matter what I've tried, he would rather hang out with that little girl. Don't get me wrong, I love Jess, and her mom, Peyton, works part-time at Linear. So, they are like family."

"But you just wish Ethan had some friends *besides* family," she finished for him.

"Exactly. I'm worried he has emotional challenges to go along with his academic ones."

"They do sometimes go hand in hand. Do you mind me asking about his mother? How long have you guys been divorced?"

She didn't think he'd married a local girl. She would've heard about that. But given Ethan's age, Finn had to have gotten married not long after her own wedding to Brandon. Maybe someone he'd met in the Army.

"We weren't ever married." Finn's words were clipped.

"Oh. Is she part of Ethan's life now?" Maybe Finn only had custody of Ethan during the summer. That wasn't uncommon. And sometimes kids had a hard time adjusting to the shuffle back and forth between parents. That could be part of Ethan's emotional challenges. Not that Charlie had really seen evidence of any in Ethan. Maybe some self-esteem issues, but those weren't uncommon in children who suffered with dyslexia and reading disabilities.

"No, she's not," Finn said, looking at the water.

Oh God, did Finn still have feelings for her? Did he want to try and work things out with her in the long run? That had never even crossed Charlie's mind.

"I'm sorry. Your relationship with her is none of my business. I didn't mean to stick my nose where it doesn't belong."

Now he looked over at her. "We don't have a relationship. She and I never did."

"Oh. Does Ethan have a relationship with her? Maybe you could get her input on your concerns about his friendship with Jess."

"She's dead, Charlie. Ethan's mother died."

Crap. She was just making this worse. "I'm sorry. I'm going to stop talking now."

Finn didn't say anything for the longest time and she wondered if she had ruined the entire afternoon. She was supposed to just be sitting here and enjoying the sun, and instead she'd gotten all into his business and caused him to withdraw.

She nudged his shoulder with her own. "Hey, I'm sorry. I, more than anyone, understand some things you just don't want to talk about. Please don't let me ruin our easy afternoon. Still want me to go in the water with you?"

~

Finn looked over at Charlie's pinched features, which just a few minutes ago had been relaxed and laughing.

Way to go, asshole. You promised her an afternoon of no worries, then turned around and gave her one more thing she thinks she needs to shoulder.

Even more, he kept wanting her to tell the truth about her life—to *trust* him with it—and wasn't willing to do the same himself.

It was hard to leave yourself open to judgment. He needed to remember that when he was expecting it of her.

"No," he finally said. "I want to tell you about Tamara. I'm sorry I was being a jerk."

"No," she rushed. "You weren't. I pushed, and I shouldn't have—"

He reached over and kissed her, partly to stop her rambling words, but mostly because it was the easiest way to make her understand he wasn't angry at her. She tried to draw back almost immediately, but he threaded his fingers into that long blonde hair and kept his mouth against hers. He didn't care who saw.

Only after she stopped all resistance and melted into his kiss did he let her go. Those blue eyes blinked open. "You're dangerous," she whispered.

He smiled. "I don't like talking about Tamara because I made so many mistakes. Ones Ethan ended up paying for. It's hard for me to tell you, *especially* you, how bad things got."

Her hand came up to stroke his jaw. "Can I remind you that until a few days ago I was living in my car? So, if this is a contest of who fell the furthest, I think I have you beat."

Finn wasn't so sure. "I didn't even know about Ethan for the first three years of his life. I met Tamara when I was on . . .leave. It was a one-night stand, a stupid mistake."

He didn't want to tell her that it had been after he'd failed to stop Charlie from marrying Kempsley. That had been why he'd taken a stranger back to his hotel room. Because he couldn't stand the thought of Charlie on her wedding night with someone else. He pulled back from her now and stretched his legs out in front of him.

But she was too smart not to figure it out. "You met her here in Wyoming?"

Finn sighed. "Yes."

She looked over at Ethan. "He's seven, right?"

Finn nodded. She was doing the math in her head.

"It happened when you came here to stop my wedding," she whispered. "I don't know how I didn't figure that out before."

He nodded. "I was reeling pretty hard."

That didn't even come close to the emotional devastation he'd been going through. And, since he'd gone AWOL, he'd had no idea what sort of future he was going back to in the Army, if he had one at all. Fortunately, that had worked out for him, largely thanks to Major Pinnock.

Finn took off his sunglasses and rubbed his fingers over his eyes. "I know after what happened against my door yesterday you're going to find this hard to believe, but I did use protection with Tamara. Yesterday is the only time in my entire life I've been too caught up to even think about it."

She gave an adorable snort. "Thank you, I think. And I'm on birth control, by the way, so we're safe."

This woman had no idea how much she splintered his focus. Always had. "Honestly, I never even thought about Tamara again. I was trying to put that entire period behind me."

"Did she contact you when she found out she was pregnant?"

"No. But in her defense, I hadn't given her any reason, or much method, of doing so. The place where I hooked up with Tamara makes The Cactus Motel look like the Ritz."

She winced. He couldn't blame her.

"She was on drugs. I mean, I wasn't actively aware of that at the time, but honestly I didn't care."

"How did you find out about Ethan at all?"

He glanced at the water. "That's what kills me the most. If I hadn't had my particular name—there aren't very many Finns from Wyoming in the Army—I never would have."

"She contacted the Army for child support?"

Finn scrubbed a hand over his face. "Worse. She tracked down my mother."

Charlie's mouth gaped open. "When she was pregnant?"

"No. Three years later. She'd already had Ethan and

he'd been taken away from her by social services. By that point she was a full-fledged junkie."

"What did she want from your mom?"

Finn watched his son playing with Jess, looking like any other healthy, happy seven-year-old. Maybe a little on the small side, but Finn had been scrawny growing up also.

"Tamara showed up with a picture of Ethan and said she needed help to get clean." He picked at pieces of grass next to the blanket, unable to look Charlie in the eye. "You know my mom. Hell, she probably would've helped for any kid, but one that looked like me in my baby pictures? I don't think she felt like she had any choice. She knew the timing of Ethan's birth coincided with when I had been here on leave. And Tamara knew stuff about me, that I was in the Army, that I had been upset about someone getting married. Tamara knew enough to be credible."

Charlie's small hand covered his on the blanket.

He kept going. "Tamara promised she would get the information about the baby and return with it, so they could get him out of foster care. She promised to get clean, with Mom's help, and get back custody of Ethan. I don't know if Mom believed her, but she didn't know what else to do. She gave Tamara two hundred dollars. But she never showed back up."

Charlie shook her head. "Honestly, she was a junkie. I'm surprised she didn't return to try and get more money, even if she never planned to provide more information about Ethan."

"She didn't show back up because she overdosed and died."

"Oh my gosh," Charlie gasped.

"Mom spent the next six months trying to find her. All she had was a first name and that picture of Ethan as a baby.

Not much to go on. Finally, she told me about what had happened. I took leave and came home to try to figure out what was going on."

He finally looked over at her. "It took a long time to find Ethan. And once we did, it was an extensive process to gain custody of him. I had to undergo physical tests to prove I was his biological father, and then it was just a long, slow system to wade through. Ethan got bounced around a lot, since he was listed as a temporary placement in the foster care system. God, Charlie, it broke my mother's heart to know her grandson had no permanent home when all she wanted to do was pull him close and keep him with her forever."

Her fingers trailed up and down his hand.

"The foster homes were a damn sight better than how he'd lived with Tamara. I can't even imagine the full truth, but I saw a picture of the shithole they were living in when Child Protective Services finally picked him up."

The place had been infested with rats—both the literal and metaphorical kind. This part of the story made him want to vomit.

"She tried to sell Ethan when he was two. That's how CPS found out about him. Evidently some other junkie couldn't stand the thought of a baby being sold, so he called the police."

He couldn't keep the agony out of his voice. He would live his whole life knowing he had failed his son in the worst possible way before even knowing he existed. Charlie's hand curled around his in silent support.

"Ethan didn't say a word the entire first year we had custody of him. I moved back in with Mom, so one of us could be with him every second, and worked at the factory."

At that moment Jess let out a squeal and Ethan a cackle.

Both Finn and Charlie looked at them. Ethan was chasing Jessica with a piece of wood, pretending it was some sort of monster.

Charlie gripped his wrist. "But look at him now, Finn. And yes, if Tamara was using drugs during her pregnancy, or if Ethan didn't get proper care or nutrition as a baby, that might affect his cognitive development. But look at him. That's a happy, well-adjusted little boy. You should be proud of him. Of yourself."

"I am proud of him. Hell, if he had never said another word his entire life I would've been just for having the strength to survive what he did. But hell yeah, I'm proud of him."

Himself? Not a whole lot to be proud of there.

"You're wrong, you know," she said without even looking at him.

"About being proud of Ethan?"

"Wrong about whatever thoughts are in your head about yourself." Now she turned to look at him, one eyebrow raised, as if daring him to contradict her.

How was it possible that she still knew him so well?

"You're thinking you didn't do enough," she continued, not waiting for him to speak. "That you somehow should've known, should've done more. You made the best decisions you could with the information you had. You acted when it was needed. That's what counts. Ethan's home life and happiness—those are the things that matter now, not what you couldn't do anything about." She picked at the grass. "Not that I'm any expert or really get any say in the matter."

Now it was his turn to raise an eyebrow at her. "Why?"

She shrugged and waved a hand back and forth between them. "This isn't important. We're temporary. I know that."

"You and I need to talk."

He expected her to make some comment about how they had been for the past thirty minutes, but instead she drew her legs up to her chest and wrapped her arms around them, as if trying to protect her vital organs from a blow. "I already know what you're going to say," she finally whispered. "And I understand, especially after what you just told me. You have to protect Ethan from people like me who won't be in your . . . his . . .life on a long-term basis."

"You don't think my son has seen us together today? You don't think he doesn't already suspect something? I haven't had any serious relationships since I got custody of Ethan. Some casual, but you're right, there's been no one he's seen me with."

She nodded. "Exactly. That's wise, and it what's best for him if you don't want him to get attached to someone like me, who means nothing to you. Better to keep it strictly on an educational level between Ethan and I."

Nothing? "Do you really think you mean nothing to me?"

She let out a sigh. "I'm not being coy, Finn, and I'm not trying to make you out as the bad guy. I just know once you get me out of your system or whatever, this thing between us will be over."

She still didn't get it. Hell, he wasn't sure *he* did. Charlotte Devereux had been *in his system* for the past fifteen years. He didn't think she was ever getting out.

"What about your system, Charlie? Am I in *yours*?"

She looked over at the kids, out at the water, down at her toes. Anywhere but at him. "Does it matter?"

"Yes, it very much does."

He thought she might not answer. Charlie was so brave, strong, and larger than life—sunshine mixed with a little hurricane—but admitting her feelings out loud had never come easy to her. He didn't know if she'd be able to now, especially if she thought he didn't care about her.

She was wrong. So, so wrong.

"What do you want me to say, Finn? Do you want the truth? That I'll take every second I can get from you? That I'll take the scraps of your time? That if you want to keep me as a hidden piece of ass on the side, I'll take it?" Her words were quiet but so passionate they felt like blows.

Now those blue eyes looked at him, pinning him. She was being sincere, no doubt. He could do nothing but sit there, gutted.

She continued, her volume staying low but her intensity growing. "Do you want me to tell you that you've always been the one for me? That I never stopped loving you even when I was married to another man? That I look over at Ethan and desperately wish he were mine? *Ours*?"

"Charlie . . ." He wasn't sure what he wanted to say to her, only that he had to stop her words. Had to stop the agony he could feel dripping from her.

She took a shuddery breath and wrenched herself under control. "You don't get do-overs in life, I know that. So, believe me, I don't expect it."

This was such a surreal conversation to be having with half of Oak Creek around them, even though no one was close enough to hear their words. But he wished they were alone so he could peel her out of that black bikini that had been driving him crazy all afternoon and show her how much she meant to him.

But those sorts of actions were part of the problem. Sweaty, passionate sex might make all the bad feelings and doubts disappear for a moment, but in the long run, it didn't do anything to alleviate her fears. If anything, it just added to them. Passion, heat, and physical connection had never been their problem.

Communication had.

"Charlie, look at me."

After a long moment, she finally turned her eyes to his.

"I used to have nightmares, you know, about your wedding day. Or maybe it wasn't really so much nightmares as it was my subconscious trying to figure out if I could have done something differently to change the outcome."

She opened her mouth, but he held out a hand and she shut it again.

"I'll be honest, five years ago, there's no way I could've forgiven you. Yeah, I probably still would've had sex with you because Christ, Charlie, I'm not sure there's anything in the world you could do to me that would make me not want to have sex with you."

She gave him the tiniest of smiles.

"So yeah, it would be exactly like you're thinking now. I would have fucked you—well and often—for a while, but that would've been it. It would've been nothing deeper to me."

He reached out and spun her whole body, which was still pretty much curled in a ball with her knees to her chest, so they were facing each other.

"Five years is a lot of time to grow," he continued. "To change. To learn that life is sometimes complicated."

"There are things I should tell you about why I got married." The words burst out of her like she couldn't hold them back any longer.

He trailed a finger down her cheek. "Five years ago, I would've taken you up on that offer. Because whenever I woke up from that nightmare about your wedding day, all I could think about was *why*. Why had you done that? I knew you loved me, Charlie. I knew you didn't love Brandon."

"He offered me—"

Finn reached over and cut her off with a gentle kiss. "Something I couldn't. I don't need to know what it was. Maybe it was money, security, stature . . .it doesn't matter. There was something you needed, and he could provide it when I couldn't."

She nodded. "It was more than money."

Finn gave her a half smile. "Good. I'm glad to hear that."

But he realized he already knew. Even when he'd thought the worst of Charlie, he'd always known there had to be more at play than just the obvious. And some day he would get her to tell him everything. But that wasn't what was important right now.

"Five years ago, I probably wouldn't have believed you, even though deep inside I never thought you left me because of Brandon's money. Seven, I probably wouldn't have talked to you at all, so it wouldn't have mattered."

"And now?" she whispered.

"Do you know when the last time was I had that nightmare?"

"When?"

"Ethan had been home for thirteen months. And he had just spoken his first words to me. Nothing life-changing, just 'Night, Daddy.' It was the first time I heard his voice. The first time anyone had ever called me *Daddy*. It was the most beautiful thing I'd ever heard." For the rest of his life he would remember Ethan's tiny voice as Finn had tucked him into bed.

"The dream about you that night started out the same, with me trying to figure out what I could say or do to stop you from marrying Brandon. I struggled frantically, running out of time, distraught. I reached the point I always did, when complete helplessness washed over me as I watched you walk to Brandon. Usually I woke up then. But that time it was different. That time in my dream, little Ethan came over to me. He took my hand and just said 'Daddy' in his tiny voice and led me away with him."

Tears were trailing down Charlie's cheeks. "Because if you had had me, you wouldn't have had Ethan."

Of course she understood. Had he really thought she wouldn't?

"I think that's when I started to let all my anger toward you go. In life, we don't see the bigger picture. We just see pieces. Sometimes those pieces are ugly. Some pieces of our past—yours and mine together—are always going to be jagged and rough and difficult to look at. But maybe, when the *whole* is finished, it might be something beautiful."

With a little sob, she brought both hands up to cover her face. Finn couldn't help it, he pulled her into his lap. Charlie's tears were always going to wreck him.

"This is twice I've seen you cry. You're starting to make me think you're not invincible."

"I haven't been invincible for eight years." But he wasn't surprised when she pulled herself together quickly.

"I don't know what the future holds, princess. None of us do. All I can assure you is that I'm not going to hold the past against you. What happened, happened. It made us into who we are, for better or worse."

She nodded against his chest. "So now we just have to find out if our jagged pieces can fit together."

"Exactly."

CHAPTER 24

THE NEXT NIGHT Finn and Charlie went out on their first date in over eight years.

With Ethan.

They'd both been a little worried about formally telling him they were dating. When they did, Ethan just looked up from his pizza and said, "So you're like boyfriend and girlfriend now?"

Finn grabbed her hand under the table, gave it a squeeze. She didn't know how he knew she needed his touch so badly in that moment, but she was glad he did.

"Yes," Finn told his son.

"Okay, cool." He then went on to ask Charlie if she'd ever seen the *Star Wars* movies—obviously much more important to him than his father's dating status.

Slightly harder had been Finn's mom, who they'd gone to see on their way home. Repairing that relationship was going to take Charlie more time. Mrs. Bollinger had been polite, but distant, when Finn had explained they were seeing each other again. She didn't want to see her son get hurt. Charlie couldn't blame her for that.

In the nights since then, they'd developed a pattern in the evenings. Charlie would come have dinner with Ethan and Finn, then hang out as Ethan got ready for bed—school was back in session, much to the boy's dismay—until Charlie had to go into work.

No more quickies at lunch at some of their old hideouts. No more sneaking in to Finn's house while Ethan was in bed and back out before he woke up. Without even really talking about it, they were doing things differently. Slowing it all down.

Their relationship was tentative, sweet, tender. All the things they had never been.

She and Finn had met her first day at high school. From that second on, their feelings for each other had been frantic. They'd been like two kindergartners on the playground: sticking out their tongues at each other and pulling pigtails. They'd been loud, they'd been passionate, they'd been feisty with each other. They'd never once been able to ignore the other—two magnets both attracted and repelled, depending on their direction.

But never in all that time had things been sweet and tender like they had for the past few days. Slow and easy and gentle . . .this new facet of their relationship was a balm for both their wounded souls. Not that there wasn't passion— there was always going to be between them. It was just less frantic, less manic. Their lovemaking was no longer trying to glue together the broken pieces of their relationship.

Charlie had no doubt all the whirlwind and quickies would return. But for right now she would enjoy the calm within the storm.

Of course, all thoughts of calm dispersed immediately as soon as Ethan was in bed and Finn's lips found hers while they sat on the couch.

Charlie giggled against his mouth. "You know Ethan is going to come down here again to tell you something about Legos, *Star Wars,* or Marvel comics versus DC."

He groaned as his lips trailed across her jaw and down the side of her neck. "Don't I know it? Remember the good ol' days when it was only our parents we had to get away from to make out?"

She gasped as he bit none too gently on that place where her neck met her shoulder. But it wasn't Ethan who stopped them this time. It was Aiden, who tapped a couple times on the door before coming straight inside.

Finn just raised an eyebrow at Aiden over the couch. "I do have a private life, you know."

When Aiden didn't crack a joke, didn't say anything at all, they both got up and walked over to him. He looked like hell.

"I'll make coffee," Charlie said softly.

Aiden nodded. "Thanks."

They all walked into the kitchen. "Where's Henry?" Finn asked.

Aiden shook his head. "He and I haven't met face-to-face since I went undercover. If anybody saw me with him, my cover would be blown. I've gotten a few updates from him, but nothing big."

Charlie had hardly seen Aiden or Henry since that morning in Finn's kitchen. Honestly, she'd almost forgotten Aiden was working undercover. She'd been distracted by other things, namely Finn.

"I know Henry took Jordan out on a date a few nights

ago. But I didn't really talk to him." She poured the water in and started the coffee maker.

"He took Jordan Reiss out on a date?" Finn asked, looking like he might jump up and yell "Inconceivable!" at any moment.

She put both hands on her hips and tilted her head at him. "Yeah, that's right. Not everybody in Oak Creek thinks she's a demon incarnate." This damn town had the longest memory and the shortest inclination toward forgiveness.

Finn held both hands out in a gesture of surrender.

"I'm glad someone involved in this has time to date," Aiden put in.

The coffee finished brewing and Charlie brought him a mug. He didn't look good. "Life at the strip club is beginning to be too much for you?"

He nodded gratefully at her when he took the cup. "I think I've fallen further down the rabbit hole," Aiden muttered.

"The NORAD stuff?" Finn asked.

"Partly. I stumbled onto something even worse last night while at a club just outside of Reddington City. Human trafficking."

Finn muttered a curse. "Are you sure?"

"The woman I saw definitely wasn't there by her own choice."

She grabbed his hand. "I can tell you from firsthand experience that some of the women who work in the clubs, dancers or otherwise, can get this sort of numb, robotic look to them. Places like that can take a toll on you, physically, mentally, and emotionally. But a lot are perfectly fine once they get out of there. I just don't want you to misinterpret a look you saw on someone. Maybe it's not as bad as you think."

Aiden just shook his head, staring down at his coffee. "Believe me, this op has cured me from ever wanting to step foot in another strip club again. I know the look you're talking about, but this was different. This woman was terrified." When Aiden looked up from his mug, there was such agony in his eyes it almost took her breath away. "She had bruises makeup couldn't cover completely. Couldn't talk because the traffickers had put some sort of transmitting device on her. I did what I could to protect her, but it wasn't enough. I tried to get her out, but by the time I made my move it was too late."

"Did you call Sheriff Nelson?" Finn asked.

Aiden nodded. "As soon as I could. The very second I could. The sheriff has somebody watching the place, but so far it's been empty."

The thought obviously ate at Aiden.

"Nelson won't let up," Finn assured his friend, "you know that. If there's something going on, he will find out and stop it."

Aiden nodded, but his eyes were still haunted. "Operation Sparrow is going down soon. Probably in the next couple days if I had to guess. But I don't know when, or where. One of the clubs they've used before, but I don't know which. And honestly even this doesn't feel right."

"How so?" Finn asked.

"Just sort of feels as if, I don't know, it's all some sort of setup."

Finn took a sip of his own coffee. "Dude, I mean this with no disrespect. But you're exhausted, and this is obviously taking an emotional toll on you none of us was expecting. Is it possible you feel like that because you're the one setting everything up?"

Aiden wiped a hand across his face. "You know I did

this sort of stuff for the team all the time and when we were on missions. I know how to separate and compartmentalize."

Finn looked at Charlie. "Aiden was our intel guy. We would send him to scout locations and gather as much data as he could. He's got an uncanny ability to blend and get people to open up to him." He turned back to Aiden. "So, what do you think is the problem? Can you pinpoint it?"

"This all seems more like a magician is distracting the audience with his left hand, so they won't look at his right. I'm missing something. I talked to Major Pinnock and Henry a few days ago, told them my concerns, and that I thought we should bring in Sheriff Nelson."

"Do you think Cline is onto you? Or what about Stellman?"

"Henry assures me Cline remains oblivious to me being undercover. He was at the club last night mingling with everyone. I swear, he's like a high school nerd trying to make himself indispensable to the 'bad' crowd. He's the reason we're at all these damn clubs every night. Probably the only way he can get some action with women."

"Anything suspicious from Stellman?"

Aiden rubbed the back of his neck. "Mostly just him not ever being around. I still have yet to see his face."

"There's something about this code." Aiden grabbed a napkin from inside his jacket pocket. It had a series of shapes and simple icons written on it. "Cline was doodling it at the club last night. I asked about it and he got all defensive, saying it had nothing to do with what he was offering. But the only time he stopped staring at it was when he was busy with one of the girls. He left it behind when he was otherwise engaged, so I pocketed it."

Aiden slid the napkin across the table. Charlie picked it up, studying the series of symbols on it.

"I've seen this before," she said. Where? Why did it look so familiar? She worked with codes so much it was hard to remember.

Finn chuckled. "You think? This looks exactly like what you do with Ethan every time you get together for your tutoring session. I've been joking to everyone that the two of you have your own language."

She smiled. "You're probably right. I've been doing so much tutoring, I see patterns in my sleep." Not that she was complaining. She would take as many sessions as she could get. She reached over and kissed Finn on the cheek. "And just so you know, in Ethan's secret language, that means 'blue baby eat just when my old dog sleep.'"

"Could that mean anything?" Aiden asked. "Those particular words?"

She shook her head. "No, the symbols matching those words are unique to what Ethan and I developed to help with his dyslexia. It wouldn't mean that to anyone else but me and him."

"So back to square one. I asked Henry about it earlier this afternoon, but he says he doesn't think it's relevant, that Gordon is a geek with numbers and computer code on his mind. I still want to check with Major Pinnock in case he's familiar with what it means." Aiden's phone buzzed in his hand. "Henry."

He read the text and muttered a curse under his breath. "Great. The Lion's Den. It's a club way on the north side of town. I'm supposed to be there at midnight."

"Speaking of, I've got to get home to change and give Jordan a ride to work." She looked at Aiden and touched his shoulder. "Be safe. Stay focused." She could already tell his concentration was splintered between his undercover work and this woman he was afraid was being trafficked. Split focus like that could get him killed. "Fight one injustice at a time."

He just nodded.

She turned to Finn. "You, I will see later."

Finn pulled her in for a kiss. "You be safe too and break the fingers of any guys who decide to get a little too friendly. Come find me at Linear when you wake up tomorrow. I'll be waiting for you."

Aiden made a gagging noise. "I don't even want to know what you two do in your office over there first thing in the mornings. Please never ever *ever* tell me."

"Why do you care?" Finn shot back. "You're never in the office anyway, even when you're not undercover. Besides, we always clean off your desk after we use it for our wild monkey love—"

She left, grinning. The door closed behind her, cutting off the sounds of the two friends play-fighting.

CHAPTER 25

AN HOUR LATER, the moment she and Jordan stepped through the back door of The Silver Palace, Charlie knew it was going to be a long night.

Everybody was crying.

Jordan looked about as nervous as Charlie felt at the sight. The dancers could be an emotional bunch on the best of days.

"You don't think all their cycles have lined up, do you? It would be like the perfect storm of PMS," Jordan said, looking around at the smeared mascara everywhere.

Charlie barely stifled a laugh. She grabbed Cinnamon, who tended to be one of the more levelheaded and unemotional women, despite her constant taunts to the audience to take the "Cinnamon challenge." "Hey, what happened? What's everyone so upset about?"

"Jade," Cinnamon said, between her tears. "She died this afternoon in a car accident. We just got word."

"Oh, my God." Charlie hadn't talked to the woman

much since that night with the scary guys, but it was hard to believe she was gone so suddenly.

That's when she remembered where she'd seen the symbols Aiden had shown her on the napkin. Those exact ones had been what she'd seen then. The same night where Jade had been dancing and had gotten Charlie out of trouble.

"She was drunk or high or something," Cinnamon said. "I'm not sure what." She shrugged one naked shoulder, her robe loosely tied and starting to fall off. "Of course, Jade was a user, so nobody can be too surprised."

Charlie was trying to wrap her head around what it all meant as she and Jordan made their way through the group of women—all reminiscing about Jade—to the back rooms. They changed into their uniforms and headed out to the bar to set up for the night ahead.

"Some of those girls are crying and I know for a fact they hated Jade's guts," Jordan said as she moved behind the bar.

Charlie nodded absently. "This place is just like high school, except with less clothing. There's a hierarchy, cliques, everything. Nobody hates the dead girl, no matter how they felt about her yesterday."

She grabbed a pad of paper and began to make a list of what she needed from the storeroom in the basement. "Hey, I don't guess you're going to see or talk to Henry anytime tonight, right?" Maybe Jordan could get a message to him about the code she remembered. He could let Aiden know when they met up at The Lion's Den.

A dreamy little smile fell over Jordan's features.

Charlie couldn't help but laugh. "Oh dear, looks like you're a little smitten."

"I had totally forgotten what it's like for someone to want me for *me*. You'd be amazed how many guys have shown up at my house since I got out of prison and offered to be the ones to help me out of my 'dry spell.'" She put the phrase in air quotes, rolling her eyes. "The other half just wants to screw the town's bad girl." Jordan shook her head. "Henry doesn't know about any of that. And he doesn't care."

Finn had talked about their jagged pieces fitting together to make a beautiful whole. She hoped that would be true for Jordan also. The other woman probably didn't even know Henry was working undercover to stop the traitors. Once she knew he was all but a hero, she would like him even more.

Charlie pulled Jordan in for a quick hug, surprising them both. "I'm happy for you."

Jordan grinned as they broke apart. "But to answer your question, no. Henry is working tonight. So, I'm not sure when I'll talk to him."

"No worries." She didn't have Aiden's number, but she would call Finn and let him know what she remembered.

She ran downstairs to fetch the alcohol they'd need to get through the shift. It was hard to tell how this night was going to turn out. If the girls were truly upset, that sometimes sent a weird vibe through the club. The audience members picked up on it and it made for a slow night.

But who knew? Maybe the dancers would decide to celebrate life, and the energy would be contagious. Lots of tips.

She hefted a crate of champagne to move it and almost didn't see the paper as it fell out.

But she damn well recognized it once she had.

The same pattern Aiden had shown her, plus another

line of code the napkin hadn't held. The symbols that in Ethan's language meant *fire his pretty chair horse.*

She stared down at the paper. She doubted anyone else would've even paid attention to it, and she knew they wouldn't instantly have memorized it. She only did because she worked with symbols like these all the time.

What did it mean? Should she take it with her? Leave it? She needed to get this paper—or at least a picture of it—to Aiden and Finn. They could check with their military guy and figure out if it was important.

She was turning to run and grab her phone in the dressing room to take a picture when the door to the storeroom opened. She stuffed the paper back into the crate where she'd found it.

"Charlie? What's going on?" Mack's voice boomed out. "We need that liquor."

"I'm coming. It's a lot."

He came down the steps. "I'll help you carry it. We got a last-minute call a few hours ago. VIP group in the back. They don't want anyone in there. Just want everything set up before they get here. And they specifically asked for every bottle of Armand de Brignac we had." He reached down and grabbed the crate that held the code. "Fortunately, this came in today, even though we didn't order it."

They didn't get much call for a three-hundred-dollar bottle of champagne at The Silver Palace. "You didn't order these?"

"Nope." Mack popped the *p.* "When I called the distributor to cuss him out about the mistake, they gave me such a good deal on it, I decided to keep it. Hell, I would've drunk it myself for that price. But I'll more than gladly sell it to the VIPs for a huge profit. Let's get them set up."

A crate of expensive champagne that just happened to

be a wrong order and had a paper with some sort of code in it? Charlie may not be an undercover guru like the Linear guys, but even she realized that was highly suspicious.

They were coming tonight.

Finn would want her to call. She would just let him know what she had found out. Even if it was just the code. She probably should've told him the whole story about how nervous she'd been the last time.

She dropped the liquor off at the bar. When Mack took the bottles of Armand de Brignac toward the back room, she rushed to the dressing area to get her phone. By the time she returned to the bar, Mack was looking for her.

"Can you set up the back?" he asked. "I have to keep an eye on the girls tonight, make sure no one gets too hysterical over what happened to Jade."

"Sure, no problem." It would give her a chance to call Finn. "How long before the group gets here?"

"Twenty minutes."

They could hear yelling from the direction of the dressing room and Mack headed that way with a sigh. Charlie immediately rushed to the back. She didn't bother to start setting it up. She just wanted to call Finn.

Her phone didn't work inside the building, but she could step out the side door from here and get a signal. She reached up and unhooked the fire alarm attached to the door and opened it, phone already in hand.

She had a bad feeling about all of this.

She was only one step out the door, not looking where she was going, when she ran straight into Rocco.

"Look who it is." His face was drawn into a sneer. "The lady with nine lives. I heard your house burned down."

CHAPTER 26

AS SOON AS Charlie left for work, Finn and Aiden stopped their banter about sex in the office. It had all been for show anyway.

He had known Aiden for over ten years and had trusted the man with his life a hundred times over. He'd fought shoulder-to-shoulder and back-to-back, and even occasionally face-to-face, with him.

He had never seen Aiden Teague so close to falling apart.

"I'm worried about you, man."

Aiden scrubbed a hand over his face, then stood to get another cup of coffee. "I'm trying to focus on Operation Sparrow. I know that situation is important. But Charlie was right. My attention is splintered at best. I can't get the woman at the club out of my mind. I left her, Finn. She was in the worst kind of trouble and I left her behind, like the creed meant nothing to me."

Never leave a fallen comrade behind.

It was the most basic part of the Army creed. Finn knew

Aiden would never break it if he had any sort of choice. What Aiden was doing was hard enough without exhaustion and guilt weighing on him.

"Charlie was also right about only being able to take down one bad guy at a time. Fighting a battle on multiple fronts is the best way to ensure defeat. That's Strategy 101."

Aiden leaned his weight on the kitchen counter, staring out into the darkness through the window. "I know, but that woman needs me, Finn. I know it sounds like some Gothic romance novel, but I can hear her crying every time I'm alone. I have to help her."

Aiden wasn't prone to histrionics. If he was feeling this way, then Finn trusted his friend's gut.

"Then I'll help you. We all will. Linear has resources and connections law enforcement doesn't. We'll use them. We'll find her, get her out."

Aiden blew out an exhausted breath. "But first I need to get to The Lion's Den."

A knock on the front door drew their attention. Finn opened it, surprised to find Sheriff Nelson on his porch.

"Bollinger." The sheriff nodded at Finn. "Sorry it's so late. Is Charlotte here?"

Finn held the door open for the sheriff to come in. "No, she already left for work at The Silver Palace. Why?"

Sheriff Nelson spotted Aiden. "Glad you're here. You were next on my list."

"Did you find anything out about the girl?" The hope in Aiden's eyes was hard to watch.

The sheriff shook his head. "No, but I'm still looking. I promise you'll be the first person I notify as soon as I know anything. Can I get a cup of that coffee?"

Aiden poured him a cup.

The sheriff took a sip gratefully. "You guys know about anything going down at The Lion's Den tonight?"

Aiden nodded. "I know I'm supposed to be there in about an hour and a half. Why?"

"Just got an anonymous tip-off that it would be worth our while to be there tonight a little after midnight. That someone named Stellman would be there."

Finn looked over at Aiden, eyes narrowed. "Wow. Someone is selling out Stellman? I thought he ruled all the local criminals with an iron fist."

"I've never heard of this guy. Who is he?" Sheriff Nelson asked.

"He's one of the people brokering the sale of the NORAD info," Finn told him, glad the sheriff now had clearance to be in on the situation. "He's bad news on multiple fronts, evidently, and not just around here. Major Pinnock specifically wanted to try to take him down. Unfortunately, nobody knows who he is or what he looks like."

Aiden shook his head. "I just can't believe someone would turn on Stellman that way. If he finds out, he'll not only kill them but their entire family. The guy is not known for his tender feelings."

"Do you think it's someone passing along false info?" the sheriff asked.

"Or it could be one of the criminals utilizing the opportunity to take out their competition. Everyone's together in one place and they get arrested," Finn said. "Maybe Stellman's not even going to be there, but they drop his name to make a bust more enticing."

Aiden nodded. "There are a lot of possibilities. And given my frame of mind, I'm not trusting my own judgment." He turned to Sheriff Nelson. "So, you should definitely follow the lead and move in. Just make sure I'm arrested with everybody else to protect my cover." He grimaced, then rubbed his eyes.

"What?" Finn asked. "Don't want to get arrested?"

"Nah. I just can't shake the feeling that this is another sleight of hand. Trying to get our focus off where it needs to be. But like I said, my judgment. . ."

"I'll contact Sheriff Holliday over in Sublette County," Nelson responded. "See if he's got a couple guys he can spare for an intercounty task force. Because whether your judgment is right or not, we've got other problems at play." The sheriff shifted toward Finn. "And it has to do with Charlotte."

Finn's jaw tightened. "What about her?"

"Found out a couple hours ago that one of the ladies she works with—a Brenda Kingston—died earlier this afternoon. She was driving under the influence. Had a shit ton of narcotics in her system, which according to some neighbors was not uncommon."

Finn shrugged. "Was she friends with Charlie? I haven't heard her mentioning someone by that name."

"She went by Jade onstage."

He shrugged again. "We don't sit around talking about all the strippers at Charlie's place of work. I'm not thrilled she's there."

"I'll admit I don't understand why Milton Devereux's daughter would be working at a place like that, but I guess that's her business." The sheriff took another sip of his coffee.

"Let's just say she has her reasons." Reasons Finn hoped to help her get off her shoulders soon. She needed to talk with her parents and let them know exactly what was going on.

The sheriff put his mug down with a thud. "I'll be

straight with you. I need to ask Charlie some questions. With Brenda-slash-Jade's death today, that makes the third in one week of someone who has connections to Charlie."

Shit. That *was* bad.

"The lady who rented her condo ends up dead in what the arson inspector says looks more and more like foul play," Sheriff Nelson continued. "A co-worker runs off the road, her toxicology off the charts."

"But she was a known drug user. So that's not suspicious." Aiden interjected.

Nelson nodded. "But with the amount of heroin in her system, the medical examiner finds it difficult to believe she made it out of her driveway, much less halfway to work."

"Are you saying someone made it look like an accident?" Finn asked.

Nelson shrugged. "We all know people on drugs do things that would be impossible to any normal person. I'm just telling you what the ME told me."

"Who is the third?"

"Ironically, Scott Fontenot, a.k.a. 'Sam,' that junkie you saved her from three weeks ago."

"Another overdose?" He ran a hand over his head.

"Yep. And before you say it, yes, I'm aware he was a user too. And they do overdose." He held his hands out in front of him. "Normally I wouldn't put many resources into a homeless junkie's death, particularly one who was already wanted for assaulting someone. Nor many more into a known drug user's DUI. Hell, I didn't even put much credence into the arson report. But when this flashed across my desk tonight, I couldn't ignore it anymore."

The sheriff took out a piece of paper, unfolded it, and laid it out in front of Finn.

"This is a missing persons report filed by a Kenneth

Lenhart. Evidently his brother, Paul, hasn't been heard from in over five days. His brother's place of employment?"

Finn knew without the sheriff having to tell him.

"The Silver Palace. He works as a bouncer," the sheriff finished. "Now all these things could be a coincidence, I realize that. Which is why I want to speak to Charlie."

Finn caught Aiden's grim look from across the kitchen. "Jade," he said. "Was that the name of the dancer she mentioned was there the night those guys freaked her out?"

Aiden nodded. "It is. We never followed up on it because I've been able to keep an eye on Rocco Christensen and didn't want to draw attention to myself by talking to her. Shit."

"What?" Sheriff Nelson asked.

Aiden walked over to the table. "That guy we're trying to take down . . .part of the reason is because after he brokers deals, he's known for making sure there are no witnesses left who can identify him. It's how he keeps the criminals he works with in line. It's also some of the reason I find it so difficult to believe he's going to be at The Lion's Den when there's a bust planned. Stellman is too highly placed and too smart to get caught in something common like that."

Finn stood. "Charlie said she saw some suspicious men a few nights before we found out she was working there. She mentioned Rocco but didn't know the others. Maybe Stellman was there that night too."

"And now you think Stellman is getting rid of people who might be able to identify him?" asked the sheriff.

"If Jade was the dancer who was in the back that night, and this Paul possibly worked there too . . ." Finn nodded. "Yeah, I think it's more than possible."

"What about the guy who attacked her at The Cactus Motel? Or Cynthia Reynolds?"

Finn looked over at Aiden. Was he being paranoid? Aiden gave him a nod—he obviously didn't think so. "Stellman was probably trying to get rid of Charlie both times, make them look like an accident to stay under the radar. Fontenot wasn't trying to rape her or steal from her. I'll bet you anything someone paid him to kill her."

The sheriff rubbed his bald, dark head. "I will give you that everyone we've talked to that knew Fontenot said he wasn't violent, although he was pretty desperate for money. Then no one saw him around for the past three weeks, almost like he was in hiding. Then a few days ago he shows up dead."

Finn could feel dread bubbling up inside him. "The explosion in her condo was meant to eliminate Charlie too. They thought she lived there. Hell, I didn't even know she wasn't living there."

Aiden grimaced. "If Stellman is cleaning house, that means whatever is going down will happen *tonight*."

Finn nodded. "And you can damn well be sure it's not at The Lion's Den. You're right, Aiden, that's a setup to distract law enforcement. We've got to get Charlie out of The Silver Palace. Once they find out the fire killed the wrong woman, they'll be coming after her."

He picked up his phone and dialed Charlie's number, cursing but not surprised when there was no answer. He looked at the other two. "I'm going to get her. I don't like how any of this is shaking out. Even if we're wrong about all of it, I want to make sure she's safe."

Sheriff Nelson stood too. "I'll send a squad car over. They can keep an eye on Charlie until you get there. I'm calling in all the help I can—we'll have to split our resources between the two clubs, just in case. I can't take the chance law enforcement won't be needed at The Lion's Den."

Finn made an emergency call to Peyton Ward, little Jess's mom, to ask if she would mind coming over to stay with Ethan. The single mom only lived about a mile from his house.

He kissed Peyton's cheek when she showed up ten minutes later, a sleeping Jess in her arms.

"Thank you," he whispered. "It's an emergency or . . ."

She smiled. "I know, Finn. You wouldn't have called if it weren't. Don't worry, we'll just crash on the couch until you get home."

He thanked her again and ran out the door. Things were on their way straight to hell. He could feel it. The last time he'd had such a huge knot in his gut, his entire team had been ambushed in Afghanistan. They'd lost two men, and Dorian had been captured, tortured, and even though they'd eventually gotten him out, he'd never been the same since.

This feeling in his gut meant trouble of the worst kind.

And Charlie was at the center of it.

CHAPTER 27

SHE'D BARELY SEEN Rocco before his fist crashed into her face. It didn't knock her out, but she fell to the ground, dazed.

Before she could even get back up, some sort of ski mask was thrown over her head, backward so she couldn't see.

"Careful, Rocco," someone whispered in a voice she didn't recognize. "It's got to look like an accident."

A gun cocked right beside her head.

Rocco dragged her forward. "Accidents happen with guns. Crazy ex-boyfriends or people trying to steal someone's money."

"You can't kill her here. It will draw too much attention to this place. We still need that last code."

The code she'd just seen? Charlie wasn't going to wait around for them to talk this out. Rocco had a grip on her arm, so she threw her elbow as hard as she could into his belly.

Then she ran like hell, ripping the mask off. She made it to the edge of the parking lot before she was tackled, her arm scraping painfully as she hit the ground. This time, Rocco not only put the mask on her but also zip tied her hands behind her.

Charlie cried out at the burn in her shoulder as he pulled too hard.

"I don't see why we have to hood her if she's going to be dead in a few minutes anyway."

"Just put her in the trunk. Unlike Stellman, I understand the value of keeping people alive in case things don't go the way you planned."

Stellman? That was the guy Finn and Aiden had mentioned.

Rocco laughed. "Good idea. Plus, I'd like to have a little taste of this" —Charlie tried to jerk away as Rocco groped her breasts, but he wrapped an arm around her waist to keep her close— "before we get rid of her."

"Let's just get inside. I've got information Stellman is going to want about some potential leaks in his organization. Not everyone is who they say they are. I just want to do the trade and get out of here."

She heard the trunk open and Rocco picked her up. If she didn't fight now, she was not going to make it out of this alive. With everyone all caught up with Jade's death it might be a long time before anyone even realized Charlie wasn't around.

She threw her body weight to the side, causing Rocco to drop her. He cursed as she got to her feet as best she could and started running again. She had no idea which way she was going but she hoped it was back toward the building.

The sound of sirens had her running faster. She prayed the police would be coming to The Silver Palace, although she had no idea why they would.

She couldn't see, all sounds were muffled, touch wasn't

an option. Charlie struggled not to panic. Her head whipped around as music suddenly blared out into the night—the door to the club must have opened. She turned in that direction, yelling through the mask, trying to get the attention of anyone she possibly could.

Then people began yelling, both in front and behind her. She kept running, her abs tensed for when she inevitably crashed into something.

The siren was louder now, obviously pulling into the parking lot. She let out a shuddery sigh of relief.

Until she heard gunfire.

She couldn't make out where it was coming from, so she ducked to the side, getting low on the ground, hoping they weren't shooting at her. She strained to see something through the ski mask, trying to make herself as small as possible as another gun went off.

There was a war going on and she was caught right in the middle of it, not sure which direction, if any, would lead her to safety.

Before she could decide, she was tackled from the side. Her shoulders screamed in agony as she rolled, trying to get as far away as she could. Was it Rocco? Had he decided to finish her off like he'd been instructed?

The hood was ripped off her, but she didn't stop her fight, kicking and bucking her weight against the man who held her down.

"Charlie, stop! It's Henry."

"Henry?" Not Rocco. "Oh, thank God."

He pulled a knife out of his boot and cut through the zip tie, dragging her behind a car. Charlie peeked around it to see what was going on.

The police car had stopped. Two officers were behind

it, using it as a shield, their weapons drawn and pointed toward The Silver Palace.

"What are you doing here?" she asked Henry. "I thought you guys were supposed to go to The Lion's Den."

"I came by to see Jordan, and then I saw someone in a mask being dragged to a car. I didn't know it was *you*."

"That guy I was telling you about, Rocco, he and someone I don't know were going to put me in their trunk and kill me later. They pulled me out of the club when I opened the door to make a call." She jerked her glance away from the police, looking behind her. Were Rocco and the other guy still out here behind them? "We have to be careful, they could be anywhere."

"One of them I took care of. That guy was about to shoot you. Rocco, I think." He pointed to a body lying on the ground by the car they'd been trying to put her in. "The other . . .you're right. He took off when shots were fired, but he might still be around."

They both ducked down as two more shots came from The Silver Palace, even though they were aimed at the police car, not them. The two officers yelled for the men to lower their weapons. A second police car came speeding into the parking lot.

She grabbed Henry's arm. "That Stellman guy you and Aiden have been looking for is inside the club right now."

"Can you identify him?"

"No. I've still never seen him. But Henry, there's some sort of code . . .Symbols. Aiden showed me some earlier tonight. He didn't know exactly what they were. He was going to ask the major."

"Symbols?" Henry's eyes narrowed. "Yeah, Aiden mentioned those."

Another shot rang out in the darkness, followed by a

third police car squealing into the parking lot. Sheriff Nelson got out, staying behind it.

"Sheriff," Charlie called. "Henry and I are back here. Some of the guys Aiden is trying to bust are the ones shooting at you."

"Guy named Stellman?" the sheriff asked.

"I don't know for sure, but I think so."

The sheriff didn't turn around to look at her but held up a hand to show he'd heard her. "We've got help coming, but it's not going to be in time if this escalates."

Fortunately, no innocent people were coming out the front door and getting caught in any crossfire, but that wouldn't last long.

There was nothing to stop Stellman or whoever was inside from taking hostages—one of the dancers, or even Jordan. The sheriff was sending an officer to cover the front door, but it wouldn't be enough.

Another vehicle came barreling into the parking lot. This one she recognized. Finn's Jeep. He pulled up next to Sheriff Nelson, but Charlie couldn't help it, even though it wasn't safe, she ran around the car and straight into him.

He tensed as he caught her weight, then pulled her into a bone-crushing hug. "Thank God. I've been trying to call you to let you know you were in danger. What the hell is going on here?" He saw the ripped skin of her arm. "Are you okay?"

There was so much she needed to tell him. "I was in trouble. But Henry saved my life."

The other man had much more safely and discreetly crawled to Finn's Jeep. Finn looked over at him and stuck out his hand to shake. "I'll need to know the whole story later but thank you. I don't know why you were here, but I'm glad you were."

Henry shook his hand and smiled. "Was just here to see my girl. Nothing more profound than that."

Charlie grabbed Finn's arm. "The people shooting from inside, I'm almost positive it's Stellman. The code Aiden showed us? It wasn't just something I remembered from tutoring. I saw that exact code when those VIPs with Rocco were in the back room. And then tonight I saw something similar in our liquor storage room. A piece of paper with some similar symbols on it was stuffed inside a small crate of champagne. I saw the symbols, Finn. I think Stellman has been using The Silver Palace to pass along a sort of code to someone else."

Finn looked at Henry. "Do you know anything about it? Is it Cline? This seems backward to me."

Henry looked frantic. "I need to see the paper. It's critical that I see it."

Finn shook his head. "What's critical is that we get the situation contained. We are going to need to get inside before things get out of control."

She didn't like that. Finn would be leading the charge.

But ten seconds later it was too late. Things were already out of control. People began running out of the doors screaming. It didn't take them long to figure out why.

The Silver Palace was on fire.

All three men around her started cursing violently. The criminals inside had created the perfect diversion. Since no one knew what they looked like, they'd be able to exit with the terrified crowd.

"You're going to have to get your bad guys another day," Sheriff Nelson said. "Right now, we've got to get that building cleared."

Henry looked completely panicked. "The paper with the code. What about it?"

Finn looked at the man like he'd lost his mind, but Charlie touched Henry's arm. "Don't worry, I memorized it. Even if we can't recover the paper, I can write down the code for you."

Sheriff Nelson and Finn were already running toward the building to help with the chaos.

"What do you mean, you memorized it?"

Why did he care so much? Couldn't they talk about this later? People might be trapped inside the building.

She glanced over at him quickly. "I work with symbols all the time when I tutor, so memorizing them was easy." She almost had to yell to be heard over the continuing chaos. "We can talk about this later. We've got to help Finn and the sheriff. People might be trapped inside. *Jordan* might be."

He finally seemed to snap out of it. "Right. Yeah, let's go help."

Henry ran toward the building. Charlie was behind him, heading to the back. If she could get inside, maybe see if the fire could be stopped—

She was near the door when Finn's arm wrapped around her waist and lifted her off her feet, pulling her back. "Whatever you're thinking? No. You stay with me."

"But I know where the fire extinguisher is. I might be able to do some good inside."

"Then we go together. Someone is trying to kill you, princess. That explosion at your condo was not an accident."

She didn't even want to think about that right now. One burning building at a time.

They ran around to the back door. She was glad to see no one was trying to get out that way, given all the smoke pouring through the opening. They were still moving closer when the whole building shook, and the roar of an explosion pierced the air.

"What was that?" she asked.

"If I had to guess, it was the flames hitting your bar or liquor storeroom. There's no going inside now."

And nobody else would be getting out. Charlie prayed everyone had made it. Finn took her arm and led her to the front of the building, where everyone in various states of shock were now watching The Silver Palace burn. The fire department was pulling in and taking over, moving everyone farther back and setting up their hoses.

Finn kept his hand on her arm, but he wasn't looking at the fire like most everyone else. He was searching the crowd, communicating with Aiden using some sort of hand signals.

Stellman might be still out here. But with the increasing chaos—paramedics were showing up now, adding to the noise and crowd—the chances of finding anyone not wanting to be found were slim.

"I want you out of here," Finn said. "Get a medic to look at your arm and go home."

She shook her head and glanced down at her shoulder. It was bleeding, but not badly. "My arm is fine, I promise. I want to stay here and help you. Maybe I could identify someone."

He stood her in front of him and trailed his hands up her arms until he was cupping her cheeks.

"Aiden is here. Zac and Dorian are on their way. We're going to sweep this area to see what we can find. Knowing you're safely at home will allow me to focus. Sheriff Nelson has a man who is going to stay with you."

She leaned her head against his chest. "I don't want to leave you. I might be helpful."

"You will be. You saw that code and you know it. That's going to help Henry and Aiden. But right now, you need to let me do my job."

She didn't want to go, but she understood his point. "Fine."

He chuckled. "You never were one to give in graciously. Do me a favor. I left Peyton at my house with Ethan. Can you relieve her? She's the only one I know who works as hard as you. She'll need to be up early in the morning."

"Sure."

"There will be an officer in front of the house. No arguments about him, okay? You are a target. I don't know how long it will take here, but I'll be surprised if I make it home before dawn. You stay put until I do."

She reached up on her tiptoes and kissed him. "I'll see you when you get in. Be careful."

He kissed her back and walked her to a squad car. His smile was cocky and reassuring.

But despite his smile, she knew the danger was closer than ever.

CHAPTER 28

CHARLIE HAD MEANT to stay awake and wait for Finn. She'd thought she would be too wound up to sleep at all. She'd sent Peyton and Jess home, waved to the officer who had obviously drawn the short straw, and made herself a cup of coffee. Then she'd sat down on the couch, wanting to see Finn when he walked in.

Next thing she knew, she was waking up with a start. She looked around, trying to figure out what was making her heart race. Was it Ethan? Had he woken up? Was Finn home? Or maybe it was just the sun starting to rise that had woken her.

She walked over to the window to peek out and saw the cop outside talking to someone. The man standing outside the squad car wasn't big enough to be Finn. She yawned and tried to rub some of the sleep out of her eyes, which were already blurry from last night's smoke. If the guys were on their way home, she needed to make more coffee.

She was turning away from the window when sudden

movement at the car caught her attention. She glanced back out, and her mind froze in shock.

The man had just stabbed the officer.

She stumbled back until she ended up against the wall, hand flying to her mouth. Someone had just killed a police officer ten yards from the front door. It didn't take a genius to figure out that person was here to kill her. Her legs felt weak and her breath sawed in and out of her chest in panicked gasps. She could feel the room starting to spin around her.

She slammed her hand against the wall. *Pull it together, Charlie.*

She had two choices: she could get her shit together and figure out a plan, or die.

"Charlie? What are you doing here? Are you okay?" Ethan was standing at the edge of the living room staring at her.

Whoever killed that officer outside with such casual efficiency wouldn't hesitate to hurt anyone else, including a child. She pushed away from the wall. They had to get out of here.

She ran over to Ethan and knelt in front of him. "Hey, buddy. Your dad sent me to hang out with you until he could get home." She didn't want to scare the kid, but not telling him at least part of the truth was going to get them both killed. She ran her fingers over his head before settling them on his shoulders. "Ethan, I don't want to scare you, bud, but there's a bad guy out front. I need you to be brave. I need both of us to be. You and I have got to run."

Those green eyes, so much like Finn's, grew big. "Really?"

She squeezed his shoulders and tried to give him a reassuring smile. "Yes, really. We've got to get away until your dad can get here and help us."

The boy nodded. "Dad will come. He promised if I ever needed him he always would."

She gave a silent prayer of thanks for all the hours Finn had taken to build his son's trust.

They both jumped at the loud banging on the front door.

"Shoes," she whispered. "Then we go out the back. Hurry."

"What about Sky?" Ethan's little face was pinched, worried about his puppy. "Will the bad man hurt Sky?"

They couldn't take him and he was too tiny to be of any assistance. "Is he in his crate?"

Ethan nodded.

"Then he'll be fine. The bad man will just ignore him, if he even notices Sky at all." She prayed that would be true.

Ethan scurried away to get his shoes and she grabbed hers, careful to stay out of the line of sight of any windows. She and the boy ran toward the back door.

"Ready?" he asked as they both arrived at it. He was calm and collected, just like Finn.

"I love you, kid." She couldn't help the words. Wished she had said them to his dad too.

Ethan just rolled his eyes, as if that was the most obvious thing in the world, and quietly opened the door.

A loud bang came again on the front door again. "Charlie? It's Henry. Finn sent me. Open up."

Henry? Oh God. And she pushed Ethan out the door. "Go. Go."

They ran. She heard the front door crash open as they rushed toward the woods surrounding Finn's house. They had a good head start, but Henry had seen them go out the back door.

"Charlie, come back!" Henry yelled. "I just need the code you memorized."

She didn't slow down. If he just needed the code, there would've been no need to stab that police officer.

They ran into the woods, Charlie praying they could lose him. But the next time Henry spoke, he was even closer. He didn't seem nearly as out of breath as a paper pusher ought to be. That did not bode well for her and Ethan.

"Charlie, you don't have to get hurt," Henry said. "I just need those codes. You said you have them all memorized, right? You give them to me and you and the boy get to walk away."

She grabbed Ethan and pulled him behind a tree so they could catch their breath. There was no way they were going to be able to outrun Henry.

The best thing she could do right now was to get Ethan away from him. Because she had no doubt that Henry was lying about letting them go, even if she gave him the codes. She grabbed Ethan's hand and began running again. He didn't complain, just ran as fast as his little legs would carry him, nearly as sure-footed as her. He and Finn must spend a lot of time together out here. She ran until they were both gasping for air, then pulled him behind another large tree.

"Ethan, you play out in these woods with your dad all the time, right?" She could barely get the words out while trying to suck in oxygen.

Ethan just nodded.

"Do you know where you are?"

Another nod.

"We need to split up," she said. "I'm going to lead the bad guy in the other direction."

Now the boy shook his head vehemently.

"You'll be okay. You can hide until your dad comes for you." She prayed Finn would figure it out and find him.

"We're not far from Jess's house," Ethan said, grabbing her hand. "We can go there. Dad wouldn't want me to leave you alone."

She snatched him against her in a hug. He wasn't scared for himself, but for *her*.

God, she really did love this kid. Just as much as she loved his dad. And knowing they were close to Peyton's house made it clear what Charlie needed to do, although she hated using Ethan's friendship with the girl against him.

"You have to go to Jess's house, buddy. To protect Jess. Tell Ms. Peyton what happened. She'll find your dad and he'll know what to do."

Ethan looked torn. "I don't want to leave you."

"I'll be okay. It's Jess who needs you now."

Ethan nodded. "Babies need someone to protect them. I always try to protect her."

She cocked her head to the side. "Is that why you like to hang out with her so much? To protect her if she needs it?"

He gave a tiny, heartbreaking shrug. "Nobody protected me when I was a baby. So, I just want to make sure she's okay."

She hugged him again. That was why he was hanging out with someone so much younger than him. Not because of some sort of stunted emotional growth on his part, but because he had so much of his father in him that he couldn't stand the thought of someone innocent getting hurt.

"You've got to go to her, buddy. Protect her."

He nodded solemnly.

"And when you get to your dad, I need you to give him this message. The symbols for *fire his pretty chair horse* and *blue baby eat just when my old dog sleep*. That's a lot. Can you remember that? Think of the symbols in your head if you have to"

He repeated them to her.

"Perfect." She smiled at him. It was the best she could do. Hopefully Ethan would be able to get the symbols to Finn. "Okay, as quietly as you can, get to Jess. Her mom will call your dad. I'll see you on the other side, buddy."

Not if Henry had anything to say about it, but she didn't care what happened to herself so long as she kept Finn's son safe. His tiny arms wrapped around her waist and squeezed. She prayed this wouldn't be her last hug. She squeezed back, and then he let her go and headed silently into the woods. Her little soldier.

She once again was so thankful Finn had taught his son skills to survive. That he had played with him out in these woods for hours, rather than just leaving him to video games.

When the small, black-haired head had disappeared, she went in the opposite direction, making as much noise as reasonably possible. Breathing like she was about to have a heart attack did not require much acting.

She ran as far as she could as fast as she could, trying to give Ethan as much time as possible to get away. Henry was catching up with her—she could feel terror eating away at her insides. Still, his flying tackle caught her off guard. He knocked her to the ground, but she scrambled away again, kicking and punching at him.

"You bitch." His fist crashed into her jaw, snapping her head to the side. "Where's the kid?"

She spat out blood where her teeth had cut her cheek. "Gone. Hiding. He's Finn's kid. Finn is a survival expert. Don't you think he taught his son wilderness survival? At least enough to get away from you."

Thank God that was true.

Henry backhanded her, then yanked her to her feet. "It doesn't matter. We don't need him. He doesn't know who I am, and even if he did, who's going to believe a kid?"

Finn. Finn would believe Ethan without a single doubt.

"Especially when I'm done spinning this to look like *you* were behind it and that you ran off with a bunch of money."

Knowing how bad her finances were, would Finn believe Henry? Think the worst of Charlie? That she'd betrayed him again?

Not that she was going to be around to know.

"What do you want, Henry?"

"I want the code you memorized."

She shrugged. "Fine. Got a piece of paper?" She'd be glad to write down some random symbols for him.

He yanked her hair back, bringing tears to her eyes. "You think you're so clever? You've been hanging out with Linear Tactical for too long. Those damn Special Forces guys, always thinking they're God's gift to humanity. Saving the world one mission at a time. Did you know Bollinger's nickname in the Army was Eagle? Ironic, considering he couldn't even see what was right in front of him the whole time. *Me.*"

"You were the one behind Operation Sparrow? Selling the information about air space?"

Henry rolled his eyes. "That intel's so small-time, I wouldn't even get out of bed for that. But believe me, Cline deciding to do it provided the perfect cover for what I've been waiting years to do."

"And what is that?"

"Those codes you have inside your head are what I need to access the override sequence for eight NORAD drones. Once I have them I'll be able to redirect them anywhere I want or sell them to someone who might like to use the United States' own weapons technology against them. Do you know how many can be killed with a single drone attack when used correctly?"

She didn't nor did she care. What she did know was that she was never *ever* giving him the information inside her head.

He yanked her to her feet. "Give me the code, Charlotte."

"Wow." She tapped her finger against her lip, ignoring the pain, the picture of nonchalance. "This opportunity to give you the code and die, or *not* to and die . . . Let me think about it." She spat more blood on the ground and glared at him. "I think I'm gonna go with *not* helping you."

That got her another fist crashing into her face. She tried not to moan but couldn't keep it in. As soon as she recovered, she tilted her chin back up. "You may as well kill me now, Henry. I'm not going to give you the information you want."

"Look at you." Henry leaned back against a tree. She guessed it was too much to hope he'd get bitten by some unknown bug that would leave him paralyzed. "You're all tough, just like your Linear boyfriend. He may have taught you quite a bit . . ."

He yanked her closer by the front of her shirt. Finn's, which she'd put on last night after a shower. She felt it rip. "Did your Special Forces lover teach you how to withstand torture?"

She didn't say anything. Refused to in case she gave

away the terror pulsing through her. Henry gripped her chin and forced her face to within inches of his. "Did he teach you the most fundamental rule of torture?"

She refused to show her fear. "What's that?"

"No matter how tough you are, how strong you are, how much training you have . . . Everybody eventually breaks. You will too, Charlotte, and you'll tell me what I want to know."

Henry pulled out a gun from a holster at his waist and she thought he was going to shoot her. She didn't even have time to throw up her arms as the gun flew down and cracked her on the back of her skull. All she could do was watch the world fade quickly to black.

CHAPTER 29

FINN and the guys stopped by Linear headquarters on their way home from The Silver Palace. They were all exhausted and frustrated. Whoever had been shooting from inside the building, whether it was Stellman or not, had gotten away. Sheriff Nelson hadn't been able to make any arrests in all the chaos.

No one had been hurt in the fire, but then again, hurting people hadn't been the intent of the blaze. *Escape* had been, and it had worked perfectly.

The only person who had died had been identified as Rocco Christensen. Finn assumed that was the man Henry had taken out while rescuing Charlie. Thank God he had, or else Charlie would've been taken or maybe already dead.

"So, we're basically back at square one," Aiden said, unloading the weapons and equipment they'd grabbed on the way out to The Silver Palace.

"Not completely," Finn reminded him. "Charlie saw the code and was able to memorize it. That's got to provide some sort of intel."

Zac took off the Kevlar vest he was wearing. Finn and Aiden stowed their firearms in the weapons safe. They may have thousands of dollars' worth around the Linear facility, but they were always kept locked away. Too many children might hurt themselves. Not to mention the much more dangerous overgrown children who thought they knew about weapons but didn't.

"Give me a couple hours to shower and to eat," Finn said. "Then I'll bring Charlie here, so we can contact the major and figure out exactly what these codes are about."

The thought of Charlie being at his house waiting for him with Ethan should've scared him, but it didn't. It felt perfect.

The others were talking about getting breakfast, Zac leading the charge since his woman was working a double at the hospital, when Finn's phone buzzed in his hand. It was Peyton.

"Hey, Peyton," he said as he answered the call. "Thanks again for—"

"Finn." The woman's voice was frantic, cutting him off midsentence. "Ethan is here and says someone is chasing Charlie."

"What?"

His friends stopped talking at Finn's roar. He put the phone on speaker, so everyone could hear. "Peyton, is Ethan okay? Tell me what's going on. Where are you right now?" He could hear a car running.

"Ethan is fine. I'm on my way to you."

"I'm at Linear."

"Shit," Peyton muttered under her breath.

"Mommy said a bad word. Mommy said a bad word," Little Jess sang from the back seat.

"Sometimes bad words are okay," Finn heard his son say, sounding like a well of deep wisdom.

"I'm turning around," Peyton muttered. "I'll be there in five minutes."

"I'll call Sheriff Nelson, so he can radio his man at your house," Zac said and walked out of the room, phone in hand.

"I'm going to your house," Dorian said. The big, quiet man didn't wait for confirmation, just turned and left. He would report back as soon as he had any info.

That might be only five minutes from now, but it was still an eternity.

"Tell me what happened, Peyton."

"She came to your house last night, I don't know, around midnight or so. Said she would be staying with Ethan until you got home."

"Right. And she was fine when you left?"

"Yes. She told me about the fire, and she had some scrapes on her arm, but besides that she seemed okay. So, I went home. I was getting breakfast ready for Jess just after dawn when Ethan showed up."

"Are you sure he wasn't just hiding from Charlie? Got freaked out because I wasn't home?" Maybe sending Charlie hadn't been the best idea. Maybe Ethan wasn't ready. Not to mention the kid had been known to go to Jess's before, although not without asking. Ethan knew the shortcut through the woods.

"No, this was different. This was not him coming to check on Jess like he always does. He ran in as fast as he could, talking about Charlie and how a bad man was after her."

Zac came back in the room, shaking his head. "Sheriff can't get his man on the radio."

"I'm pulling up now." Peyton disconnected the call and Finn ran outside. He had the door to the car open and his son in his arms in seconds.

Ethan started to cry. "I didn't want to leave her, Daddy. But Charlie said I had to protect Jess."

Finn didn't know what was going on, but he knew his son wasn't at fault. He set him on the ground and crouched down so they could see eye to eye. "And is Jess safe?"

Ethan nodded.

"Then you did the right thing. When Charlie gets back, I'm sure she'll say the same."

That reassured the boy enough to get a small smile out of him.

"Can you tell me what happened, buddy?"

Everyone listened as Ethan told them about a man knocking on the door and Charlie telling Ethan to run.

"Where were you when Charlie told you to go to Jess's house?"

"Almost halfway to the creek, heading south."

Finn nodded. He had always made sure Ethan understood directions—it was something everyone should know. It was paying off now.

His son looked at him, the bit of accusation in his eyes clear. "I don't think Charlie knows the woods as good as us. You need to fix that. I'm afraid she'll get lost."

Finn wanted to crush his son to him. The fact that Ethan cared so much about Charlie warmed every part of his heart. "I will, buddy, I promise. Even better, we'll fix it together. You and I will teach her all about the woods near the house. Do you remember anything else?"

Finn's phone buzzed. A text from Dorian to the entire Linear group.

Cop dead in patrol car. Stabbed. Tracking Charlie into woods.

Shit.

He glanced at Zac, then Aiden, and both had the same concerned expressions. Zac began responding to Dorian, probably to provide the information Ethan had just given them.

Ethan tugged on Finn's shirt. "The man was yelling about a code. Charlie wanted me to tell you about it. *Fire his pretty chair horse* and *blue baby eat just when my old dog sleep.*"

They brought Ethan inside, so he could write it down using symbols instead of the words.

"I'll be damned," Aiden muttered. He pulled out the napkin he'd taken from Cline. The first part matched perfectly.

"And we need to get the major right now. And Henry too. He was freaking out about the code at The Silver Palace, so he must have some idea what this is."

Ten minutes later they had the major on a video conference call. They'd already sent the codes. The look on the man's face did not reassure any of them.

Major Pinnock didn't beat around the bush. "This is bad in some of the worst possible ways. The code you sent is in two parts that should never have been together in one location."

"They weren't, really," Finn said. "Charlie saw the second set inside The Silver Palace. She thinks someone— Stellman, maybe—was using the club to pass along information."

"It wasn't Cline, I can tell you that," the major said. "This is definitely not info he had access too. Or at least not both parts. The second code is from a contractor we use, an engineering company."

"Do you know what it is?"

The major scrubbed a hand over his face. "The first section is the computer override access for eight UCAVs with their full weapons capacity."

Unmanned combat aerial vehicles. Drones.

Full weapons capacity meant the consequences could be devastating.

"The first code alone doesn't really mean anything," the major continued. "It has to be used at a particular terminal at a particular time."

"Then why is someone after Charlie?"

"Because that's what the second code is. The terminal and access time."

Finn whistled through his teeth. "So, what you're telling me is that inside Charlie's head is everything needed to access eight UCAVs to be used at will?"

The major nodded over the screen. "But the good news is, without the specific laptop the code refers to it's all useless—" The major stopped talking as someone came up to him and whispered in his ear. Finn watched the color drain from the man's face.

"Is Henry with you?"

Aiden shook his head. "I haven't seen him since the fire last night."

"Then, gentlemen, we have a huge problem. I think Henry has played us from the beginning. I've just been notified that the terminal the codes belong to are for one in his possession. A remote terminal. Again, not problematic in and of itself."

"But if he gets the second code from Charlie, he'll have

everything he needs to hijack eight drones. Is that what we're saying?" Finn asked.

The major nodded. "Affirmative."

Shit.

Finn was thinking this was about as bad as it could get when a text came from Dorian.

I found signs of struggle. Definitely Charlie, long blonde hairs. Blood, but not life-threatening. I tracked them back toward your house where he moved her to a vehicle.

In other words, where Dorian couldn't follow. The man was damn near a genius when it came to wilderness survival and tracking, but no one could track a moving vehicle on foot.

"It's going to take at least twelve hours to contain this and change the codes in our system," Major Pinnock said. "Henry was smart. He distracted us with the whole Cline/Operation Sparrow stuff. Pretending to work with you provided all the cover he needed."

"He's been playing the long con," Aiden said.

Aiden's instincts had been right all along.

"Once he has those codes from Charlie, he'll have no reason to keep her alive." Finn didn't give a shit about how or why Henry had been able to fool them. Charlie's blood was on the ground and Henry, someone who had been lying to their faces for weeks, had her life in his hands.

Zac's hand landed on his shoulder. "Charlie will know that. She's smart."

"That's what I'm afraid of. She'll figure out what Henry wants and that he'll use it for acts of terror. She won't tell him. That just means he's going to use force to get it from her."

Going to? Henry was probably already using whatever

method necessary to get the information from Charlie. Agony swallowing him, he turned to Zac.

"Zac, she thinks she's so strong. She thinks she'll be able to withstand . . ."

He couldn't finish the sentence. Zac's hand squeezed his shoulder again. They all had personal experience with torture. The thought of Charlie going through that . . .

"Focus, Eagle. Her survival is the most important thing. We'll get to her."

Finn pushed down the terror threatening to swamp him.

"If you can get him on his cell phone, we can track him," Pinnock said quietly.

He wanted to slam his fist on the table. "What good will that do? He could have her anywhere. Be on the move."

"Not if he's trying to obtain intel by force," Aiden said. "Henry has to have her somewhere he can control outside factors. We get his location. We extract her as a team."

Aiden and Zac were already moving, gathering the weapons they would need for their impromptu strike team.

"Henry has no reason to think we know he's a traitor," Aiden said. "If we play it cool, we can keep him on the line. But you're going to have to focus, no matter what he does."

Finn nodded. He might want to rip that bastard apart piece by piece, but he would hold it together until Charlie was safe.

The major gave them the info needed to track Henry, then disconnected the call to handle his own crisis within NORAD.

In under five minutes Finn, Zac, and Aiden were in Finn's Jeep, ready to pull out in whatever direction the tracker led them. Zac would be driving, with Finn and Aiden in the back so they could talk to the other man.

Henry wouldn't be able to see the GPS feed NORAD was sending them.

"Focused," Aiden whispered to Finn. He nodded. He had never been more focused on anything in his life. The only thing that mattered now was getting Charlie back alive.

Aiden made the call to Henry, keeping it on speaker.

They needed to keep him on as long as possible. After one minute, the GPS tracker would at least give them a direction to head in. Three should pinpoint Henry's location.

Of course, this would only work if Charlie hadn't already given up the information. If she had, Henry would have no reason to pick up at all. Finn held his breath as the phone rang once.

Twice.

A third time.

His hands clenched into fists.

In the middle of the fourth ring, the call connected. Henry's voice rang out. "Aiden, what's up, buddy?"

Finn let out a silent sigh of relief even as he wanted to jump through the phone and strangle the other man.

"Hey, Henry," Aiden responded with a smile. "We lost you at The Silver Palace. We're all heading out to breakfast and wanted to see if you'd join us. Figure out our next plan of action and see how many problems we caused by not being at The Lion's Den."

"Finn there with you?" Henry asked.

"Yeah, hey man." Finn forced his tone to be as neutral as possible as Aiden eased the phone closer to him. "I've got to eat something before I go home. I'm starving."

"Did there end up being a big bust at The Lion's Den or did nobody show? You're headed over there, right?" Aiden asked. "We didn't find anything useful around The Silver Palace."

"But thankfully nobody was hurt in the fire," Finn continued. They were talking a lot but at least it was keeping Henry on the line.

Zac eased the Jeep forward as the GPS kicked in with a general direction. They only needed to keep him on the line for a few more minutes.

"Where are you guys now?" Henry asked. Aiden's eyes met Finn's. Was the other man getting suspicious?

"Almost to the Frontier Diner," Aiden replied quickly. "How about you?"

The man paused for so long Finn was afraid he'd disconnected the call. Only the fact that they still had the GPS feed gave him hope.

"Just running down a few leads of my own. Listen, I can't meet you guys right now, but I'll take a rain check. Why don't we meet up this afternoon? Talk details."

They were going to lose him. Zac held his finger up and spun it around signaling that they needed to keep him talking. No shit.

"Hey, Henry," Finn interjected before the other man could hang up. "I didn't get a chance to thank you for saving Charlie's life. She said you took out that guy who was going to kill her, Rocco."

"Don't worry about it. I've got to go. I—"

"Finn!" Charlie's strangled cry rang out, cutting Henry off.

He kept playing his role, hoping to keep Henry on the line. "What was that, Henry? Was that Charlie? Is she with you? What's going on?"

The line went dead.

CHAPTER 30

"PLEASE TELL ME THAT WAS ENOUGH." Finn could barely force the words past his throat.

Zac had the Jeep speeding out of town in the direction the tracker sent them. "It's going to get us close, but not an exact location."

"How close?"

Zac grimaced. "Maybe two square miles."

Finn wanted to slam his fist against the window. Henry could kill Charlie a hundred times over before they found her in a two-square-mile area.

A desperate fear unlike anything he'd ever known coursed through him. Sitting in this vehicle were three of the most highly trained men in the greatest military in the world. But all their training, all their knowledge, all their skills . . . none of it was going to be enough to save Charlie.

And then Aiden's phone beeped again.

"Oh please, God," Finn whispered.

"The clock restarts," Zac said. "We still need him for three minutes." It was a video call this time. That would be more dangerous, trying to make sure Henry didn't know how close they were. Aiden hit accept.

"Henry, what the hell is going on? That sounded like Charlie," Aiden said.

Henry's face came into view. "I didn't want it to happen like this, but there doesn't seem to be any way around it. Give the phone to Finn."

Finn took a breath. He had to hold it together. Aiden handed him the phone.

"What's up with all the games, Nicholson? Is Charlie with you or not?"

"The two of you are close, right? I know she spent the night with you." Henry was keeping the screen close to his face, so they couldn't see anything around him. "I need you to do me a favor, Bollinger. Talk some sense into your woman."

Henry turned so the camera was facing Charlie. He heard Aiden's sharp intake of breath and felt cold sweat breaking out along his own spine.

Oh Jesus. Charlie was tied to a chair, her small body barely upright, her breathing erratic. Her eyes were swollen almost shut, her face already bruising. Her nose had clearly been broken. The T-shirt—way too big for her, it must be his—was ripped and hanging off one shoulder.

Holding it together took every bit of control he had. Keeping Henry on the line, not letting him know how close they were, that's what was most important now.

Killing that bastard would come later.

But when Henry reached over and yanked Charlie's head back by her hair, making her cry out in pain, Finn nearly lost it.

"What the fuck, Henry?" he roared. Both Zac and Aiden shot him concerned looks, but he didn't care.

"I need the other part of that code. You're going to talk Charlotte into giving it to me, or you'll watch her die very painfully."

"What code?" He tried to buy more time. "What are you talking about?"

"Stop with the games, Bollinger. You know exactly what code. The one she memorized before The Silver Palace burned." He watched in helpless rage as Henry backhanded Charlie.

Charlie's tiny moan of pain broke his heart. He knew that sound, that feeling. It was the sound of someone close to breaking. Someone who had reached their limit. Any other civilian would've reached it long before now and would have already provided Henry the info he wanted.

Finn would give everything he owned to be the one in that chair right now rather than her.

"We all know what I'm talking about so quit screwing around. Charlotte has put up a noble fight, but it's time to stop playing games. Tell her to give me the code." He pressed the phone right up to Charlie's face.

"Finn?" The word came out of her mouth so softly he almost couldn't hear it.

"I'm here, princess."

"I won't tell him. He can go to hell."

If Finn's heart wasn't shattering into a million pieces, he would've smiled at Henry's scream of rage. The man really had no idea what he'd started. In a battle of wills with Charlotte Devereux, Finn would bet on Charlie every time.

"What is it with you Special Forces people?" Henry yelled. "What, did you train her to withstand torture on your first date? They desked me, you know. No more combat-controller missions after I blew out my knee. Then the military fast-tracked me for retirement since I wasn't of use to them anymore."

That's right, you bastard, keep monologuing. Zac was nodding as he glanced at the GPS tracker. They almost had the location.

"Yeah, well, I'm sure if the military could see you now, beating the shit out of an unarmed woman half your size, they would ask you back as fast as they could."

"I'm just taking what was owed to me. You guys are the Army's golden boys—the beloved Green Berets. You have no idea what it's like to be thrown aside like trash."

"The military is a machine, Henry. Anybody in for longer than a year, no matter which branch or what job, knows that. If you can't do your part to make the machine run smoothly, you're replaced. That's how it works."

Finn had no idea how he was managing functional sentences while seeing Charlie in this shape. They just needed another minute at most.

"Well, they shouldn't have replaced me. They're going to realize that when they see what I've done. How I fooled you all. I'm done messing around, Bollinger. The codes in Charlotte's head are time sensitive, and I need them now."

To everyone's amazement Charlie started to laugh. It was the most heartbreaking sound Finn had ever heard.

"Well, you really shouldn't have told me that, asshole." The words were so garbled through her swollen lips they were difficult to understand.

Behind the screen, Zac gave Finn a thumbs-up. They had Henry's location.

Henry yanked her back by the hair again. "And why is that?"

"You said it yourself: everybody eventually breaks. But

now I know I don't have to withstand all your torture. I just have to make it past your deadline."

Henry had just been out-interrogated by someone with no military training whatsoever.

This woman. Finn was getting her out of this and they were spending the rest of their damn lives together. He didn't care what she'd done in the past. She was the most amazing person on the planet.

Zac was communicating through their shared hand language. They were three minutes out. She just had to survive that long.

"She's strong," Henry said, almost sadly. "I'll definitely give you that, but she doesn't really know how bad torture can be, does she, Finn? I didn't want it to come to this. Honestly, I don't really have the stomach for it. I was hoping she would listen to you. But I guess not."

Bile pooled in Finn's gut when Henry pulled out a small blowtorch.

"See? She doesn't understand how bad it can get."

"Don't you fucking do this, Henry." Sweat started beading on his brow.

No, God, please.

Zac pushed even harder on the gas, trying to get the last of the speed out of the Jeep even though he'd already had it at its maximum.

Henry shook his head. "I don't *want* to. She doesn't have to go through this. Explain that it's okay for her to tell me. I promise, one ex-military man to another, that she will not die in any pain, if she tells me."

Zac signaled with his hands. They were less than one minute away.

It wouldn't have mattered if they were an hour away. Finn still would've said the same thing.

"Princess, look at me."

One of her eyes cracked open.

"You've done your part. Now it's time to let someone else take over this fight."

"I don't want to tell him," she whispered.

He rubbed his fingers across the screen, as if he could touch her skin. Comfort her in some way. "I know you don't. But you're not in this fight by yourself anymore, okay? Any of it. You and I are in this together. I need you to trust me. Tell Henry the code."

"Listen to him, Charlotte," Henry said off camera. Charlie's swollen lips tightened just the slightest bit in mutiny. He wanted to tell the other man to shut the hell up. Henry wasn't helping his case.

"Princess, I love you. I need you to trust me."

Henry snatched the phone away. "I hope that works and she'll listen to you. Otherwise it's going to be a very painful way to die."

"You trust me, Charlie Devereux! For once in your damn life, please trust me!" He yelled it, wanting to be sure she heard him. She had to believe him. The damage Henry would do, even if they got to her in a minute, would scar her forever in every possible way. It wasn't worth it, even if he did get control of the drones.

"Was nice working with you, fellas."

The call went dead again.

Whatever last bit of composure Charlie had disappeared with Finn's face as the phone blinked off. She'd tried to be strong for so long, even after she'd passed out because of the pain, but now she had nothing left. She could barely focus enough to even remember the code.

Henry turned the blowtorch on and held it in front of her face. Close enough for her to feel the heat, but not burn her.

"Time is up. Decide."

Finn had said to trust him. Maybe it meant she was weak. Maybe it meant she didn't want to die a horrible death. But she was going to trust him. If he said it was okay to tell Henry the codes, she would believe him.

"I'll tell you."

He turned off the blowtorch, thank God, and walked to the laptop on the table nearby.

"I only get one shot at this. If you give me the wrong code, I swear to God I will burn off every inch of your skin before you die."

Charlie was too exhausted to even respond with a sarcastic comment about his melodrama. God, everything hurt so badly. She couldn't see, could barely hear. She'd long since lost feeling in her arms, which were tied to the chair. She had swallowed so much of her own blood she was afraid she might vomit it up again.

"Code, Charlotte."

Should she give him the wrong one? If she was going to die anyway, should she try to do what was right, despite what Finn had said?

Trust me, Charlie. For once in your life, please trust me.

He'd sounded like he was begging. Had she done that? Had she reduced that strong, powerful man into begging for her trust? Made him beg *again*, the way he had before, when he'd told her not to marry Brandon? She hadn't trusted him then.

This time she would.

She gave Henry the code. Perfect and complete, praying she wasn't making a mistake that would get thousands killed.

She trusted Finn.

Henry typed it in and waited, riveted to the screen in front of him, oblivious to everything else. Charlie felt a hand wrap over her mouth, touching her so gently it wouldn't possibly stop any noise if she really tried to yell.

Then she heard him. "I love you, princess."

Finn was here.

He kissed her temple, then stepped away. Zac lifted the entire chair, with her in it, and moved silently back, Aiden and Finn now standing between her and Henry. She couldn't stop the moan of pain that fell from her lips at the movement, but those had been so frequent it didn't even draw Henry's attention.

He laughed, still staring at the screen. "I'll be damned, I didn't think you would do it. And honestly, I didn't think Bollinger would tell you to give me the codes either. Some people just can't see the bigger picture."

"Oh, I think I can see the bigger picture just fine," Finn said. "It involves you spending the rest of your life behind bars for treason."

Henry straightened and spun, reaching for his gun, but the guys were expecting that.

Zac stepped in front of her, another line of protection, so she couldn't see what happened. But a moment later, three shots rang out. Somebody fell to the ground, but not any of the three standing in front of her, between her and harm's way.

Now that Finn was here, and she knew she was safe, staying upright and conscious was becoming more and more difficult. If her hands weren't strapped to the chair so tightly, she would've already fallen out of it.

Then Finn was next to her, his large hand holding her head, so she didn't slump any farther to the side. Aiden crouched beside him, and a few seconds later her wrists were free. Finn eased her from the chair onto the ground, cradling her head in his hand the whole time.

"He's dead," Zac said from across the room. "I'm calling it in and requesting an ambulance."

"I'm glad he's dead." Her words came out all mushy. She knew she shouldn't feel that way about someone dying, even Henry, but she did.

Finn slid a little piece of hair back from her eyes. "I'm glad he drew on us first so that I didn't have to commit cold-blooded murder."

She wasn't sure if he was joking or not, so she didn't ask.

Agony was spiking down her spine and white dots floated in her vision. It hurt to swallow, to breathe, to think.

"Go ahead and rest, princess, you deserve it. I'll be right next to you when you wake up. Trust me."

"I do. I'll always trust you." The words hurt. Everything hurt so bad. But she wanted Finn to know that. There was so much more she wanted to tell him too. She tried to get the words out.

"I-I . . ."

He laid beside her so they were face-to-face and pressed his lips in the most gentle of kisses against hers. "Hold that thought, princess. I promise, we've got all the time in the world to say the things we have to say to each other."

She held on to those green eyes—eyes that held the promise of *everything*—until she couldn't hold on any longer and the pain pulled her under.

CHAPTER 31

THE HOSPITAL PUT Charlie in a medically induced coma almost immediately upon her arrival. It was for the best, Finn knew that. It was a precaution to make sure the swelling from all the blows she'd taken to the head didn't do any further damage. Her concussion was severe.

Henry was damn lucky he was already dead. Because seeing Charlie so silent and still was unbearable—so much worse than when Finn had her in his bed a month ago when she was sick. He wanted his hurricane back. Even though he may never get a moment of rest or peace, he wanted her in full force.

The tiny, battered, still woman on the bed wasn't his hurricane.

Zac and Annie had stayed with Charlie while Finn had gone home to shower, change, and see Ethan. They'd had an important talk before going to Grandma's house, so Finn would be free to stay at the hospital.

When he got back, Mrs. Devereux was in Charlie's room. Of course, she would be; Sheriff Nelson knew how to get in touch with her now since Charlie's condo had burned down.

He took a deep breath and stepped inside the room, praying the older woman wouldn't kick him out. He wouldn't be able to bear it. "Hello, Mrs. Devereux. You probably don't remember me, but—"

"Finn!"

The small woman stood and pulled him into her arms for a tight hug. "I'm so glad you're here. Of course, I remember you."

"Oh." He couldn't figure out anything else to say. He'd always thought Charlie's parents hated him.

"Can you tell me what happened?" she asked. "Sheriff Nelson called to say Charlotte was in the hospital, but he didn't have many details. That nice Dr. Griffin explained that they were keeping Charlotte asleep to help with the brain swelling and to give her body a chance to heal, but look at her, Finn."

He already had, and he knew what Mrs. Devereux was feeling. "It's hard to see her like this. But she's strong. Dr. Griffin—Annie—is confident Charlie will wake up with no problems once they begin tapering down the meds."

Mrs. Devereux sat back down and patted the chair next to her. "Tell me what happened."

During his time in the Army, he'd been a part of missions where a fellow soldier had been hurt or died. When Finn had come to offer his condolences or well wishes to the families, sometimes months afterward, he'd never been able to talk about specifics because of security. He'd never dreamed he'd be in a similar situation involving Charlie. But he couldn't give Mrs. Devereux the whole truth.

"There was a crazy person at her work," Finn finally settled on. "He attacked her."

"Did they arrest him?"

"I understand he died during the altercation." He hoped Henry was burning in hell.

"This happened at her school job?"

"No, not at her tutoring job. Charlie's other job."

"Other job?" Mrs. Devereux's lips pushed together into a thin line. "I knew it. I knew she'd been working somewhere else besides just teaching. Where?"

Shit. He wasn't trying to blow the whistle on Charlie. But damn it, if she was working this hard to help provide for her parents they probably deserved to know that.

"Mrs. Devereux, I think we should wait until Charlie wakes up and talk about it then."

"Ha!" she scoffed. "Have you met my daughter? Do you honestly think she's going to give up information to me without some sort of knockdown, drag-out fight?"

No, he didn't. He just didn't want to be in the middle when it happened.

But then all the energy seemed to drain out of the woman. She watched him with the same blue eyes he saw every time he looked at Charlie. "It's not fair for me to be upset about her having another job. I haven't asked. I knew she was working hard, but I deliberately haven't asked. Every month the medical bills get paid for Milton and that has been what's most important." Her voice dropped to a whisper. "But I look at her now, beyond the bruises, and I see how wrong I've been to just live with my head in the sand. I see how tired she is. How thin."

Three weeks ago, she'd been worse, but Finn wasn't about to mention that. Charlie had been wrong not to let her mom know how desperate things had gotten.

"She has a second job as a bartender." He didn't mention The Silver Palace specifically in case Mrs. Devereux was familiar with the place. Because although he wanted some of the burden off Charlie's shoulders, he wasn't stupid.

"The care for Milton is expensive. It was necessary for him to be at that facility when he was part of the experimental drug trial eight years ago. But now he doesn't need to be anymore. There's nothing they're doing for him there that we can't do ourselves with just a little bit of help. He and I talked during his lucid times about moving back to Oak Creek, to be closer to Charlie. And because this has always been where we considered home." She sighed tiredly. "Milton was always the one to make decisions in the family and I was happy to let him. But I think because of my unwillingness to make decisions, Charlie has paid the price. Literally."

"She loves you," he responded, because it was nothing less than the truth. "She wanted to provide for your needs the way you always did for hers. You raised her to be that way and it's commendable."

But commendable or not, he had no intention of letting Charlie continue to shoulder all this.

Mrs. Devereux sighed. "I'd like to move into her condo, but I know it's not big enough for the three of us."

Oh shit. *Again.* "Um, actually, there was a fire a couple of weeks ago and it burned down."

She looked at him in shock. *"What?"*

"Charlie moved out a few months ago, so it didn't really involve her." Except for the whole somebody trying to kill her part, which was probably better left out of the story. "She's living with a roommate now on the east side of town."

He'd rather cut off his tongue than mention her being homeless for nearly eighteen months.

They sat in silence for long minutes while Mrs. Devereux processed it all, both staring at Charlie.

"It's difficult to see her so still, isn't it?" she asked.

"Almost impossible."

Mrs. Devereux was holding Charlie's hand, so Finn reached over to rest his fingers on her ankle over the blanket. Just touching her made him feel better. The movement did not go unnoticed by Charlie's mother.

"How about you two? Considering she didn't tell me she was working two jobs, or that her condo burned down, I assume she wouldn't tell me if you two were dating."

"I'm not sure that what we're doing could be called dating, but I can promise you my intent toward your daughter is serious and long-term." The longest of terms.

He prepared himself for an argument, but it didn't come. "Good. It was obvious to everyone you two were meant for each other, ever since you were teenagers."

Finn couldn't keep the shock out of his tone. "I thought you hated me."

"Why would you think that?"

"Honestly, I thought it started when I gave her the nickname. Then it just grew when you guys decided I couldn't provide for her the way Kempsley could."

Mrs. Devereux shook her head slowly. "Well, first off, I think we both know she's always been closer to a Charlie than she ever was a Charlotte. I definitely never hated you for the name." She stroked her daughter's hand. "You were always the eye of her storm, Finn, not Brandon. Never Brandon. Do you know why she married him?"

He shrugged. "Honestly, it doesn't matter. I plan to marry her now. As soon as I can talk her into it."

That had been the big talk he'd had with Ethan. They were a team now. Finn couldn't make these sorts of decisions without input from his son. He explained that he loved Charlie and if Ethan didn't mind, Finn wanted to marry her. For them to be a family.

Ethan had agreed.

Then his son had proceeded to explain to Finn that he loved Jess and planned to marry *her*. That he would take care of Jess because she didn't have a dad and babies needed a dad to protect them, like Finn had come and protected Ethan. Since Jess didn't have a man around to protect her, Ethan was willing to fill in.

So evidently both he and his son were basically engaged to females who didn't know it.

Could be worse. And it also explained Ethan's desire to hang around the younger child so much. Because he wanted to *protect* her.

Could be a lot damn worse.

Tears filled Mrs. Devereux's eyes. "It should've been you. It should've always been you. And while I truly appreciate that you've gotten past it no matter what, I want you to know that she married Brandon because he offered to get Milton into the experimental drug trial for his prion disease. Milton would've been dead years ago if it hadn't been for that. Just another time when I let Charlotte carry the load rather than telling her to do what was best for her."

Finn waited for the relief to come at Mrs. Devereux's words. Relief that there had been a legitimate reason for Charlie to marry Kempsley rather than him.

It didn't come.

And that's when he knew he had truly forgiven her. Because it honestly didn't matter to him why she'd done it. All that did was that they were going to be together going forward. Charlie. Finn. Ethan. And all the other babies he could talk her into having.

"Thank you for telling me. She probably never would've."

Mrs. Devereux grabbed his hand with the one not holding Charlie's. "She needs someone strong like you. A boulder who won't get blown around by her winds."

He would be what Charlie needed. And the first thing on her mind when she woke up would be the job and revenue she had lost.

Mrs. Devereux sighed and looked back at her daughter. "Charlie tries to shoulder too much. I can't continue to let her be a little dictator."

He had the perfect solution. "In that case, as soon as we can get someone here to sit with Charlie, I was wondering if I could invite you to my house to plan our own coup d'état."

CHAPTER 32

IN MOVIES, the hero gets the shit beat out of him, then a few hours later, he pops up and is back at it—jumping through buildings, saving all the kittens, sprinting across rooftops with a smile and a wink.

Charlie could attest, that was not realistic at all.

She wouldn't be doing any of that—not even the winking part—for a long time.

Waking up was slow. Slow and *painful*. And no matter how much she wanted to, she couldn't seem to keep her eyes open very long.

But every time she did, Finn was there.

There was a rotation of people with him—Mama, Aiden, Jordan, Zac, and Annie, others—but always Finn.

She wanted to talk to him, to ask a million questions, but her voice didn't seem to work, and she couldn't quite remember them anyway. So, when he reached over, kissed her forehead and whispered, "Trust me," she did.

She was content to just lie in bed and look at him. His big body sitting in the chair beside her while he held her hand. His smile as he talked to people coming in and out of the room.

His green eyes as he took care of her every need, from a sip of water to shifting her weight on the bed.

For two days that was enough. To just lie and be and heal.

By the end of the third day awake, she was feeling much better . . .and much worse. Her body, despite how crappy every single part of her felt at this moment, was going to recover. But she had responsibilities. Bills. Lying around in the hospital for any longer than absolutely necessary was not an option.

"I have to get out of here," she said to Finn.

She expected an argument, but he just grinned, then leaned over and kissed her. "There you are."

She kissed him back—as much as her damaged lips would allow—but didn't relent. "Finn, I can't stay here. You know the situation with my dad. I need to get back to work. Really, I'm feeling better."

He sat back down and grasped her hand in both of his. "I'm glad you're healing, and you're right, you won't need to be here for very much longer. But, princess, you can't go back to work, at least not to the jobs you had. The Silver Palace burned down, remember? And until some of that bruising on your face heals, tutoring probably isn't an option either."

She closed her eyes, panic bubbling up inside her. He was right. But what was she going to do? Every day she didn't work was a day less of income that she needed to survive. Plus, she was now going to have hospital bills to worry about.

"Princess, look at me."

She didn't want to. She wanted to be childish, keep her eyes closed and the world far away.

But when his fingers stroked her cheek, she couldn't help but turn into his hand and do what he asked. She opened her eyes and found his face right next to hers, just like he'd been at the warehouse when he'd rescued her.

"You are the most amazing woman—hell, *human being* I've ever known. Standing up to Henry like you did, holding out under that sort of physical duress, takes an awe-inspiring power of will. Most people would've buckled long before you did. You're a hero in every sense of the word."

She gave him the tiniest of shrugs. She hadn't felt like any sort of hero. She'd just felt agony.

"But you know what?" he continued. "I wasn't the least bit surprised you were able to go toe to toe with Henry. Because every second since you walked back into my life has served to prove how strong you are. How faithful. How selfless."

"Finn . . ."

"You, Charlotte Devereux, fight for the people you love."

Even though she didn't know where Finn was going with all this, what he said was true. She would always fight for the people she loved, no matter what it cost her. "Yes."

He stroked her hair away from her face. "Will you fight for me, Charlie? For us?"

"Yes. Always, yes." Whatever she had to do.

"One thing I learned in the Army was that sometimes to win a battle I had to lay down my weapons, even when it went against all my instincts to do so. I had to trust my team —the people fighting with me for the same goal—to have my back."

Now she knew where he was going with this. "Finn, I

love you, but I can't allow you to pay my bills."

He didn't get mad, didn't make an argument. Just reached over and kissed her gently again. "I'm not planning on doing that. You trusted me in that warehouse, Charlie, and I'm so glad you did. Will you again? Will you fight for us, this one time, by laying down your weapons and allowing your team to have your back?"

It wasn't really trust if she didn't have a choice, but she did have one. She could leave here, probably tomorrow, and find another job, part-time at first until she could handle more. She could make a deal with her father's treatment center to pay a little late for the next few months. She could do it herself. Carry the burden herself.

But Finn was asking her to trust him. To fight for their love in a way that was unnatural for her. Difficult. But she loved him.

So, she would.

∾

Six Weeks Later

"You're a sneaky bastard, Finn Bollinger," Charlie said, sitting out on his porch, sipping coffee. "Just in case I forget to tell you that every day, I want you to know."

And by *sneaky bastard* she meant the most fabulous man in the entire world. They both knew it. He just grinned and winked.

His engagement ring was on her finger.

Her parents were living very happily in the back section of his huge house. They had their own bedroom, bathroom, living room, and kitchen—plenty of space, private, and free.

All she had to pay for now were any medicines her father needed that government insurance didn't cover, and for the nurse that came in a few times a week to assist her mom. All in all, about one-tenth of what she'd needed to earn before. It made only having one job much more bearable.

She was still living at Jordan's house and would be back and forth until her wedding to Finn six months from now. The service would be held in the same chapel where Finn had once argued she shouldn't be marrying anyone but him.

He'd been right.

Maybe best of all was dinner last night with the whole crew: her, Finn, Ethan, Finn's mom, Baby, Wavy, and Charlie's parents. They'd all sat around the table, eating burgers the men, including her dad, had cooked out on the grill, when Ethan had very casually asked Charlie if he could call her *Mom* once she and Finn got married.

She had been too choked up to do anything but nod. Vehemently. The conversation had then launched into what Ethan should call her Mama and Dad. Finn's mom was Grandma, so it was decided that Charlie's parents would be Nana and Papa.

She had just sat at the table and stared.

This.

Everyone speaking all over each other, laughing and joking about Oak Creek gossip and upcoming events. Talking about school, work, and home. With every person she loved safe and here with her, *this* was what Charlie had always dreamed of having.

This was what she would fight for every single day for the rest of her life if she had to.

Last night after everyone had gone home and her parents and Ethan had gone to bed, she had spilled the last of her secrets to Finn. Mama had already told him how she'd married Brandon to get Dad into treatment, but she finally explained how the Kempsleys were blocking her from getting a full-time job in education.

They'd agreed they would fight it, figure out what had to be done, and stand shoulder to shoulder. Together.

Until then, she was more than happy to continue with her tutoring job. And as a private tutor for Ethan, of course. Her goal was to have him reading *beyond* grade level by the end of the school year.

She looked at Finn now, still smirking sexily at her as he sipped his coffee. Ethan was already at school and her parents had gone into town for breakfast.

Maybe it was time to get a head start on making some future kids she could tutor.

If she could stop Finn from treating her like she was precious and breakable. The precious part wasn't so bad, but . . .

The shape she'd been in after Henry's attack had scared the hell out of Finn. He'd admitted it. Even now she still had some residual problems: headaches and dizziness from her concussion, occasional numbness in one hand due to nerve damage from being tied to the chair.

She and Finn had made love a few times since she'd recovered. And, admittedly, that feat hadn't been as easy as before, since there were so many people around all the time —parents, kids, friends.

But Finn had yet to really let himself lose control with her. It was just about time for that to happen. Finn needed to realize she wasn't breakable.

No time like the present. They were alone, unsupervised. It was time to get into trouble. They'd always excelled at that.

She put her coffee cup on the table, then stood and walked until she was between his legs, leaning over him, resting her hands on the arms of his chair.

"I love you." She reached up with one hand to trail her fingers down his cheek. "You know that, right?"

He raised an eyebrow as his hands gripped her gently on her hips. "I thought you just said I was a sneaky bastard."

"Oh, that's very definitely true. How else can you explain that I ended up engaged, with my parents living in your house, and currently planning all the future kids we're going to have?"

That eyebrow rose even farther. She couldn't help it; she leaned closer and kissed it. "You're *currently* planning our future kids? As in, right at this moment?"

"I haven't been on birth control since my stay in the hospital. So, I was hoping maybe we could start trying for a brother or sister for Ethan as soon as possible. As often as possible. As hard, fast, and dirty as possible."

His fingers tightened on her hips. *Yes.* That's what she wanted.

"Starting right now. Right here in this chair while no one's home but the two of us."

"You're not going to get any argument from me."

She smiled then reached down and grabbed the elastic waist of his sweatpants, yanking the material past his hips, just enough for his erection to spring free. She trailed her fingers up and down the length of him, smiling at his hiss. "Repeat after me, soldier: hard, fast, dirty."

"Charlie . . ."

She kissed him. "I'm not breakable, Finn. I needed you all sweet and gentle for a while. But now I need you to remember my fire. My strength, not my weakness."

She hiked up her skirt to her thighs, then stepped over

his chair until she was straddling him. "Hard, fast, dirty. Got it?"

She began easing herself down on him. Now they were both hissing.

"You're not wearing any underwear." His voice was strangled, just how she wanted it. "Now who's sneaky?"

"Can't handle it?"

He rocked his hips and she slid farther down, felt the wonderful burning stretch of him. "Once I let go, I won't be able to haul it back. You know that," he whispered.

She nipped his lip with her teeth. "I *want* that."

He didn't say anything further, just sat up straighter in the chair, curved his arms up and around her back until his hands cupped her shoulders, then pulled her down onto him.

Hard. Fast.

He moved his hands to her waist, lifted her up, and slammed her down on him again. Over and over.

This heat and fire and storm was them. Had always been them.

Forget gentle.

Her head fell back as he reached his hand under her skirt and swept his thumb across her clit in firm, brutal strokes. She was gasping his name a few moments later as her orgasm crashed over her in waves.

She hadn't even caught her breath before he had his hand fisting in her hair and was yanking her face up to his. "I have never, from the moment you stepped into this town and caught both my eye and heart, thought you were weak. You got that?"

He punctuated each word with a thrust of his hips. All Charlie could do was wrap her hands around his shoulders and hold on.

"I think we've covered hard and fast," he said. "Let's move on to dirty."

Before she could even figure out what was going on, he picked her completely off him and spun her around, so she was still straddling him, but facing away from him on the chair.

She gasped as he slid back inside her, this angle making him so much deeper.

"You want babies?" He whispered in her ear, hand still fisted hard in her hair. "I'll give you as many as you can handle. I'll give them to you in whatever way you want. Soft, gentle, hard, fast. Ride me, dirty girl. I want to feel you come apart all over me."

One of his hands pushed between her shoulders, forcing her to lean forward until she had to catch her weight on his knees. Her eyes rolled back in her head as every movement now drove him against that spot inside her that made everything burn.

"Ride me, princess."

She did. Hard, fast, and dirty. When his fingers slipped around to add to the madness, she keened his name as colors flashed behind her closed eyes and all she could feel was him. Distantly, she heard him call her name as his hands gripped her hips with bruising force and he emptied himself inside her.

He eased her against his chest, her skirt keeping their naked skin hidden. They just lay there, draped around each other for long minutes until their breathing finally returned to normal.

"You are very definitely a sneaky bastard," she said when she could finally pull a coherent sentence together.

"I'm sneaky enough to keep you on your toes for the next fifty years or so."

The way he'd just blown her mind? She didn't doubt it for a second. "Promise me, Eagle, that it will always be you and me, no matter what."

"It was always us, princess. Maybe we had to be apart these years, so we could understand how right we are together. We might have never truly appreciated that otherwise. But from here on out, yes. You and me, no matter what."

She snuggled closer to him, feeling his strength surround her. She was a fighter, she always would be. And their love was worth fighting for.

OTHER BOOKS BY JANIE CROUCH

LINEAR TACTICAL SERIES
    Cyclone
    Eagle
    Shamrock
    Angel (2019)
    Ghost (2019)
    Echo (2019)

INSTINCT SERIES
    Primal Instinct
    Critical Instinct
    Survival Instinct

OMEGA SECTOR SERIES
    Infiltration
    Countermeasures
    Untraceable
    Leverage

OMEGA SECTOR: CRITICAL RESPONSE

Special Forces Savior
Fully Committed
Armored Attraction
Man of Action
Overwhelming Force
Battle Tested

OMEGA SECTOR: UNDER SIEGE

Daddy Defender
Protector's Instinct
Cease Fire
Major Crimes
Armed Response
In the Lawman's Protection

ACKNOWLEDGMENTS

Just like a mom with her kids, I know an author is not supposed to have a personal favorite book... But I've got to admit, Eagle is mine. (shhh! Don't tell!)

But there are many people that deserve my gratitude for making this a beloved book:

First and foremost, still and always: my husband, aka Captain Awesome. New seasons in our lives have brought challenges, but we always manage to handle them. I don't care what the variables are, as long as the constant is us.

To my kids, now all in high school and one in college. Thank you for sharing me with the voices in my head.

Again, my undying gratitude to my tribe: Marci, Girl Tyler, Anu, Stephanie, Regan, Nichole, Julie, Beth, Lissanne, Elizabeth. Every time you spot something I missed, or encourage me about something you liked, or just bully me to get one more page written...you're a blessing.

To my editors and alpha readers: Elizabeth Nover, Jennifer at Mistress Editing, Marci Mathers, Elizabeth Neal, Stephanie Scott, and Aly Birkl. Thank you for your patience, consistency and hard work. I depend on you so much and you never let me down.

And to my readers, especially the Crouch Crew: THANK YOU. Thank you for your emails, your messages, and your support. It means everything. I promise I will always endeavor to write the stories that keep you enthralled from page one. Life's too short for boring books!

With love and appreciation,

Janie Crouch

ABOUT JANIE

"Passion that leaps right off the page." - Romantic Times Book Reviews

USA TODAY bestselling author Janie Crouch writes what she loves to read: passionate romantic suspense. She is a winner and/or finalist of multiple romance literary awards including the Golden Quill Award for Best Romantic Suspense, the National Reader's Choice Award, and the coveted RITA© Award by the Romance Writers of America.

Janie recently relocated with her husband and their four teenagers to Germany (due to her husband's job as support for the U.S. Military), after living in Virginia for nearly 20 years. When she's not listening to the voices in her head—and even when she is—she enjoys engaging in all sorts of crazy adventures (200-mile relay races; Ironman Triathlons, treks to Mt. Everest Base Camp) traveling, and movies of all kinds.

Her favorite quote: "Life is a daring adventure or nothing."
~ Helen Keller.

facebook.com/janiecrouch

twitter.com/janiecrouch

instagram.com/janiecrouch

Lightning Source UK Ltd.
Milton Keynes UK
UKHW012026211221
396040UK00003B/951